Jihad!

Dale L. R. Lucas

PublishAmerica
Baltimore

First printing

ISBN: 1-4137-5140-7
PUBLISHED BY PUBLISHAMERICA, LLLP
www.publishamerica.com
Baltimore

Printed in the United States of America

7/1/05

To a great mentor and friend

Hall

— 1 —

Caribbean Sea
Tuesday, October 11, 9:32 p.m.

The silence of the night was surprising when considering the enormity of the liner as it slid through the vast expanse of the ocean under a full moon and clear skies. The only evidence of the movement of the ship was the constant low tone vibration that started somewhere in the bowels of the vessel and emanated throughout the superstructure in a calming but powerful surge. This power emanated in a slight vibration one could feel in the soles of one's shoes or from the palms of the hand if contact was made with the grey metal that was a constant in the marine vessel. Even the waves had chosen this evening to calm what would normally be an endless vision of white caps as the tides flowed to some nondescript destination that would never be reached.

The *Corona Princess* was a product of the insatiable hunger for petroleum and reflected the enormity of this desire by its size. The ship had been constructed at Liverpool during the mid-eighties and was, therefore, considered a neophyte in comparison with her sister ships making the countless cycles from the oil ports to the destination ports and returning on what was a well planned calendar of events.

Due to the modern construction and equally modern electronics systems of the ship, it was only natural that the owners had been allowed to be selective in the choosing of a crew. Not less than thirty candidates had responded to the quest of filling the captaincy of this beautiful vessel. The selected candidate was given latitude in the building of a crew that would match the quality of the hardware that would be operated at optimum capacity during the next three to five decades with only rare shutdowns to perform scheduled maintenance.

It was only expected that the sea would maintain calmness in respect of the enormity and perfection of the ship passing through it. In fact, the ship had been built to withstand the worst that a raging sea could offer and still keep a steady and uninhibited passage that would occur under normal conditions. This mastery of the ocean had been proven on more than one occasion under the equal talents of her captain.

Captain Oleg Uberhausen was sitting in his favorite chair located in the corner of the command center. His meerschaum pipe had a slight red glow and produced an aroma that the crew had come to take delight in. His first officer was at "the conn" and was scarcely conscious of the captain being on the bridge since Captain "O" was frequently found sitting in his selected position rather than retiring to his quarters when his presence was not required on the bridge.

The brightness of the moon reflecting upon the calm seas had a soothing effect that was designed to reinforce the reason most seafaring men choose the life. Oh sure, the snow-capped peaks on a mountain range, under a full moon, could produce a beauty of its own, but to ride the surface of a never-ending expanse of sea under the same conditions was one which any member of the crew would have chosen for himself many times over.

The only contact was another ocean liner some thirty miles away whose presence was more readily discerned from the screen in the pilot house than by the lights on the distant ship which lost their luminance due to the brightness of the night. Only the tersest of hails had exchanged between the vessels as they made the common courtesy calls to each other. Long conversations did not take place as a rule between men of the sea. Of course, this did not spill over to the shore crowd one would encounter after leaving international waters. Those guys operating within the twelve mile limit seemed to have an insatiable desire to hear themselves on the radio with endless weather checks at night or fishing reports by day.

Ten days earlier the *Corona Princes* had lifted anchor in the Persian Gulf and made its way south to the point where it could once again reverse directions north into the Red Sea and ultimately through the Suez Canal. From there it had been smooth sailing as the huge vessel crossed the Mediterranean from east to west and finally, into the Atlantic for its crossing.

The voyage would take them through the other manmade passage into the Pacific before the cargo was unloaded up in Richmond, California, at the north end of San Francisco Bay. Maybe he would lay over for a couple of days and give his crew liberty in San Francisco. It was a great city to visit and the ships compliment certainly deserved the R & R.

But right now the night was clear and he could let his mind travel to the various places he had visited during his decades of seafaring. Whenever he allowed himself this reverie it always caused him to return to his native Norway and the wife who had devoted herself to making him happy. In a couple more years Oleg would hang up his skipper's hat and join his bride back home in Oslo, where they would reap the bounty that had been amassed during his career at sea. That thought brought a smile to his face.

Western Indian Ocean
Wednesday, October 12, 8:32 a. m.

Halfway around the globe was another ship of similar size and cargo making its way in far less comfortable seas. Even with the enormity of the ship's bulk, the swells and monstrous waves kept up a steady barrage against the vessel determined to impede its forward progress. The attention of the crew could scarcely be one of concern, as seas like this were a common nuisance in the lives of seagoing men. The maturity of the crew evidenced itself in their calm demeanor and professionalism as they moved in a practiced caution about the pitching vessel. Like the *Corona Princess,* the *Valhalla Express* was making its one hundred twelfth passage across open seas with a common cargo between the two.

"Sure glad we have full holds for this blow, huh, Cap'n?" was the comment of the watch officer on the bridge to his sage, old leader. Captain Roberto Sanchez scarcely acknowledged the query, as he recognized that his junior officer was somewhat new to the maritime life and was looking for assurance that all was well.

"Take a look fore and aft to make sure everything is staying shipshape, Mr. Wainwright," the captain directed his nervous bridge officer. Might just as well keep him busy for a while and teach him to accept the inevitability of rough seas. He'd be safe since the crew was already making inspection tours for the stated purpose involved in the order issued by the chief executive of the ship.

Mr. Wainwright would make a fine officer once he got used to the numerous personalities of the oceans. You never failed to understand that the seas were the most unforgiving if you failed to respect them, but fear was never to be condoned when gaining this respect. You learned that you must first learn to react to the realities of sailing and once you accomplished this task, you began to read signs that would prepare for contingencies before the fact. Captain Sanchez was an accomplished and highly respected captain with enormous experience to back it up. This was, after all, a somewhat mild storm they found themselves in today. And it was true that the cargo holds being full of oil would keep the ship from pitching in the wild seas.

The storm would end in a few hours and they would continue on and make the turn up through the Red Sea and the Suez passageway to the Mediterranean and on to Athens. It was fortunate that the storm was here in the Indian Ocean rather than when they were making headway through the "Med." Storms in the Mediterranean were more severe than others due to the shallow bottoms that magnified the storm activity.

Captain Sanchez was hardly concerned with the storm of the past few hours as his mind was filled with the five men who had jumped ship just prior to departure from Kuwait. Without any warning, these men had simply vanished off the crew a mere twelve hours before departure. Two members of the group had been relatively new, but the other three had been with him for over three years and had never been the cause of any incidents during the past.

The Kuwaiti Police captain had been quite positive in his description of the five men who had commandeered a sedan and drove off in the direction of Saudi Arabia. Reportedly, they had asked directions to Yemen from one of the local service stations. Fortunately, the policeman had been able to locate a total of six able seamen to replace the missing crewmen and gave strong voucher as to their quality of character and ability to work well under orders. Captain Sanchez had considered just going back to his home port in Athens before replacing the ship jumpers, but the pending weather and need for full manning caused him to welcome the new members of his crew. They did, in fact, seem to be fine men who were well disciplined and sober. All in all, it had been a good choice as they immediately fit in with the rest of the crew and were learning rapidly the intricacies of sea life aboard the *Valhalla Express*. They even seemed to be excited to learn the ship and its operations.

Captain Sanchez hoped that the storm would pass before they entered the Red Sea and on up through the Suez. Although the waters within the canal would remain calm, the winds could cause problems as the huge tanker made its way through the narrow locks. Although the ship had double hulls and would be able to withstand any bumping that might occur during the passage through the canal, it was something that no self-respecting ship captain liked to have happen aboard his vessel. Yes, the Egyptian pilot would be in control of the ship during the passage, but again, a ship's captain never really gave up complete control of his charge.

From the time Roberto Sanchez had been a small boy growing up in his native Chile he had always been fascinated with the sea. His father had encouraged his bent in this direction and purchased kits from the local hobby store for his son to build with all the care of a heart surgeon. When Roberto was nineteen he had left home and joined the crew of a cargo ship. The eagerness of this young man and his willing spirit had caught the eye of each succeeding ship's captain and before long he had worked his way up to the bridge. After that he had taken shore leave to complete the studies necessary to attain his own captaincy.

Because of his total dedication to the sea, Roberto had never taken the time to court the ladies and, although he certainly had the normal desires of any young man, his devotion to his chosen profession had just not made time to pursue this avenue.

Alaska
Wednesday, October 5, 11:17 a.m.

It was bitter cold. Even the locals here in Anchorage were complaining about the sudden cold snap that seemed to show up at the most unexpected times here on the south coast of this great state. After all, Anchorage is located along the Humboldt Current that flows in an eastward arc along the Aleutians and then follows the coast line down to the lower forty-eight. This pattern caused the south coast to have more favorable weather than the interior parts of the state, but there was that occasional pressure from the north that seemed determined to let the inhabitants of the milder climate know that they were, after all, Alaskans.

Fernell Suffort suffered more for two very obvious reasons: He was Indonesian and from the tropics. The coldest days in his homeland would have been welcomed in this part of the world in the summer months. His team had arrived by air only two days before and all nine of them had been kept busy by renting trucks and autos needed in their mission assignment. You just couldn't walk into the local Anchorage Ryder rental *en masse* to rent four trucks and two automobiles when your nationality was Indonesian. Each

9

individual assigned the task of making the rental had been carefully selected with the ability to pass themselves off as Native Americans. This meant that the each one had to be fluent in the English language, but with just enough accent to reflect their "Indian heritage."

After spacing their rentals over a period of the past two days and from the four rental agencies (the two autos were rented at the airport to take the pressure off the local availability), the vehicles were relocated to different locations to create dispersion and dispel any queries as to why so many trucks were parked in the same area. The same care would be exercised when it was time to go to the Port Authority to pick up the incoming cargo that had been shipped much earlier.

It was now time to conduct the loading operations and make the necessary preparations to move out to the various designated locations. It was decided that the point of departure should be from Fairbanks, so the loaded vehicles would be required to make the long trip north in what could end up being inclement weather.

Their cell leader had made the decision that the trucks would move in pairs with the autos a convenient distance from each of the sets of trucks. If there were problems with mechanics, weather, or even police encounters, it would be best that there would be sufficient personnel to handle any one of these contingencies. The best manner of addressing these situations was accommodated by the makeup of each team in the convoy. The chance of some road patrol discovering the nature of the vehicles and their cargo would be eliminated by immediate termination of any such discoverer.

The cargo pickup was to occur at Homer, situated some one hundred miles to the south of Anchorage, down the Kenai Peninsula. The drivers were to leave Anchorage and travel the distance so as to arrive at the Port of Homer at staggered times ranging from 10 a.m. to noon. Inquiry at one of the local gas stations revealed that the trip would take them approximately two and a half hours if they didn't encounter any problems. This meant that each driver would add a full hour to his planning and that way there would be a period of rest just north of town should the trip be uneventful.

On the designated morning the vehicles had arrived at the Port of Homer; traveling from separate directions so as to preclude any pattern if anybody were watching. Of course, the chances of that were so remote that it really had not even been necessary. However, discipline and thorough training caused one to be always careful even when the situation did not call for it. It was always the unexpected little things that tripped up individuals involved in the business of intrigue. Fernell was not about to overlook a single detail on this most important mission.

The loading of the trucks went so smoothly as to cause the cell members to wonder if they had been set up. Two of the longshoremen had been eager to assist their fellow Native Americans around the normal "red tape" and the trucks were loaded with the "generators" in less than half the normal time required. The Indonesian Muslims attributed all this as an omen from Allah that He was "making their paths straight."

Once the vehicles were loaded they were to immediately head back up north to Anchorage and to their designated holding area to await the arrival of the rest of the cell members. When all the vehicles were back in Anchorage, Fernell directed each of them to go to separate service stations and top off their fuel tanks. He didn't want to stop until absolutely necessary on the way north.

The entourage went to their designated start points and was on the road in less than half an hour from the time the last of the cargo transports had been reached by the last truck. In order to avoid any contact absolutely unnecessary, one member from each cell section had gone into the local fast food establishments and purchased for the entire crew—to go. They would have plenty of time to consume their meals while on the road. The members had been careful to carry an abundant supply of the strong Indonesian coffee in their personal baggage. It would be welcomed in the next couple days to both, keep them alert, and provide some relief from the bitter cold they would encounter.

The travel to the northern destination would require them to get onto Highway 1 out of Anchorage and switch to Highway 3 just south of Wasilla, some fifty miles north of Anchorage. From there the convoy would continue on through Talkeetna to Chase and on to Cantwell much further in their travel. From there it was a short distance to Healy and Anderson before reaching Fairbanks. The total distance was in excess of 320 miles in a land that could produce any number of difficulties, especially at this time of the year.

Occurrences mocked their attention to detail and contingency plans as they encountered not a single incident in the long drive to Fairbanks. This route was one of beauty, but presented several areas where disaster could result, and there was a chance that no one would ever notice it due to the rarity of traffic at this time of year. Arrival was ahead of schedule as the roads had been recently snow-plowed and the low temperature had frozen solid the occasional bog they might have had trouble negotiating. One of the vehicle convoy entourage had to halt for a short time to give a cantankerous bull moose the right of way in crossing. Even that was a welcomed sight as the members of that sub-cell would have quite a story to tell at some future date.

Much of the discussion among the various members of the sub-cells had centered on the short daylight in this part of the globe. The sun had risen in a clear sky at approximately 10:30 in the morning and had set a mere three hours later. Even at its peak, the sun was very low on the horizon and gave the day an eerie twilight atmosphere. As they continued on toward the northern destiny there would be a pronounced shortening of the daylight hours. The people who lived here must be a very strange breed indeed!

Arrival in Fairbanks was not to change their existence to any degree. Hotel accommodations in that city were so sparse that their comings and goings would be certain to draw attention, so the participants made the best of situations in the vehicles available and had slept in them as best they could. They dare not try to sleep without the engines running and the efficient heaters working. Anyone doing so would have been frozen to death before midnight. With the pending mission they would need to get as much rest as possible, but it is an impossibility to "bank" sleep. Further, the excitement of the mission and the approaching hour of its onset were designed to keep them semi-conscious throughout most of that night.

The team had been instructed to be very careful when going outside at night, as the occasional grizzly bear would still be delaying hibernation in pursuit of one last meal. For that reason, there was a mass exodus of the vehicles once the entire team had risen for the day. It gave a new meaning to "yellow snow."

Two hours later the cell members had begun to disperse toward their designated positions, but not before a lengthy session of morning prayers to ensure their successful accomplishment. The travel from this point would be challenging and arduous.

The first and second sub-cells took Highway 6 toward the northeast as they headed toward Circle Hot Springs. The latter two sub-cells would head to the southeast on Highway 2 from Fairbanks in the direction of Big Delta. There the two elements would split up with the fourth group taking Highway 4 to the south of Big Delta. Each member of the parties was well schooled on the routes to be taken and had conducted extensive map studies of the area in order to conduct their respective missions without a hitch.

By the prescribed times each of the four groups had negotiated the distances necessary to reach their appointed area of operations. Everything was going smoothly. Praise be to Allah!

Damascus
Thursday, September 8, 7:34 p. m.

Abu Bin Hadj was in a foul mood. Normally, a friendly sort, he had gone for nearly four days now without sleep and his demeanor was the victim of a large burden of fatigue. Early in the developmental stages of "The Movement" it had been determined that compartmentalization was the key to success. Patriots involved in the Movement must be kept completely isolated from the rest of the brotherhood. There were bound to be casualties in this just cause and no individual could withstand the examination by torture without giving up other members of the group. While this proved to be a wise decision, the downside was the fact that larger areas of responsibilities would be required from the operatives.

Every plan had to be broken down into group tasks. In the international movement there were nine separate area groups operating in areas of ethnicities and geographies. Within each of these groups were teams specializing in various technicalities based upon their abilities brought to the movement during examination and recruitment. Within the teams were cells with the capability of operating independently while supporting an operation they probably had no idea of the target or desired outcome. The important element was the fact that nobody even knew who members of peer cells, teams, or groups were. In fact, they could not divulge even their own chain of command, as all assignments were passed by dead drops and blind passes. A cell would be given a set of tasks to be accomplished and a schedule for the events. No deviation in either case was tolerated. Infractions of even the slightest detail were dealt with on a permanent basis. There could be no failures!

It was during the last weeks that Abu Bin Hadj had been given a series of tasks by the Patriarch. His responsibility was to select the team (or teams) to accomplish these tasks. It was in the assignment of the tasks that protocol had been set aside by the Patriarch. Rather than just pass along the mission, the emir had taken the time to relate the significance of the operation to the four area commanders involved. Abu had an almost uncanny ability to hide his emotions at any given time. However, he had left the meeting with the weight of the world on his shoulders.

Time has an ability to become flexible. Some periods of our lives are measured as rapid when others are seemingly lengthy. It is not the elapsed time that determines the speed with which it passes. Instead, it is the circumstances or events that take place during that period which give rise to the duration of the time. It was only about one hundred hours ago that Abu had risen from his bed in a suburb of Damascus to see that his "trip" had been activated.

He had dressed quickly and left his home in the usual meandering walk that would lead him to several of his known drops until he found the one which would produce the message he needed to retrieve. He would never take the time to read the instructions until he safely returned to his home. The walk would continue in a meandering manner, just in case anyone was observing his activities.

He was somewhat surprised to find that he was to go on a trip of some length. He would drive to Damascus International Airport and catch a flight to Athens. From there he would fly to Cairo and finally, board a third leg of the journey to Morocco. He was unsure if that would be his final destination and, other than normal curiosity, he didn't really care. His focus was fixed upon his duty to follow his instructions to the minutest detail. It did not matter if the mission was of high importance or "housekeeping" matters. He would not deviate his attention to detail as long as there was breath in his body.

Abu arrived in Morocco in time for evening prayers and was anxious to reaffirm his devotion to Allah since he had missed his two other obligations while en route. He would take his time to honor his faith before he returned to the hotel he was told to check into. Although he was famished, he waited until after prayers to attend to his personal desires. Somehow it made him feel refreshed to acknowledge his devotion to Allah by fasting.

Travel accomplished as it was today seemed draining. Each leg of the trip had been under a different alias. He was well practiced in changing identity by appearance and in name. He left Damascus as Doctor Mohamed Said, with the appropriate credentials of an Egyptian physician. When he boarded the plane in Athens he had become Ahmed Wahid, a respected engineer from Yemen. The man arriving from Cairo on the last portion of the flight was Mahmud Abdul Zaki, a distinguished member of the diplomatic corps of Egypt. He would be in Morocco to study irrigation techniques.

His accommodations had been taken care of by the *charge d'affaires*, who in reality had been a member of a local cell who had no idea why the hierarchy had decided it was in their interest to make arrangements for some Egyptian diplomat with very low credentials. Regardless, the orders had been received and it was the duty of every patriot to follow the direction without a thought given to the sanity behind it. After a leisurely dinner at a delightful restaurant, Abu (or Mr. Zaki) had gone back to his room to find a comfortable bed and uninterrupted sleep.

Abu was awakened by the morning calls to prayer and, although it was approximately 5:30, the bright morning sun was cutting through the draperies of his suite. He arose from his bed and went through his ritual of purification (shower and personal grooming) before he began his early morning prayers. He had scarcely accomplished this when there was a knock on his door. Approaching the portal, he discovered an envelope had been passed under it and he didn't even bother to open the door. Instead, he moved directly to the table and opened the seal on the envelope.

Abu had been summoned to a meeting that would begin at nine o'clock that morning. A car would come by the hotel and he was to be ready to immediately enter the back seat, where he would be taken to the meeting site by the driver. This would give him ample time to go down to the hotel restaurant and have a leisurely breakfast before he had to depart the hotel. Since no instructions had been made with regard to checking out, he assumed he would be returning for still another night. This was more than strange, since normally such meetings were limited to short duration and the attendees dispersed before any pattern could be established.

Precisely at 9 a.m., the vehicle pulled up in front of the hotel and he was gestured to get in. Almost as soon as he entered the vehicle and before he had fully closed the door, the car lurched ahead and made a series of rapid turns and backtracks to shake any would-be tails, which were unlikely. Once the driver had assured himself that he was not being followed he became relaxed and began to concentrate on an elaborate route planned with intricate detail. The trip took nearly an hour, but as near as Abu could ascertain, did not cover a distance of more than fifteen kilometers before pulling up a long driveway of a villa straight out of a movie set for the rich and famous. The driver pulled up to the front and, after a prearranged signal from the entry way, continued on to the rear entry of the mansion and came to a stop.

"You are to go directly into the back door and go into the second room on the right as you enter. Go into the room and you will be given further instructions." The driver was as poker-faced and unemotional in this script as if he were teaching his child to tie his shoes.

Abu found the back door open and proceeded directly as charged, closing the door behind him once he entered the prescribed room. He was the only occupant of the room. Nearly half an hour lapsed with no sound or indication of what the purpose of his mission was from Damascus. The only piece of furniture in the room was a basic kitchen chair, which he availed himself to await further developments.

When he had just about given up on anyone acknowledging his presence, the door opened and two very large men came in. Without a word, the men placed a blindfold over his eyes and then placed a cloth bag over his entire head. That accomplished, the two men positioned themselves on each side of him and lifted him to a standing position, conducting him from the room and into the hallway he had been in when he entered the back door.

He became aware that there were others in the hallway and discerned that others were being led in the same manner as he from other rooms in the hallway. Several turns were negotiated and he was once more deposited into a chair that was probably a match with the one he had been sitting in the previous half hour. He sensed as well as heard the others being seated much in the same manner. Once the movement stopped, his head cover and blindfold were removed.

Once his eyes became adjusted to the low level of light he noticed that he was seated in a cubicle that was enclosed on both sides and the back by heavy curtains. Noise coming from either side indicated that there were people in matching cubicles on his left and right. Indications were that there might be more individuals in similar situations beyond his immediate neighbors. The number of participants was impossible to determine, but he suspected that there were at least four, and even maybe a couple more.

In front of him was another cubicle that was placed in a manner to be visible from all the other enclosures as well. However, the front of the cubicle was covered with a semi-transparent curtain of gauze which was designed to allow visible verification of a man seated in a large chair with heavy arms. The location of the light source was such that no features of the seated member could be ascertained, but when the voice came from the veiled enclosure, there could be no doubt whom it was. He was in the immediate presence of the Patriarch.

A hushed silence fell over the room as each of the area commanders present recognized the eminence of the patriarchal presence of their Holy Leader. As far as Abu was concerned, this was the closest anyone knowingly had ever been to the Patriarch. This fact alone made it apparent that something of gigantic proportions was about to occur.

"My brothers," the voice from behind the curtain began, "you are about to become a part of the greatest event since the Movement was inspired by Allah. For over four millennia now we have been denied our rightful position as the firstborn of our Father Abram. The patriarch, Ishmael, was the rightful heir to the blessings due from Father Abram. It was only through the deceptiveness of his younger half-brother that the birthright was pilfered.

"It was only in the last century that the infidels gained their foothold in our lands. They had their willing backers from the satanic West and were able to infiltrate our ancient lands and make a mockery of Allah. I am here to tell you that they will not prevail!

"The evil empires of the West have become powerful because of their ill-gotten gains in the financial world. In so doing, they have become drunk on the fruits of the Holy Land. They have become totally dependent upon oil to maintain their evil intention to keep the people of Allah from achieving their rightful place of leadership in the entire world.

"Well, all that is about to come to an end. You brothers in this very room will be the soldiers of Allah in this great victory. During the next few weeks you are not only going to witness the fall of the West, but you will become the instrument by which this glorious day will become a fact."

If the room was quiet before, then the silence became deafening at this point. Although every member of the Movement was well versed on the historical facts of the Sons of Ishmael, to hear it coming from the very lips of the Patriarch gave a new and fresh perspective. Before long, Abu could feel the tears of emotion streaming down his cheeks as the old cleric continued to pour out his heart and soul before them. He went on to tell how the infidels of the West had come to their lands and wreaked carnage in the name of their God. The Crusades by the hated Catholic Christians had almost decimated the true believers a mere five-hundred years before.

After a lengthy dissertation of the histories of their people, the tenor of the Patriarch's voice began to change as he laid out his plan to bring the hated West to their knees. The economy of the West was more fragile than they would like to admit. It seems that the least of changes to the prevailing conditions could cause the stock market to dive to disproportionate levels. Well, they were in for a catastrophe that they would never forget. Although the impact would affect the entire world, it was just deserts to countries like Japan and the European lackeys who had stood by while the hated Americans had dominated the rest of the world. If someone could just interrupt the economic balance for a period of half a year it would take a decade for them to recover. By then it would be too late.

The rest of the time in Morocco was filled with detailing the attack and assigning specific tasks to the attendees. The organization was so well controlled that not a single participant ever made contact with another and the secrecy of the organization remained in tact. The enormity of the requirements that faced Abu was mind boggling. To add to the frustration was the fact that not a single note had been taken during the entire three days before departure. Each member was grilled repeatedly by the "instructors" as to the intricacies of their specific tasks. Not only was the assignment critical, but the timing of each event was geared toward the entire mission. Each element had to be performed at precisely the right time. This was no small undertaking, since the actions required would fall into whole spectrum of time zones. Only the initial times were to be local in nature; after that the operation would proceed as a military operation using "H" hours to maintain control.

Abu could scarcely remember the return trip to Damascus, but was aware that it was a retracing of the original trip and identities, in reverse order. It would have been helpful to have cat-napped on the return, but the enormity of the burden placed on his shoulders required his full attention and would not allow the needed sleep to come.

He arrived back in Damascus International just after 1400 hours and had to undergo the delays that were ever present in the world's airports before he finally returned to his automobile for the drive home. Regardless of where "home" is, there is always an uplift of the spirits when one reaches it. The familiar surroundings cause a certain comfort to come over the occupant and allows for total relaxation.

But there was no time for relaxation just yet. Abu began a systematic review of the tasks and personnel required to ensure success. He was tempted to put pen to paper, but the admonishment from the Patriarch had placed a burden of guilt that could only come from the throne of Allah for any person who did so.

His wife was excited to see him and wanted to discuss the happenings of his sojourn, even though she had always been rebuffed in all his previous trips. She just never gave up. His firm response to her seemed to be taken as a personal attack when he would not even discuss where he had been and his accommodations. It was always the same. She would leave the room with the same hurt look on her face and from somewhere in the reaches of the house he would hear her scolding one of the children. Well, she would get over it and he would find some time in the next few days to show her his devotion to her.

As was his custom, he organized his thoughts into compartmental areas and concentrated exclusively in that area until he had explored every facet to the minutest detail before moving to another compartmented area. He would need to schedule his meetings with the necessary "assets" on a scheduled basis. To maintain compartmental requirements would necessitate going through the normal blind drops and secret contacts. Finally, the task member would need to hear directly from himself the intricacies of the mission. This was always accomplished by telephone with elaborate counter-surveillance techniques. The tasked agent was not even allowed to inform his chain of command concerning any aspect or reason for the mission. After the action was completed, the leaders involved would draw their own conclusions as to the role played by their charge, but the matter would never be brought up in the future.

After he had addressed each task in the operation he began to think about individuals qualified for the activities. He could not resort to personal recognition, since he had never breached the requirement to remain anonymous to others in the Movement. His selection would be based upon past successes (or lack of) from the various elements of his command. Without relating the mission details, he would relate the skills needed and would allow the subordinates to determine who would best fill the requirements. It came as almost a surprise to discover the number of individuals this matter would require. He could only imagine what his peers would be developing in their planning cycles. He was, however, certain that each one would go about this phase with the same dedication as he was determined to give.

Once he was certain that he had all the details worked out in his mind, he finally gave in to the fatigue that was coursing through his entire body. It was important to get some rest and then to recover his thoughts of the evening. His head hardly met the pillow before he was in a deep sleep. His complete expenditure of all his strength and emotions was such that he didn't even dream. When he once more opened his eyes it was evening of the following day.

— 2 —

Alaska
Saturday, October 8, 6:12 a.m.

Before leaving Fairbanks, each of the trucks had gone to separate locations to top off the fuel tanks and fill the "jerry cans" with additional fuel that would be required while completing the missions each sub-team was to fulfill. There were a total of four separate destinations, so each truck and its two-man crew had been on their own from their individual points of separation. The full cellular team would not reassemble until they were safely back in Jakarta and there would be no need to do so then.

Fernell had decided to accompany the vehicle with the least distance to travel and selected the various vehicles and crew members to assign to each mission. He elected to have one of his two crewmates drive the vehicle and was quite pleased with the seriousness on the man's face as he maneuvered the truck with the skill of a professional driver. Even though the destination of his vehicle was the shortest in distance and travel time, it would still take a minimum of seven hours to negotiate the distance. Before leaving Fairbanks he had once more admonished the other drivers that there was plenty of time to reach their destinations and still exercise the required caution determined by the terrain and weather conditions. He went over the preparations and expectations with renewed attention to detail as he sat in the right hand passenger seat of the truck jostling its way cross-country.

The Alaska Pipeline is one of the marvels of modern technology. Tasked to move tremendous amounts of oil across heretofore thought impossible distances and through some of the worst terrain and conditions imaginable, it had operated for more that two decades with results even better than the engineers had expected. The environmental achievements had been more than met and yet delivered a continuous supply of the crude to various parts of the world with reliability.

Oh yes, there had been that nasty incident when the drunk sea captain had run his vessel aground and caused the "tree huggers" to go ballistic way back in the past, but the safety record and enhancements to the ecology by the fact that the pipeline had been built had, for the most part, silenced that crowd long ago.

It took the planned seven hours to reach the designated point of the pipeline and, although it was quite dark when they did, the huge profile of the pipe with its supporting columns loomed out of the darkness like a giant tree lying on the ground waiting to be cut into logs for transport to some distant sawmill.

The three men decided to wait until the following day to complete their activities and took advantage of the camping equipment they had brought along to establish their home for the next few days. This proved to be more of a task than they had anticipated, because the tent had frozen to its own image even though it had been stowed in the back of the truck. It took some time to clear out a place to set the tent up, but the energy that it took to do so helped to keep their bodies from freezing in the extreme weather conditions.

There was, however, no way that you could keep your face and hands from icing up and becoming painful to the touch. If you tried to work with the heavy mittens on it became impossible to secure the tent loops and pegs. It became an assembly line operation. One person would doff the gloves for a couple of minutes and work at a feverish pitch and then the next member of the team would take over and then rotate repeatedly until the campsite was satisfactorily in place.

The camp was placed some distance from the pipeline and in an area with cover and concealment. This was to prevent the accidental discovery by some inspection team that might come out to check the pipeline. This was highly unlikely, but no possible contingency was left to chance. The actual work to be accomplished would take less than an hour. The team members did mention that it was a good thing that they had the chance to exercise a work effort when the camp was set up to provide a basis for timing the work to be accomplished.

Now that the camp had been established there was little left to do but to wait for the appointed "H" hour to arrive. None of the team members could figure out why it was so important to accomplish their task precisely at the specified time and date; however, they had long ago learned that there was a definite reason for every detail of every mission. It was not necessary for them to understand why; they must obey completely every facet of the mission as given.

The other team sub-cells had performed in the expected professionalism learned in many months, or even years, of servitude. Each team was expected to arrive at a certain point along the pipeline and establish their base camp in the same manner as their leader had instructed them. This was actually a positive situation as far as they were concerned. They did not have to improvise for any situation that might arise. There was a plan for any situation, regardless of how remote the chance of such a contingency.

It was only the team to the south who had to exercise any of the contingency plans. They had scarcely set up their camp when a forest ranger appeared out of the blue before they had any opportunity to observe his approach. He simply strolled into their campsite and entered their tent unannounced.

"You boys sure picked quite a set of weather conditions to be out here huntin'," he grinned as he gestured to their weapons lying around the shelter. "I guess I need to check yer huntin' licenses just for the record," he continued to the startled two men in the tent.

The ranger was packing a pistol on his waistband but, from the looks of it, it only came out for cleaning and storage.

"Since when did us Indians have to get a license to feed our families?" the taller of the two men queried the official in as good-natured humor as was called for in this situation. "Aw, heck, Buckley, guess I'll have to get out my reservation card for the nice man." With that he reached into his backpack and pulled out a .357 magnum revolver and, in a clean and deliberate move, brought the pistol around and fired twice directly into the ranger's face.

Blood sprayed all over the end of the tent and the ranger seemed to stand frozen in time for nearly a second before his lifeless eyes understood the shock of his ended life. Without hesitation, the two men dragged the dead man's body out of the tent and over to a crevice some fifty meters away and casually rolled him into the gap. As concerned as they might have been in carrying out the garbage, they went about the task of hiding his corpse before they returned to the tent.

"Do you think he was all alone out here?" one of the men voiced.

"I don't know, but we better find out," his cohort answered and immediately both men got up and began seeking the footprints in the snow in order to backtrack the approach of the forest ranger. It didn't take long to discover the boot prints of the officer, and they warily made the distance some two-hundred meters to where there was a large four-wheel-drive Hummer. A cursory inspection indicated that the ranger had been all alone when he arrived and had probably smelled the smoke from their camp stove in their tent. A two-way radio and microphone were dangling from a make-shift hook near the console.

"Do you think he might have given a radio call before he came to our tent?" one of the men queried.

"I doubt it, but there's one way to check—Field to base, over … " the man stated into the microphone in a manner that sounded authentic. A long pause was allowed and the call was repeated. There was a faint breaking of the squelch, but no discernable message came over the receiver. It was obvious that the radio was in a position where no contact would have been possible.

"Allah be praised!" the second man nearly shouted as he cast his eyes heavenward. "It would have been tragic if the ranger's whereabouts were known to his headquarters. The other team member was being more pragmatic and began an investigation of the journal lying on the passenger seat. The only entry in the journal for today was a terse "09:00—inspection of quadrant #4." The time was now 17:00, so he had probably been negligent in his contact reports.

Besides, it was Sunday and the infidels always went to church because their Pope had told them to. It was unlikely that anyone would miss the guy before a couple of days and by then it wouldn't matter.

The other two teams had little difficulty in negotiating the rough roads to their designated points. Set up was routine and they had been in place a full day before they were to begin their actual mission.

Three days after their departure from Fairbanks each of the four sub-cells arose from sleep and began the task of placing huge charges of plastic explosives on the pipeline. Not only did they place their charges at the strategic points of the pipeline, but huge explosive devices were set on the adjacent pilings upon which the pipeline rested. When the explosion occurred there would be large craters created to prevent any rapid repairs. It was estimated that a minimum of one hundred feet of the pipeline would be vaporized and the craters would attain a depth of approximately twenty feet. These craters and the local area would be filled with crude oil and make excavation of the blast site nearly impossible without major equipment being in place. During this time of year the movement of such equipment would be nearly impossible, due to the elements. No, this pipeline would not begin to operate again for the greater part of a year. H-hour had been established as midnight on the October 12—tomorrow night!

The Panama Canal
Wednesday, October 12, 7:52 p.m.

The *Corona Princes* was under the direct control of the Panamanian pilot who had boarded the vessel just northeast of the canal entry. Years of skillful steering of all types and sizes of seagoing vessels could have made him complacent in his moving of the huge oil tanker through the lakes and locks of the canal, but his professionalism caused him to exercise the same preciseness as was his custom after twenty-three years in this service.

That fact did not completely dispel the certain tenseness of Captain Uberhausen. Although he tried to hide the fact, he never relished the relinquishing of command to some unknown, regardless of the capabilities of the pilot. To ease his tensions, he had relocated to his personal quarters to wait the time when the ship would be returned to his personal control. That would be approximately two and one half hours from now, so he might just as well relax and take advantage of the opportunity to catch up on his letter writing.

His wife, Helga, had long ago learned to accept Oleg's periods of departure as a norm of life. They had been married for nearly half a century now and she had learned to accept his love affair with the sea. He would come home after two months at sea and dote upon her every whim for ten days before it was time to leave again. The first two days would be spent getting reacquainted and then they would honeymoon for the next week. In fact, Helga seemed to enjoy her lifestyle and used his periods of absence to get involved with her love of painting. She always enjoyed his letters and shared much of the general information with her neighbors.

He had just begun his latest letter home when there was a knock on his cabin door. When he turned the latch a sudden burst of energy hit the door from the other side and nearly threw him across the cabin. Before him stood two of his crew members, but they were no longer part of that crew. Each of the men were carrying AK-47s and pointing them directly at his head and chest. He started to protest when one of the men hit him on the side of the head with what appeared to be a small baseball bat.

"Shut your filthy infidel mouth, you son of a pig, if you want to live five minutes longer!" one of the brutes said to him in a manner of complete contempt, but leaving no doubt that every word he said would be backed up with action at the slightest provocation. Captain Uberhausen was no coward, but he was no fool either. It was better just wait and see what they want and not make a bad situation even worse, he thought to himself.

His absolute surprise at these happenings was obviously apparent and his captors seemed to delight in his confusion.

"So, how do you like us being the new captains of this miserable bucket, you filthy swine?"

The man making the comments had been one of his best men for well over half a year now. He had been ready to promote him when they reached home port and the sea captain could not believe that these words were coming from one of his most favored deck hands.

The other man seemed somewhat frightened but was exhibiting signs of demonic possession. His eyes held a cruel stare and there was a hint of a smile coming from the corners of his mouth.

"C'mon, lets just kill him and get it over with," the second man said in a high-pitched voice that indicated his fear and, at the same time, lack of any conscience. Fortunately, the first man seemed to be in control and a swift backhand across the face of his cohort produced the silence that he desired.

"You will stick to the plan!" his leader hissed in his direction with all the authority of a Marines drill sergeant.

He turned to the captain and began to address him in a more civil manner now that his authority had been gained.

"You are not so bad for an infidel, but you have been a part of the system that has exploited our people and Allah for too long now. It is not my desire to kill you, but you must understand that I will do so without the slightest remorse if you do not immediately comply with every order I give you. Do you understand?"

All that Captain Oleg could do was nod his head in a reassuring manner.

"Good, now you are to remain here with my brother and not give him cause to kill you before I come back. I can assure you he will do just that if you give him the slightest cause to do so." With that, Mr. Amood left the room and closed the door.

Amood had already put into practice a plan that had been in the making for a long time now. His cohorts had subdued various members of the crew without alerting anyone on the bridge and were actually in control of the vessel as it glided into the world-famed Panama Canal. As the water craft continued on its way there were locks to be negotiated and lakes to cross as the ship made its way—northwest to southeast—from the Atlantic Ocean to the Pacific.

No one on the bridge was aware of any reason for caution or fear. That is the reason that there was a brief moment of time when the reason for that fear and the actual realization that it was there lapsed. Suddenly, the entire vessel shook violently as a huge explosion erupted from somewhere in the vessel. Simultaneously, a huge gap opened in the bottom of the hull, spilling the entire contents of oil into the narrow confines of the canal. The ship immediately sank to the bottom of the canal. The depth of the canal and the size of the ship allowed for the main deck to remain above the water line but the tremendous blast had only served to ignite the ship's cargo and now all that was left was an inferno that contained a mixture of black smoke with fierce flames. Not a single soul was left alive aboard the ship, nor for some one hundred meters surrounding the canal. The Panama Canal was closed and could not be opened again for several months of monolithic efforts.

At precisely the same instant, the *Valhalla Express* was in the narrowest portion of the Suez Canal. Captain Sanchez had relinquished his stewardship of the vessel to a fine young Egyptian pilot who treated the former with the utmost respect and even apologized for having to make the transition of leadership. Neither the polite young officer nor the ship's captain had the slightest idea of what was taking place a few meters away.

The new crew members had accomplished the same mission as had their counterparts halfway around the world. The only variance was the fact that each of them had completed their individual task and managed to leap over the side of the vessel and land on the edges of the canal before the tremendous explosion took place. They might just as well have stayed onboard since the fireball created by the explosion of the *Valhalla Express* placed them well within the kill zone when the charges deep in the ship exploded.

Once more, there were no survivors within one hundred fifty meters of the doomed ship. Like the *Corona Princes,* the *Valhalla* went immediately to the bottom of the canal. Like its sister ship, there would be no rapid removal and it would be months before world shipping did not have to circumnavigate the Cape of Good Hope or the Straits of Magellan. The world's shipping had been drastically changed in a matter of a few minutes.

Alaska
Wednesday, October 12, 11:33 p.m.

During the past twelve hours each member of the Indonesian Muslim cell had been going about their tasks with a deftness that extolled precision. The charges had been placed in exactly the manner they had drilled on back in Jakarta for a full week prior to the trip north. All was accomplished. Every piece of equipment had been picked up and accounted for. There was no evidence that anyone had ever been camped in the area. The only evidence of foul play, the ranger's corpse and his vehicle, had been moved to the direct impact area of the cratering charge. There would be no remaining evidence that he or his vehicle had ever existed in half an hour. To cap it all off, there was a snow storm beginning to cover their tracks as the last vehicle began to depart the area. The last task before departure—the setting of the timer for midnight—was set and rechecked before pulling out.

Fernell had settled down in the middle of the front seat so as to allow the second member of the sub-cell to literally act as "shotgun." Although he had managed to get some sleep, his total hours of rest had been less than half of what he normally required. The snow falling into the glare of the headlights seemed to have a hypnotic effect upon him and after a short distance his teammate jabbed him in the ribs to silence his snoring.

To the north and south of Fernell and his cohorts were brothers doing exactly the same as his team. The points of attack were situated approximately twenty-five kilometers apart and at locations selected for their inaccessibility. This was going to be one monster of an attack upon the hated United States and their willing lackeys.

At precisely midnight a series of huge explosions rocked the countryside around the Alaska Pipeline. No living human even heard the blasts, but they would certainly feel the concussion of it for months to come. Some low-level engineer down in Valdez would be the first to notice the abnormality when the flow of oil came to a gradual halt over a short period of time. At first he would check all his gauges to ensure they were working properly, but before long he would be on the "red phone" to alert his superiors to God-knows-what. By then the members of the Indonesian Muslim cell would be well on their way out of the area. The sudden snowstorm made it certain that no aircraft would be checking the area; much less for vehicular traffic.

As it turned out, it was the team farthest south that was to encounter problems during egress from the blast site. The storm had intensified in the southern sector and was causing large snowdrifts to build up in numerous areas. The truck was having difficulty in maintaining forward momentum and still keep the vehicle on the makeshift roadway built by the Forest Service years earlier. More than once the rear duals had slid dangerously close to the ditch parallel to the roadway and the snow continued to fall unabated. This condition was not one that allowed the driver to fall back on past experience. You just didn't get much practice driving on snow down in the tropics. The driver and passenger were experiencing charges of adrenalin in sufficient capacities to completely dissipate their drowsiness.

This nerve-wracking situation continued for mile after mile and the snow, which had previously been called a blessing by covering their tracks, was now the subject of much prayer to Allah. It wouldn't do for them to become stuck or be in an accident now that they were so close to success. The thought entered their minds for the dozens of times when the vehicle suddenly jerked to the left. The driver, being unaccustomed to snow driving, turned the steering wheel violently to the right and slammed on the brakes.

There are certain things you must avoid doing when an automobile begins a skid on ice or snow. The same things apply doubly when you are driving a truck. Proof of this physical law was immediate and unavoidable. The truck attempted to do a series of three-hundred-sixty-degree turns but was prevented from doing so because the spinning vehicle left the roadway and began to roll sideways and end-over-end several times before it came to rest, nose down and upside down in a raging stream.

Both doors were blocked by huge boulders and all the glass had become splinters when the truck was making its way down the steep embankment. The injured occupants had tried to crawl out of the hole made by the missing windshield, but there was a large tree trunk wedged in the way. Both occupants were severely injured but might have made it were it not for the freezing water and having no one to assist them for miles away. Both men managed to stay alive long enough to give their final praises to Allah, but in the end both ended up cursing their miserable death.

No one would be there to mourn their passing. Their families had no idea that they were on this mission and would never even be told what happened.

"Tell me about those seventy virgins in paradise again … "

Each of the remaining trucks made the return trip to Anchorage and was turned in without fanfare. The managers of these facilities were used to high mileage since anywhere you went in Alaska was of great distance. The fact that each vehicle was subject to high mileage was looked upon with glee since truck rentals in the winter months were slow and, at best, for local runs only. This is probably why the renting "Indians" had not been checked too thoroughly when they rented the vehicles. Before turning the trucks back to the rental agencies, the drivers had carefully washed them inside and out. While the rental agent certainly appreciated his vehicles being spotlessly clean, it was not done for his benefit. The leasing parties did not want to leave the least identifying mark to trace back to them.

When the driver returned the truck to Ryder, the manager of the agency asked him if he had seen another of their trucks while coming back to town. "No, we saw very little traffic on the road and we would have noticed another Ryder truck. I don't know if we even traveled the same route anyway. Sorry."

By happenstance, two of the sub-cell teams observed each other while waiting for boarding out of Anchorage International. Neither team gave any acknowledgment to each other. All four of the Indonesian Muslim cells were dressed in much the style of the local Native Americans and made attempts of avoiding any situation where they might be forced to encounter one of their "Indian brothers." That could have been very embarrassing at the least and dangerous at worst. All four faked sleep while they waited for departure. One sub-cell would fly directly to Tokyo and the other to Seattle on the first leg of the trip. Neither knew, nor cared, what the other would be doing en route to their homeland.

As the Muslim men were waiting in the Anchorage airport, CNN was covering the huge news stories coming off the wire. It seems that both the Suez and Panama Canals had been the subject of huge accidents. Teams of experts were en route to the scene of both catastrophes and reports were continuing to come in from both locations. The scene switched to Washington, D.C., where there were reports of some significant catastrophic event occurring in Alaska. It seems that the huge Alaska Pipeline had been shut down for the first time on an unscheduled closure. News was sketchy but the look of concern on the face of the secretary of energy indicated that this was more than insignificant. He informed the journalists in the room that he was personally on top of it and would keep them informed as developments became known.

— 3 —

Washington, D.C.
Thursday, October 13 8:00 a.m.

The State Department of the United States was operating at crisis level and contacts between the secretary of state and the secretary of defense were seen heading into the White House well before the morning rush in the nation's capital. It was rumored that the entire cabinet had been at 1600 Pennsylvania Avenue since late last night. So far, the president had not addressed the nation but the major stations had been requested to provide air time at 8 p.m.

It seems a tight news blackout was being affected and the major networks were, for once, not speculating but reporting the obvious without much comment. The worried looks on their faces were enough to raise the spectrum that something enormous had just taken place and equally apparent that no one at this point was up to the task of deciding what to do about it.

This was not something new to the world. The events of September 11, 2001 had provided ample opportunity for the public to understand the lengths to which enemies of the West would go to inflict harm. Most people on the street were convinced that it was the enemies from the Middle East who were responsible for the terrible events that had taken place during the previous night, but government officials were not ready to comment formally regarding the matter. Leaks were coming with machine-gun rapidity that everyone in government was leaning toward the same conclusions.

Ambassadors from the entire Middle Eastern bloc were coming and going at the White House and seeking any air time they could manage to "assure the American people that we are your best friends." The United Nations Security Council was called into emergency session, but with only sketchy information it had about as much significance as if the Boy Scouts had called a high-level meeting.

It wasn't until nearly noon that a picture was developing to determine the magnitude of the attack. By now all the major networks were calling it just that. The chance that these three major events would occur at precisely the same minute, on a world-wide basis, left no doubt that this was a coordinated attempt to disrupt the entire world's oil supply. The impact was just now beginning to emerge to those who would take the time to discover it.

By the time that the evening drive was starting to develop, gas stations had already increased the cost per gallon by nearly forty cents. The networks were already talking about gasoline rationing, and talk show hosts were discussing the upcoming winter months and how heating oil would be in short supply. Due to the nature of the events it was apparent that no deterioration of the military stocks of petroleum could be allowed to occur. People were just plain scared.

At exactly 8 p.m. the president of the United States came before the entire world. The nation stood still and watched as President Marshall related the events of the past twenty-four hours. His tone was determined, but the anger behind it was scarcely concealed.

" ... my fellow Americans, we have been attacked by terrorists who are determined to end our way of life. Last night at about this same time, three major targets were hit in a coordinated attack with the goal of bringing a halt to the world's flow of oil. The Suez and Panama Canals were effectively closed for some time to come when this cowardly enemy caused two super tankers, laden with full hulls of crude oil, to be sunk in locations where the choke points would block the channels.

"At the same time, four enemy teams of terrorists penetrated the United States and blew up the Alaska Pipeline in isolated regions of Alaska. Their attack on this vital American asset was affected in a manner to cause a lengthy period of time before the flow of oil may once more be available to us and our Pacific Rim allies.

"It appears that the actual culprits, in the case of the two super tankers, paid for their misdeeds with their lives. The size of the detonations was such that no person could have escaped the carnage of the incident. Unfortunately, that is not the case of those who attacked the Alaska oil pipeline. Governor Atkins has mobilized the Alaska National Guard and I have authorized FEMA and support from our military sources to assist him in any way possible.

"The Central Intelligence Agency, the Federal Bureau of Investigation, and all the Cabinet secretaries are working full time to get to the bottom of this terrible crime against humanity. You can be certain that we will get to the bottom of this cowardly act. I have directed my national security advisor to work directly with the governments in the area of the sabotages to gain and give as much support as possible. Tomorrow I will ask the Congress to approve an emergency budget to get us through this time of peril.

"Now let me turn to the international community. Over the past months much of the world has been aware of the war on terrorism being waged by this and like-minded nations. Repeatedly we have asked for, and received, much from our friends around the globe. There have been, sadly, those nations who have neither assisted nor taken steps to impede these criminals who cause such pain for so many. Early in this war it was stated, 'If you are not for us, then you are against us.' That statement is truer today than ever before. I am directing the secretary of state to contact all the major sovereign nations' leaders to determine the support we can count on at this time. Those who continue to ignore these requests for assistance will be considered to be in the enemy camp and will be dealt with accordingly. Those nations who are harboring these international criminals will be treated with the same actions as the individuals we are pursuing, and we will bring those responsible to justice.

"And now, to my fellow Americans, once more we have been attacked by those same elements that bombed the towers of the World Trade Center and the Pentagon, and caused valiant Americans to chose to give up their lives in a Northern Pennsylvania field rather than to allow these terrorists to fly their commandeered airplane into the White House. The manner in which you demonstrated your courage and compassion to the entire world is an indication of what America is all about. Once more we are being called upon to show our resolve in overcoming the greatest challenge we have faced in the life of our beloved country. I am confident that I can count on you to exhibit that same courage and compassion that you so vividly demonstrated in the past. This nation is like a beautiful quilt. We have assembled the very cream of the crop to build a nation united in purpose and dedicated to honor. Among us are diverse members of society. We come from remote places and our language and appearances are equally diverse. I encourage you to be kind to one another during this terrible time. Many of our citizens come from a part of the world where the Muslim faith is paramount. It would bring us shame if we were to lump our own patriots in with the cowards who are the true enemies.

"And finally, to my fellow Americans of Arab decent, I know I can count on you to assist us and enlighten us to those areas where we can pool our resources to defeat this common enemy. I want you to know that no decent American would hold these acts of cowardice against you. Your contribution to our country has been unfaltering and freely given. We applaud you in this effort. Should any of you experience any personal animosity during this time of pulling together, I want you to immediately report such activities to the "800" number you see at the bottom of your television screens at this time. You have my promise that the matter will be dealt with both timely and effectively.

"May God, by what ever name He is known, bless you and the United States of America. Good night."

"Well, there you have it, ladies and gentlemen. Fox News has learned that the three coordinated attacks were led by the same group of psychopaths who have been plaguing the civilized world for the past four decades. Reports out of Fairbanks, Alaska, indicate that one of the saboteur teams was killed in an accident as they were making their way out of one of the pipeline detonations. Documents found on the bodies indicate they were from Indonesia and are part of the infamous al-Qaeda. The fact that all three terrorist actions came simultaneously can only underscore that a single organization was behind the entire act of war. Our correspondent in Kuwait has learned that the government of Kuwait has opened an investigation of one of its top police officials in regard to this matter. Not much is known at this time, but Fox will continue to keep you updated as developments come forward."

The major networks continued discussions with all the same familiar faces in the news world for the remainder of the evening. Much of the commentary was speculative and continued only because it was expected, even though not much was known at the present time. "Experts" ranging in expertise of every aspect of the various fields even remotely tied to the situation were brought before the cameras to enlighten those who continued to pay heed. The one who should have drawn the most attention was the president of the New York Stock Exchange. His face was grim as he explained in incomprehensible language the possible impacts this disaster could have upon the economic picture internationally. At the same time, members of the European and Japanese stock exchanges were making their own comments to members of their community.

The bottom line was that nearly ninety percent of the world's oil was going to have a difficult time being distributed to the end user. While the majority of the supply remained unaffected, the transportation problems were enormous. All oil coming from the Middle East would have to be moved around South Africa to reach the European and Western Hemisphere countries. The choices left for the Pacific Rim nations were to ship eastward through the Indian Ocean or the Atlantic and Pacific. The time element in this transport would be nearly impossible to live with but, out of necessity, would be required. No relief would come from the Alaska Pipeline for months to come. Japan and the Koreas would be devastated by these conditions. China would come out of this pretty well since they had built a direct pipeline to their Western neighbors some time earlier.

When the "lifeblood of modern technology" is removed from the scene, the impact can only be disastrous for the economies of the industrialized world. All manufacturing and development is determined by the fuel to keep "the machine" in operation. Yes, the economies of the O.P.E.C. countries would suffer, but the peoples of these nations were used to lower standards of living and would adjust as they always have in the past. The New York Stock Exchange decided to remain closed for the next three sessions to allow calm to return to the market.

The Department of Homeland Security was operating at full tilt. If airport security was tight in the past, it was now laboring under intense scrutiny. Lines at airports were long and flights were being delayed more often than not. To their credit, the passengers completely understood even when the delays became annoying. So infrequent were any incidents attributed to this heightened situation that the few who became belligerent became the subject of national news reports. The enormity of the task before the department became evident when the major networks began to show the number of ports around the United States. Added to this was the large number of airports around the country to demand the close scrutiny of the law enforcement types. Border security had been the least controlled area of responsibility in the past. Suddenly, executive orders were issued to reinforce the sovereignty of all borders.

Of course, there were the small groups parading in front of the White House with placards denouncing the administration for being the cause of all the recent woes. Unlike the past, however, a group well over three times that number had formed a hasty counter-group of protesters to denounce the former group. A few fistfights had broken out and, without much fanfare, the protestors decided that they should make their getaway while it was still safe. The normal liberal press corps was left standing in shock with their collective mouths wide open.

The Pentagon was manned around the clock with reinforced staffs engaged in all those activities one might expect in such circumstances. The contingency plans and operations war room was buzzing with intense activity. Officers with specialties in various hot spot countries were dispensing information as fast as could be accomplished. Overflights from aircraft and satellites had been adjusted to those targets which deserved further attention due to the latest developments. Military air controllers had concentrated their attention on any air traffic approaching Indonesia or the Middle East. Not one single airplane would land without the full knowledge of these individuals with uplinks to the full armada of A.W.A.C. aircraft. Teams of international policemen had been in place to meet each airplane when the passengers emerged from the gates.

Indonesia, the only country from which proven terrorists had been determined at this point, was anxious to show its complete cooperation with the international community. For this reason any passenger arriving in Jakarta for the next couple of weeks could expect to be detained for not less than one hour before leaving the gate to retrieve baggage. Persons whose national origins were from the host country could expect even longer delays as the interrogations continued around the clock. The terrorists who were en route home from their evil deeds would join the ranks of those who were in for intense questioning. Every statement made or lead given would be checked fully before the incoming passenger was allowed to pass. The chance of escape for the guilty was going to be extremely difficult.

The South China Sea
Saturday, October 15, 18:00 hours

Unfortunately for him, Fernell Suffort was completely unaware of the conditions some two hundred kilometers from the front of the aircraft he was a passenger in. He had finally succumbed to his fatigue after the refueling stop in Honolulu and began to feel rested after his multiple stops on the legs of his trip.

After departing Anchorage his Alaska Airlines flight had landed in Seattle. Leaving SEATAC after a two-hour layover, his next destination had been San Francisco. The delay in SFO was short and gave only enough time to travel from one gate to the departure gate for Southwest Airlines that would take him to Los Angeles. His layover in LAX was nearly four hours; too short to risk going to sleep, but too long to fill with meaningless "busy activities."

The United Airlines flight to Honolulu allowed him to relax and recuperate with some actual sleep periods. He normally traveled in business class, but the aircraft was so overbooked that he had been upgraded to first class. The comfort of this overindulgent spoiling of the infidels was, for the first time, welcomed by an exhausted Muslim traveler.

Looking down upon the southern ocean surface gave him a feeling of comfort in the knowledge he would soon be home and would have the time and ability to completely relax. He would not have been quite so complacent if he were aware that a gauntlet was waiting for folks just like him. He would have been aware of this had he taken the time to listen to the continuous broadcasts emitting from the multiple television sets located at each stop along the way. The network of choice in the international airports is CNN. To fill the time of broadcast, CNN had run and rerun the story about the processing in the Indonesian International Airport. Fernell had made it a point to not watch the news channel. He had determined that it would not fare well to be an Indonesian traveler coming from the Western Hemisphere, showing interest in the reason for the recent situations. He had to fight back the desire to watch and inwardly gloat over the tremendous successes of the Movement.

A smiling and beautiful young flight attendant had come by to pick up his beverage container and announce arrival in fifteen minutes—ahead of schedule. He decided to make one last pit-stop at the lavatory to freshen up and wash the "sleepers" out of his eyes. There was no time to shave, but that would come later. He returned to his seat to find that the attendant had raised the back of his seat to the forward position. She smiled as she gestured toward the lighted seat belt sign, and he acknowledged with his most pleasant grin in his present tired state.

The pilot brought the plane down with anticipated, but still appreciated, smoothness and left the active runway onto the taxiway leading to the appropriate gate. They had traveled a short distance when the airplane came to a halt well out on the tarmac. Murmurs of complaint began to emanate from various points around the cabin as passengers were anxious to deplane after a long flight.

"Now what's the problem? Let's get going … "

All of the two-hundred-fifty passengers were trying to gain the attention of the flight attendants to address the obvious queries concerning the delay.

The voice of the captain finally came over the cabin speakers to announce that there was a backup in the arrival gates and it would a few minutes before "our" gate became vacant. The captain graciously thanked all the passengers for their cooperation and consideration during this unavoidable delay.

"A few minutes" turned out to be a full thirty-seven minutes. There was the expected cheer when the airplane engines revved up once more and the brakes were released. Another seven minutes elapsed before the airplane came to a halt at the gate. The flight attendant was trying desperately to inform the passengers that they should remain seated, with their seat belts connected. She could scarcely be heard over the standing, pushing and opening and closing of the overhead storage compartments. Fernell, being one of the first class passengers, was one of the first ones to enter the tunnel of the gate and make a hasty move toward the safety of the airport terminal.

"Excuse me, sir. Please come with me, if you will."

The polite tone could not hide the fact that something was very wrong. *How could they possibly know it was me?* he thought. Did one of his cohorts get caught and talk? He could not fathom a situation where the latter would become possible. Hopefully, the police official did not see the slight drop of his shoulders during the confrontation. If he did, there was no discernable acknowledgment of it. When Fernell heard other passengers being accosted in the same manner, he decided that he might be OK after all.

The officer escorted his charge to a small room a short way from the gate and gestured for Fernell to enter. There was a small table in the center of the room with a chair on each side of the table. There was a mirror on the side of the room that didn't even disguise the fact that it was one-way glass. There was no manner to discover if others were observing on the other side of the glass. It was disconcerting.

"Where are you traveling from, Mr. Suffort?" the inspector questioned in a manner that indicated that he already knew every aspect of Fernell's itinerary.

"Vancouver, Canada," Fernell responded with as much a relaxed voice as he could muster. Prior training in both Afghanistan and Iraq had been devoted to much of what he could now expect to endure. "That place is really beautiful—have you ever been there?" he continued with feigned enthusiasm for the fictitious visitation.

"No, I haven't. I see here that our records show you traveling from Anchorage. Why would you travel to Anchorage from Vancouver? It's so far out of your way."

Well, Fernell was now sure that his departure point was a matter of fact, so he had best be extremely cautious in his responses.

Fernell laughed amicably and slapped his knee. "You wouldn't believe what I had to go through just to get out of Vancouver. You'd think that it would be quite easy to fly out of Vancouver and land in Seattle. That is not the case. I could have taken a ferry or even rented an auto and driven to Seattle, but the arrival would have left me missing my connection flight, so I had to buy a ticket from Vancouver to Anchorage and then back to Seattle and even then it was questionable if I could make my connecting flight. I thought it was quite ridiculous, don't you?"

"Yes, it sounds ridiculous to me," the inspector stated without any indication as to what part of the report he was referring to. "Do you have any documents, with photograph, that indicate your present address?"

Fernell managed to keep his controlled demeanor on the surface and immediately reached in his jacket to retrieve his passport. He casually handed the document over to the police official and made no comment as the passport was opened and examined. The photograph was not only carefully examined, but the policeman took extra effort to examine the edges of the snapshot to ascertain whether the picture was the original, or had been a replacement after the fact.

"What is your telephone number again?" the officer asked in a casual manner. Fernell began to answer the question before he realized that there is no requirement in the passport for that entry. He continued to provide the number requested without pointing out the fact that he had not given the number previously.

When one has been trained by the very best you can easily determine when the demeanor of the interrogator has changed from casual to concern. Where could he have gone wrong? This guy was no amateur and he didn't care that his target audience knew it. He was enjoying this! Maybe Fernell was being too cool during this interrogation. Wouldn't an average citizen become more nervous during such a session? He decided to gradually shift to a more frightened projection.

"Why are you keeping me here?" he blurted out in a manner to appear frightened and worried. "I didn't bring in any smuggled goods and you can search me and my bags for any drugs or illegal items."

Wasn't that the way a normal citizen would react? This attempt to recover some semblance of normalcy seemed to fall on deaf ears and caused contempt to build in Fernell's attitude. He would try another approach.

"I'm tired and haven't done anything wrong! I insist that you either charge me with some infraction or allow me to go to my home and rest. I don't know of any reason why you would want to hold me here. I am a true follower of Allah and don't deserve to be detained like a common criminal."

The reference to Allah would inform this detaining officer that he was a fellow believer. After all, Indonesia was the largest Muslim nation in the world.

"I prefer to call Him 'God' or 'Jehovah'," the officer stated without looking up from the passport he had been examining. "Could you provide me the address of the office building you went to when you picked up your passport?"

There was a single office building in Jakarta that issued passports. Any passport issued to an Indonesian would be issued from this office. Unfortunately, Fernell had no idea where this building was located since he had never been there. His passport had come from one of the greatest forgers in the known world of espionage and had been delivered via blind drop at some location well out into the countryside. He tried to feign forgetfulness, but the inspector would not buy it.

"Surely, you would know the whereabouts of such an important governmental office if you ever went there," the policeman stated. "Think hard—this is important!"

The redness in his face could be felt by Fernell as he had let a triviality expose his guilt. There was no escaping this obvious breach of plausible conduct. He made a few feeble attempts to provide the information, based upon his limited knowledge of government offices. In his profession, he was not about to frequent such places.

"Wait here," the policemen ordered and left the room to confer with his superiors. From the look on his face, which showed complete contempt for his prisoner, Fernell Suffort would not be sleeping in his own bed this night, and probably never again.

— 4 —

Jakarta, Indonesia
Sunday, October 16— early morning hours

Fernell Suffort had just been thrown (literally) into a cell somewhere in a city where such occurrences were little noted, nor apt to be remembered. He was hurting in places where he had never experienced pain at any previous time. Although there was a cot within arms reach of where he lie, he was unable to gather the strength or will to take advantage of it. When a person is arrested in the United States there are certain rules strictly enforced when it came to the humane treatment of the accused. This definitely was not the United States of America!

Within a few minutes of the departure of the investigating officer at the airport, Fernell was handcuffed and dragged from the room by three huge men and hauled in the most embarrassing manner through the airport to a waiting police van. Two of the men got in the back with him while the third took over driving responsibilities in the front compartment. The new law enforcement officers were not as professional as his initial interviewer had been. Instead of desiring him to talk, the slightest vocal sound out of Fernell brought immediate corporal punitive action. The journey to wherever it was they ended up took a matter of ten minutes.

The three thugs in charge dragged him from the van in a manner to let him know that his personal comfort was the very last thing on their mind. He was dragged up the stairs to a grey building and through the front lobby and down a narrow stairway through several flights of stairs. Once there, he was taken down a dank hallway and ushered unceremoniously into a carbon copy of the room in the airport. Already seated in the chair of authority was the interrogator from hell. The escorts slammed him down in the chair and moved to the corner of the room.

"You have disgraced your country and Allah!" the man across the table from him almost screamed in his face. He made it abundantly clear that this statement was one which needed no response or comment from Fernell, and he reached out and cuffed him with the heel of his hand in a manner that indicated he had practiced this move many times. "As of this time you are being held indefinitely while we sort out your mischief to bring before the magistrate. While you are in this capacity you are going to curse your mother for ever giving birth to you."

To add emphasis to his last comment he once more lashed out with a bone-jarring cuff to the side of Fernell's face. He felt the blood spurt from the tearing of his flesh over his left eyebrow.

"Now, you son of a pig, tell me everything and it will go easier on you. If you don't do this the easy way, and I truthfully hope you don't, I will garner every fact from your blood-drenched lips as you long for death. You may begin … "

Fernell had been trained by the very best his Middle Eastern brothers had to offer. He had crawled in the desert sand with barbed entanglements over his head, while machine guns had been fired all around him. He had negotiated infiltration and obstacle courses under the most intense fear known to any man while in this training. His body had been wracked with pain due to the intense physical challenges over days of the toughest training, in the worst possible conditions imaginable. That, however, was a picnic compared to the mental challenges leveled at him by his trainers, the Arabs. He came out of that school with a conviction that there was no manner in which he could be forced to talk or give up his comrades. His trainers had failed to consider the man he was faced with now.

Colonel Harmon was not a sadistic man. He simply could not abide any person who broke the law or brought discredit upon himself, his country, or Allah. His disgust with these so-called followers of Islam who had not ever become acquainted with the teachings of the Koran brought his emotions to rage. Here, in front of him, was one of these terrorists who defamed the Great Allah and the teachings of Mohammed by committing the most unspeakable

41

crimes and using the Creator as an excuse for doing so. Allah needed men like Colonel Harmon to bring such slime to His infinite justice.

Fernell managed to hold out for just over forty minutes (a new record) before he made the first crack in discipline. Within the next three hours Colonel Harmon had managed to extract every shred of information known to Fernell Suffort. That didn't mean that it came easy. Fernell had sacrificed his fingernails to the pliers before he divulged the first bit of information. Next came the bones of three fingers before he could no longer hold out. Once the first valuable details had come out, it only took an occasional prodding of a boot placed in a particularly vulnerable part of his anatomy before he completely divulged his entire knowledge about the mission.

Once the information came out regarding the operations within the Indonesian organization and all the known activities conducted to date, it was not a great leap to discover the secret workings of al-Qaeda in other theaters. Of course, all this information was expedited to the American Embassy for dispatch to Washington. From there it would only be a matter of time before all the pieces of the puzzle were matched to form a clear picture of not only the present actions, but to sort out the very structure of the entire terrorist organization. It was wonderful that the break in this case would come from Jakarta, even though it was the Americans who discovered the intelligence in the wrecked Ryder truck.

As it turned out, Fernell was the first of his cell members to return to Jakarta. The survivors had a rude awakening awaiting them upon their arrival. As it turned out, Fernell was unaware of the accident and deaths of his cohorts. Had he been aware of it he certainly would not have returned to Indonesia as he had. The entire world organization was in jeopardy because the driver of the rental truck had been driving beyond his capabilities.

Now that his identity was known to international law enforcement agencies, his life would have been inconsequential to the Movement. In fact, if there were any opportunity to do so, it would be the Movement that would extract the maximum penalty for this breach of secrecy so vital to the organization. He was certain that if he were to be sent to any prison in Indonesia he wouldn't survive the first week. Even prisoners were Muslim and there was bound to be some of them committed to the Movement. In the movies he would have been provided a lethal pill to bite down on, but unfortunately this was not the movies. He would have to find another way to take his own life rather than await the excruciating pain that would be sure if he waited for another to take the necessary action. Surely Allah would not hold his confession against him as he held out far beyond any normal expectations before losing control. That thought was upper most in his mind at this point. His life on earth must end soon.

Jakarta
Sunday, October 16, 9:41 a.m.

It was uncanny that the six surviving members of Fernell's cell had been aboard the same aircraft from Tokyo when it was making its final approach to Jakarta International. The circuitous route each of the three remaining sub-cells had used to arrive at Tokyo caused the merging of travel in such a manner. Of course, the three sub-cell teams took great precautions to avoid each other and managed to find seating in separate sections of the cabin. At this point they had felt a complete gratitude to Allah for his safe conduct for each of them as they were returning to their beloved country. The fact that they had accomplished so much in the support of so valiant a mission caused a sense of intense pride to well up from the pit of the stomach. They would never be able to mention their role in the matter, but self-pride would follow each member of the unit to the time they joined Allah in paradise.

As the wheels made contact with the runway it was as though the safety net was no longer required and now it was time to bask in success. Unlike the earlier arriving airplanes, there was no delay in bringing the craft to a skillful halt at the prescribed gate. There was no need to hurry, so each of the team members waited until nearly half the plane was empty before they rose and disembarked into the gateway tunnel.

Emerging from the tunnel it was strange to see so many uniformed policemen in the area of the gate. It must be due to the beefed up security they had been witnessing on each leg of the trip. As each sub-cell of two emerged from the ramp, a team of officers broke off from the group standing around the gate and followed a short distance behind them. The officers were engaging in a discussion and didn't seem to be the least bit interested in them until they reached the exit for arriving passengers. Only then did they move to each side of the travelers.

Almost in a whisper the officers said, "you two, continue to walk and don't make any sudden movements. Keep your hands in front of you and walk directly toward the police van right in front of you." Each of the three groups of two were handled in exactly the same manner and ended up being placed in the same van as the first two. Once inside, the culprits were all handcuffed in a continuous chain of retainers and ordered to sit down and "keep their filthy mouths shut."

The vehicle went directly to the same location where Fernell Suffort had been taken and down the same stairway to six separate rooms. Their ankles were shackled and their wrists were cuffed behind them at this point. Rather than seat them in the available chairs, a very large man knocked them to the floor with a vicious round-house right. In each case, the velocity of the punch caused severe bleeding to erupt from the face of its victim. In at least two of the cases, the recipient was knocked unconscious.

In turn, Colonel Harmon came into the separate rooms, not so much to question the men but to rub their noses in the fact that their miserable leader, Fernell Suffort, had ratted them out the first chance he had. He had even gone so far as to blame these men for the entire attack and said he had tried to talk them out of it to no avail. The police officer related all this and laughed at their stupidity to place their trust in such a vile person. Colonel Harmon gave them just enough information to let them know he was completely aware of the whole matter and said, "If you want to cooperate with me now, I'll do what I can to help your case."

The sadness and disillusion of the cowardice and conniving of this trusted leader was more than they could stand. In each case, the six men were more than willing to tell all. In the case of two of them, they were capable of adding the names of other members of al-Qaeda heretofore unknown. Every tidbit of information known to the six men was extracted in a matter of two hours from the time they came into the police station. Only then did Colonel Harmon inform each of them that it had been only under the most severe torture that Fernell had divulged the slightest bit of information. He went on to tell them that they had been detected from a completely different source and Fernell had been loyal to them to the very end. It gave Colonel Harmon great pleasure to see them crumble in complete despair when they learned they had given up the entire organization without any torture whatsoever.

"This is beautiful," the police commander was heard to say as he left the room of the sobbing terrorist.

Armed with the wealth of information gleaned from the interview with the Suffort cell of al-Qaeda, the military and police officials were busily planning a sweep to gather up the entire Indonesian branch of that organization. This would require a coordinated operation that took place in a very short period of time. The government did not want elements of the vile organization to have an opportunity to warn the various cell groups once the net was closing in on them. This operation would require the trap door to open and close in a simultaneous manner to prevent any escape by members of the hated enemies of the state.

In that it could not be ascertained how deep the agents of al-Qaeda might be in the government organizations, it was decided to limit knowledge of the planning stage to only those of proven credentials. The leadership of the police and military were screened and re-checked to provide a current evaluation to the situation at hand. If there was even a hint of a doubt with regard to the officer being considered, his name was struck from the list of planners. This did not mean that the particular individual was suspected of anything, but it did provide the basis of investigation at a later date.

There was a necessity to conduct the planning in a short period of time. Certainly, the seven remaining members already in custody would be missed by someone, so it was imperative to strike while the iron was hot. With that in mind, an emergency meeting was called with a slate of attendees being given individual summons. Once the summoned party was notified they were required to immediately accompany the courier to the meeting site. No contact with anyone was permitted post-notification. The wives and family members would just have to wait for their loved one to come home after the operation was conducted.

Prior to the meeting a team of skilled people had been busy locating addresses of the names of individuals on the list to be apprehended. Investigators had already been put in places of surveillance at each location where a suspect was living or known to frequent. This had placed a tremendous load on the limited number of people who had been screened for that purpose.

The planning committee members were ushered into a large room and asked to be seated to await the speaker, who would come before them and explain why they were here. Much speculation was being passed back and forth by the crowd as they sat in their respective seats. None of them had any idea as to the actual reason for their being here, but before long that, too, would become clear.

"Ladies and gentlemen, you are about to embark upon a mission that will place the entire world, and especially your country, in your debt. This day will be remembered for many generations to come as the day when our citizens were cleansed of a scourge so vile that it must be the pet project of the very devil himself." Heads turned to each other in an attempt to discern the full impact of the statement just made by the president of their country standing before them.

"For hundreds of years now, Indonesia has been a loyal follower of the Prophet Muhammad. We have prided ourselves with the devotion of the citizens to the will of Allah. Our schools have been blessed with a curriculum that includes daily reading from the blessed Koran. We know the difference between good and evil. That is why it pains me deeply to discover that we have those among us who have blasphemed the name of Allah by despicable acts.

"In recent days all of you have learned of the terrible acts of terrorism committed in Panama, Egypt and the United States. What you didn't know, however, was that the crime committed in the state of Alaska was perpetrated by citizens of this country. These dastardly and evil men were part of an international crime organization known as al-Qaeda. This cowardly organization has the audacity to claim that they are the true followers of Islam.

"In accordance with Allah's perfect plan, He has caused these evildoers to be exposed. All the members who actually took part in the destruction of the Alaskan oil pipeline have either been captured or are dead. Providence has granted that those captured are in our hands and not in some place where the execution of them would be denied. Nine individuals were on the team that went to Alaska; two are dead and the remaining seven are incarcerated right here in Jakarta.

"But there is still more to be done. We know of over two hundred people, by name and location here in Indonesia, who are full-fledged members of al-Qaeda. At present time, each one of them is under close and covert surveillance. Your task will be to formulate a coordinated plan by which we can collect every one of them in a single blow that will exterminate this contaminate from our lands forever. You have been quarantined so that the operation will remain totally silent and deadly. Unfortunately, we will not be able to contact each of your families to assure them of your safety. Suffice it to say that their pride in you will overcome any hardships during this temporary time."

The president continued on for several more minutes setting the tone of the pending operation without getting into specifics. Once he had completed his address, he turned the meeting over to the chief of staff of the Army to discuss the actual mission. The general description of events of the preceding week and the part played by the Indonesian contingent was related in all the facts known. There were gasps heard at several points of the presentation as the audience learned the full extent of the carnage.

After the completion of the general's presentation the members of the assembly were assigned to the various sectors of control that would complete the operations plan and those who would be in charge of the physical execution of those plans. Half an hour later the various meetings were called in order to deal with the entire aspect of this historic enterprise. The individuals on each staff element took a few minutes to introduce themselves and discuss their specific qualifications to be members of the particular team they were on. Once the plans of these sub-elements were finalized they would assemble with the entire body to coordinate their plan into the whole concept for operation.

The highest emphasis was given to those who would be conducting the arrests. Since this was to be a combined operation between the military and national police, it was important to organize the field teams in the same manner. There was not going to be any "turf wars" in this operation—period!

It took only a day and one half of marathon planning to put together the final product. In that the finest minds in the country had been responsible for the OPLAN, the results were of extraordinary perfection. There would be no glitches to explain when the after-action report was conducted. All those with the responsibility to do so were in complete agreement that not a single soul on the infamous list would be free by tomorrow morning.

The White House
Monday, October 17, 7:43 a.m.

What in the world was behind the secrecy and selection of Todd Martin, by name, to be summoned to the Oval Office? Todd had been by the White House on numerous occasions but had never set foot in the building. He had been personally appointed to the State Department by his former boss while he had been in the Army. He had served on the personal staff of General Harold M. Croft over at the Pentagon some years before and had made quite an impression on the General. When General Croft was selected as assistant secretary of state shortly after his retirement, Todd was called and asked to join the team over at "State."

The General was not disappointed, as Todd had jumped into the assigned task with the same energy that had been the hallmark of his entire military career, cut short by his present duties. Although he really missed the regimen of Army life, he understood that the work he was now involved in would be instrumental in keeping his former cohorts from having to put into action all those Operational Plans (OPLANS) that were in continuous revision to suit the latest hot spot in the world.

When General Croft had been called to head up the State Department by the current administration, the secretary of state did not forget those who had made him look so good in earlier positions. Todd was one of those who had the complete confidence of his long-time leader and was pulled along on the secretary's coattails. But that still did not prepare him for the surprise of being called in by "The Chief," as old acquaintances were prone to call him.

"Todd, your country needs your services at a level that far exceeds your present grade and rank. I could go on and tell you all about it, but it should not come from me. Suffice it to say, you will probably hate me for recommending you once you get going on this assignment. I'm going to ask you for blind trust in me and your understanding of the commitments I made to serve our great nation four decades ago as a young plebe over at the Point.

"You don't have to accept this appointment, and should you decide to tell me no, I will continue to have the same respect for you as a dedicated and true patriot. With that assurance from me, what is your answer?"

In normal situations, the chief would have allowed him some time to think over his reply, but there was some reason for the need for expediency in this matter. This man in front of Todd was the finest officer and gentlemen he had ever had the pleasure to serve with or for. There could only be one answer.

"Sir, I have no idea what you are getting me into, but you know that I have a loving wife and two children; and further, you know that I love my country with the same intensity as you have demonstrated since the day I first met you. I accept!"

That was just an hour ago. Now Todd was turning into the enclosure that surrounded the home of our chief of state and commander in chief. What was he supposed to say to the guards at the gate? Before he had an opportunity to address that matter, one of the guards leaned into the driver's window and said, "Mr. Martin, welcome to the White House. If you will just park your car right over there in the executive parking lot, one of the guards will escort you to the right place."

After parking his car, Todd crawled out and was somewhat embarrassed as from force of habit he locked the doors. The Marine guard had suppressed the smile that was doing its best to cover the face of this disciplined service member.

"I think it will be safe here," the young man stated and managed to turn smartly before his humor could no longer be suppressed. No further comments were made as the two of them stepped out to the side entry of the mansion.

The entry was protected with the usual governmental building security system. Todd had to go through the passage twice before realizing that he had his cellular telephone in his trousers pocket. Once he had made the satisfactory disclosure of his metal objects and change, he was taken in tow by an officious young lady who would take him directly to the Oval Office. The palms of his hands were sweating profusely and he was sure that he would be greeted by the president with outstretched hand. Trying to be calm, he began rubbing his open hand on the seam of his suit pants. It was only then that he remembered that he had worn that hideous tie his daughter had given him on his last birthday. Just great—the president would be greeted by Pooh Bear!

"Come on in, Todd," the president stated in a pleasant voice and with an equally pleasant smile. "Hey, great tie! My kids gave me one just like that for Father's Day. Bet you didn't expect to be coming here today ... be sure and tell your kids that the president has one just like it." No wonder this guy had won by such a landslide. You just couldn't help but like him immediately. The tie was now a forgotten matter.

"Gentlemen, ladies, let's get started," the leader of the free world said as he took his place behind the most beautiful desk Todd had ever seen. "Todd, why don't you sit in that middle one so we can talk?" the president said as he gestured toward the identified chair.

The president began to reiterate all the facts concerning the recent terrorist attacks and gave an overview that was unnecessary but served to direct everyone in the room to the subject matter at hand. Once the recapitulation was complete, he began to address the steps that would be necessary in order to restore order.

"Todd, you probably wonder why you are here today."

Without waiting for a response, he continued, "Mr. Martin, I need a ramrod to assist me in addressing this matter and I want that person to be you. Secretary Croft has already told me that you have accepted this challenge. Last night I had the opportunity to study over your dossier, and I must tell you that I fully concur with Hal's recommendation. I see you were a Green Beret down there at Fort Bragg in your earlier years—good show, man! Also, I notice you graduated in the top of your infantry advanced course down at Fort

49

Benning. Before you had an opportunity to go off and get yourself killed, General Croft grabbed you for his personal staff. Says here that you were the finest officer he had ever commanded. Not bad, 'cause I know that Hal is a demanding leader who has the ability to uncover true talent. Do you still make those morning runs of five miles?"

Todd went on to answer in the affirmative and was somewhat embarrassed as the commander in chief went on for several minutes expounding upon the obviously impressive record Todd had built for himself. This was done primarily for the entourage in the office at the present time. When he had finished this part of the meeting, he turned directly to Todd and began giving him his mission orders.

Todd was to be in charge of all aspects of the current investigation and liaison with foreign governments and domestic agencies, including the CIA and FBI.

"You have access to me at any time you may need it," President Marshall stated and peered over his half-frame glasses to look at each member present in the room in an unspoken message that said, "Don't mess with this guy."

Over the next half hour, the specifics of the office were discussed and parameters, what few there were, noted. Generally, Todd was the direct representative of the government of the United States on all matters pertaining to the recent terrorist act, the ensuing investigation of the incident, and resulting actions of restoration and any punitive actions against those responsible. Of course, Todd was to keep the President fully informed by attending the daily morning briefing or providing updates if he were absent from Washington.

Once they had left the Oval Office, the White House chief of staff invited Todd to his office to help him get started on the various elements necessary to do his job. Todd was grateful for this obvious gesture of kindness for "the new kid on the block." Armed with all the necessary information to be gleaned from 1600 Pennsylvania Avenue, Todd soon returned to his automobile and was rewarded by a smart salute from the Marine guard, who had certainly been told that this new guy was high on the list of dignitaries authorized to be in the White House.

Todd drove over to the State Department and pulled into his reserved space, and as he was locking the doors to his car, recalled his *faux pas* of locking his doors when he was parked inside the gate of the White House. No doubt every guard on the premises had a great laugh over that one.

As he got off the elevator on his office floor he was greeted by a large contingent of his fellow workers, who made a great show of bowing and genuflecting with tongue-in-cheek humor and acknowledgment of his obvious huge promotion. The greatest majority of them were happy about the new assignment and wished him well.

"You're not getting rid of me quite that easy," Todd laughed. "I've been told that I may keep my old office since I know where the pencil sharpeners and bathrooms are here in this building. Hope you guys don't mind having me hang around for awhile?"

When he entered his office he was pleased to see that his in/out boxes were removed so that some other poor slob would have to take over his previous responsibilities. He would be sure to inquire if there would be any necessity of doing an "overlap" with the new individual responsible for his caseload. He was further delighted to know that he would retain his former secretary, as Mrs. Johnson was an absolute genius at detecting Todd's needs before he had the opportunity to voice them to her. Mrs. Johnson was waiting for him when he opened the door and could not hide her delight over the most recent developments.

"Congratulations, sir," she said with as much enthusiasm as she could muster. She was taking obvious pride that her boss was getting the recognition he so richly deserved. He was the most considerate man she had ever had the pleasure to work with. He had always treated her with great respect and dignity and always took the time to show genuine interest in her welfare.

"They told me that I could stay with you if that's what you would like … " He cut her off mid-sentence and put his arm around her shoulder and said, "Young lady, you just try to get away!" With that she broke protocol and gave him a firm hug.

"I plan to be out of the office for much of the time, so I will be counting upon you to 'man the fort' a lot of the time, Mrs. Johnson. Heaven knows, you're the brains behind this outfit anyway and your security clearance is equal to mine. I think, anyway. If it isn't, I'll get that fixed 'cause you will need to know what's goin' on around here." With that he gave her a briefing on what was to transpire while this operation was ongoing. When he finished, she let out a loud, "whew!"

"I'll do my very best not to let you down, sir," she said with her usual ring of professionalism that he knew would hold her in good stead. If the rest of Washington, D.C., had people of her integrity and dedication then the country would always be in good hands.

— 5 —

Indonesia
Tuesday, October 18, 23:00 hours

The sudden crash of the front door being broken down and the loud voices heard coming from downstairs had roused Ahmed El Jamaal from his sleep. He had just made the transition to deep sleep after retiring for the night only half an hour earlier. He bolted straight up from his bed and reached for the pistol he always had at the ready on his night stand. He scarcely had the pistol in hand and the lamp next to his bed turned on when three armed men had burst into the bedroom with weapons pointed at both Ahmed and his wife. His wife was screaming at the top of her lungs while the intruders were maneuvering into positions surrounding the pair. Ahmed sized up the situation and immediately allowed his pistol to dangle freely from his hand. This scenario was being played out all over the nation at precisely the same time.

The spouses and family members of each member of al-Qaeda were included in the round up and by 0100 hours the last arrest had been completed and the wanted individuals in custody. A total of nearly five hundred individuals were in custody, counting only the adults. There were numerous children who were taken to places already established to care for them while this sad adventure was playing out. Caretakers were selected for their known compassion and willingness to care for the displaced children in this terrible time. Beds had already been made up for the children due to the hour of the operation. In anticipation of the upsetting conditions caused by the arrests of parents, abundant numbers of mothers had been on hand to comfort and hold.

The remainder of families had been taken to a holding area behind fences and the intended targets of the arrest were moved to another building on the south side of town. Many of those arrested were being transported from remote areas and would not arrive until morning. The sweep had been complete and all those on the wanted list and several who were in meetings with members on that list were brought in as well. The only description for the operation was total success!

Within a matter of hours, dispatches were sent to the appropriate offices in Washington, D.C., with complete details of the operation. Invitations were extended to interested parties of that nation should they desire to conduct interrogations with the detainees. Of course, the response from Todd Martin's office came back as affirmative and rapid.

In the meantime, trained interrogators were busy doing their own interviews in a manner that was alien to that which would be done by the Americans. Individuals awaiting their turn to be interrogated were forced to remain silent while the echoes of wailing and cries could be heard coming from other parts of the building. Some of these voices were merely recordings being played to get inside the head of the al-Qaeda members. It was having the desired affect. The looks of fear in the holding cell were infectious and wearing upon the entire group.

Before the rising of the sun that morning, the list of others who were missed in the previous round-up were known and arresting teams dispatched to ruin their day. It was shocking to know the extent that this cancer had grown in the nation. If this was the situation here in Indonesia, then what must be the toll in Arabia? It was decided best to use the State Department of the United States to pursue this avenue, as it was not conclusive that the Arab states would be as enthusiastic at rounding-up their conspirators with al-Qaeda. The Americans and Israel were better equipped to handle that aspect, but they would have the full backing of the Indonesians. This new office and it's department head were really on the ball and had already gained the support of every available asset to the Indonesian government.

Before the end of that day there were swarms of U.S. personnel at the detention site. As promised, full access to the arrested persons was provided to the allies and much was being accomplished with regard to the international aspect of the terrorist group. Along with this intelligence came certain decisions as to how the information would be dealt with. Syria and Iran had been implicated beyond any doubt. The gathered intelligence pointed directly to the leadership of both nations. Along with that were the expected alliances with certain members of nations supposedly closely allied with the Western world. The leaders of these nations were not implicated, but officials from several key positions in those governments were undeniably up to their eyeballs in bed with al-Qaeda. Diplomacy would be exercised in dealing with those situations; however, there would be no compromise in the disposition of such individuals.

"I can't believe, after all we did to free Kuwait, that their national police chief is involved," was commented by one of the ranking members of the interrogation team. "I want to be there when they take that S.O.B. down. My son was killed in that war!"

The permeation of the corrupt organization extended into all the governments of the Middle East—even Israel! There was going to be hell to pay when this hit the fan. Some of the Arab countries had been straddling the fence long enough. That day was over. In the words of an ancient national leader, " ... choose you this day whom you will serve ... " The United States of America had been hurt once too often and they were mad as hell. With the military might to back up this anger, it would not be wise to oppose them right now.

The United Nations was bogged down in its usual ineffectiveness. Fully one-third of its membership was from totally corrupt nations and another third from dictatorships. The hypocrisy practiced on a continual basis was well-known to the enlightened world and used as a tool by the rest. In a complete disregard of protocol, the president of the United States had just "requested" that the secretary general come to the White House for discussions. The message was clear that the charter member of the organization was not only ready to pull completely out of the organization, but would probably expel the organization from the United States. The secretary general was quick to respond favorably and acknowledged the breach of protocol as a casualty of the busy schedule of "one of our most cherished member nations." The more colorful translation of the message came from behind closed doors when a member of the Cabinet said, "Tell that raghead to get his ass on his camel and haul ass down here to Washington while he still can."

The Panama Canal
Monday, October 17, 7:33 a.m.

The composite team from Bechtel, Morrison Knutson, and the Army Corps of Engineers had been rushed down to the attack site to provide on-site inspection of the damage caused by the recent catastrophe. It was even worse when seen firsthand than was noted by the television pictures sent back to the States. The vessel had exploded with such force that it caused it to rise up on its left side in a grotesque manner and exposed a huge hole in the hull where the main blast had emanated. The carnage was not just limited to the actual canal and ship but spilled over to the equipment surrounding the canal for nearly two hundred meters around the ship. Everywhere was bent and twisted metal that had been subjected to intense heat, both from the initial blast as well as the ensuing fire from the ignited cargo in the hold. It had taken a full two and one-half days just to put out the raging fire. At least two firemen had died in the quest to put out the fire and a third was not expected to survive another day.

The actions required would be to first remove the hulk of the ship from the canal. This would be an enormous task since the ship was broken in several places and was still submerged in the waters remaining in the canal. It was going to be a major effort just to pump the water from that section of the canal since the locks had been destroyed both fore and aft of the ship. Once the water was pumped out a further assessment of the damage to the canal walls could be accomplished to determine the amount of repairs necessary. A great amount of damage was sustained on the port side of the oil tanker when the full force of the initial explosion caused a cratering effect deep into the walls of the canal. Full testing of the soils surrounding the site would be required to ascertain the damage.

Anyone who has ever visited the Panama Canal is aware of the rail system adjacent to the waterway. These locomotives are used to assist the ships in their passing between the various levels created by the locks. One of these engines had fallen directly into the canal and was resting on the hull of the ship. The railroad tracks were twisted like strings of spaghetti and would need to be replaced as well. Much of the soil compaction would be required before the heavy equipment could be moved canal side to remove the ship and locomotive. Estimates from the consortium of engineers were that it would take a minimum of three months to remove the debris from the canal. After that would come the rebuilding process. It seemed unlikely that part of the requirement could possibly be completed before mid-summer. Divers were already in the water but were finding it nearly impossible to see anything because the crude oil was still present, even after the huge fire.

The Suez Canal
Monday, October 17, 09:00 hours

When you build a canal in a desert country the challenges are astronomical. Although the terrain is nearly level surrounding the construction site, the soil is mainly sandy loam. If you dig a hole in the ground you must remove twice as much dirt as normal, since the sides continue to fall back in the hole you are digging. If one desires to construct a canal in such an environment, the shoring of the walls is the primary concern. The walls must be sufficient to hold back the pressure of the encroaching sand. Further, the base of the dig must be reinforced as well to keep the sand from flowing under the retaining walls and back up into the existing canal. Dredging is a constant necessity to keep the desert from reclaiming the project and returning it to the original state.

The same entities as were to be present in Panama were on-site at the Suez. They were there "to augment" the Egyptian government in making a bomb damage assessment. Once more, the on-site scene was awesome when observed firsthand. The huge remains of what had recently been a beautiful oil tanker were lying in a twisted and ominous angle only imagined in a horror movie.

The bow of the ship had risen up and was resting upon the former right bank of the canal while the remainder of the twisted and broken ship lie submerged in the mud and water. The entire surface of the ship was covered with a heavy coating of black soot from the burned oil. The fire crews had not been able to put out the fire and had merely attempted to contain it to the proximity of the blast site.

As evidence of the reclamation of the desert, there was continuous caving on both sides of the canal both fore and aft of the ocean liner. The walls of the Suez, now breached, were falling back into the trench at an alarming rate. The longer it took to begin repairs, the more that would be required to put the edifice back into service. Estimates of the cleanup were nearly the same as for the Panama Canal, for much different reasons. Before the stricken vessel could be removed there would be a requirement to build a platform for the huge derricks to rest upon. Once these were in place the cutting teams could come in and chop the vessel up into movable sections. Like the Panama, there was a necessity to remove the water from the canal so that the work force could gain access to the lower sections of the oil tanker. There would also be the danger that some of the fuel was still in the vessel and to use normal cutting torches would be prohibitive.

Once the removal of the wreckage of the ship had been accomplished, the remainder of the task would be much easier than that of the sister canal. That did not mean that the operation was simple, but it sure was much less a headache than those engineers would be facing on the other side of the world. The assessment team collected sufficient data to return to the comfort of the Cairo offices and developed the plan of attack for reopening the Suez Canal. The team was more optimistic when they were able to sort out the individual tasks necessary for that end.

Alaska
Thursday, October 13, noon

As suddenly as the snowstorm had developed over much of the state, it had been pushed to the south and east and was dumping a new layer over the western part of Canada and as far south as Juneau. The rest of the state provided clear skies and a high pressure system designed to keep it that way for some time.

With clear skies and unlimited visibility due to the recent cleansing effect of the previous storm, it was great weather for flying. In consideration of the recent events, there were numerous aircraft conducting aerial observation sorties over the entire length of the Alaska Pipeline. The pilots were in awe of the damage that had been wreaked upon the much-touted line. Whoever had made this attack certainly knew what they were doing. The blast sites were in some of the roughest terrain when it came to access and difficulty in building. It was impossible to make a clear assessment by fly over in a fixed-wing aircraft, so "choppers" from Forts Wainwright and Richardson were the vehicles of choice. The "hueys" were able to land sufficiently close to the trouble spots and deposit the assessment crews as soon as they were known.

At one of the sites they located the burned-out wreckage of a Forest Service vehicle and discovered that it was one being sought by that agency for the past two days. The Forest Service personnel asked if there was any evidence concerning the driver of the Hummer. The surveillance team was unable to help there but offered to shuttle a representative out to the site to retrieve the auto. They mentioned that the truck was in such a state of damage that it would never be of service again. Still, the forestry guys might want to get it out of the area during the cleanup phase.

The news was not so rosy at the blast sites. Not only was the pipeline completely wrecked for a distance of nearly one hundred meters, but three of the pedestals upon which the destroyed section stood were completely vaporized. The places where they had once stood were large craters purposely designed to cause real problems to anyone who desired to reconstruct them. By taking measurements, it was discovered that these craters averaged a depth of twenty-two feet deep and a width one and one-half that distance. The craters were full of oil that had coagulated to the consistency of thick syrup. The ruptured pipeline had taken some time to spill its contents onto the exposed terrain and filled the craters and mixed with the surrounding snow to create a muck that ended up engulfing anything in the proximity. The pilots of the Army aircraft could not keep from frowning as the returning engineers re-boarded their helicopters for the return trip. There would be a lot of unhappy crew chiefs back at Wainwright and Richardson.

Like the two other disaster areas, it was going to take a major effort to conduct the cleanup of the "ground zeros" of the blast sites. Whoever it was that would draw that assignment had better be willing to work in the biggest gunk hole in the world. Once the spilled oil was cleaned up from the sites, the work could begin on filling the craters with the appropriate land fill of choice. The reconstruction of the pillars would be no more difficult than it was the first time and then the damaged pipeline could be replaced. The latter would take a much longer section than just the obvious damaged portion. Miniature hairline cracks might be present in the pipeline for as much as a quarter mile away. A minimum of half a mile of new pipeline would be required at each damage site. Of course, the tree-huggers would insist that the old pipe be removed and the landscape re-seeded and reforested before the project was completed.

The initial assessments of the terrorist sites were analyzed and turned in to the appropriate agencies by the end of the first week after the explosions. While the damages were terrible, the engineers gave their assessments in very positive terms and provided a general time period for each step to be completed. Although this provided a certain amount of comfort to the governmental agencies, there was still the inconclusive impact that these terrorist acts would have on the economic environment. The fact that the damage could be repaired was good news, but the imminent approach of winter meant that there would be a tremendous shortfall of heating oil for the Northern states. It was absolutely imperative that this crisis be eliminated before it occurred. At the bidding of Todd Martin, the president made a call to the president of Venezuela and requested a diversion of exported oil directly to the United States as a measure to prevent disaster. After bargaining on "goodwill" gestures being returned in the future, President Diaz agreed. Of course, he failed to mention the fact that the United States had bailed his butt out on two occasions recently when he had gotten his nation on the brink of bankruptcy.

The American president was thinking, "OK, you jerk, you have our feet to the fire this time, but we'll remember how you treated us the next time you need a favor."

The next area to be addressed was in the area of transportation. The first priority would be toward the trucking and rail systems in the United States. Immediate concerns surfaced by Todd's teams showed that food had to be shipped. Manufacturing materials and goods needed to be moved to the factories and then to the consumer. The shippers needed even more fuel for their vessels now that they would be required to forgo the two canals and add thousands of miles to each transoceanic crossing. It would be a time to put extreme pressure upon all those so-called friends in the OPEC to give a break on pricing as well as increase their output during the lapse of the Alaskan Pipeline. God pity any one of them who used this unfortunate time to play oil blackmail. Right now, there was a reassessment being made as regards the policies toward the Middle Eastern Arab bloc. In case they didn't understand it, their value as assets to the United States was undergoing the most thorough re-examination that has occurred in half a century. *OK, you guys have the oil, but try eating or drinking it. You need our food products a heck of a lot more than we need your oil.*

At Todd's suggestion, the president had been conducting a daily briefing on all the major networks since the night of his first announcement. The goal was to shore-up confidence in the economic future of America and instill a "can do" attitude in all of us. Initial assessments were that he was being very effective on both fronts and, as of each close of the business day, the markets continued to maintain a status quo. This would not last forever, so there had to be continuous reinforcement coming from the White House to make it a reality. One or two congressmen had attempted to use the situation to degrade the administration and polarize politics a couple of days ago. News that a recall drive from their constituents was in the offing quickly changed their comments from that moment on. Newscasters had reflected upon their lack of judgment and left no doubt regarding how this maneuver would impact upon their next run for office.

Unfortunately, the same economic news had been exactly the opposite in the other foreign markets. Japan was in big trouble. The leadership had done nothing initially to bolster the public and when they decided to do so, it was too little, too late. The streets were beginning to be grid-locked with vehicles that were out of gasoline. The utilities were scheduling "blackouts" in the major cities to maintain only the basic needs for power. The people of Japan have long been admired for their peaceful tolerance, but now there were acts of disobedience occurring on a more and more frequent basis. The prime minister was being asked to step down, although he was powerless to do much to correct a situation he certainly had not caused.

The European Common Market was not fairing much better. While most Americans thought this to be poetic justice for at least two of its members who had "stuck it to us" during the conflict in Iraq, there were the close friends in the remaining nations that we certainly wanted only the best for. Like the Japanese, the Europeans were asking assistance from the president of the United States. Being the statesman that he is, he assured them he would seek ways in which he could honor that request.

As it turned out, his help came in an unexpected way. His speech to the Americans and inspiring message was played in both Japan and in the European capitals. The president had made his remarks in a manner that included all the peoples of the world. Almost overnight, a new attitude was growing internationally that this major crisis was one that would be overcome because it had to. Instead of whining and complaining, he called upon the citizens of the world to unite in the just cause of eliminating terrorism and institutions which gave them sanctuary. He called upon the major powers to approach the United Nations with a demand that they perform the duties expected by every peace-loving citizen of the world. They would no longer be allowed to kowtow to those who obstructed in moral leadership. Those dictators and unsavory individuals who were causing intolerable conditions in their homelands had best make an immediate turnaround, or seek asylum where they could no longer practice their oppression.

The whole world was buying into this and a silent revolution was beginning to evidence itself in places where it had never shown up in the past.

There was a mass demonstration in Damascus that threatened to turn violent if the president did not immediately replace his entire cabinet and military leadership. He went on national television and tried to placate with some moderate reforms, but it became obvious that he was not really in control in the first place. Several senior government officials and at least two army generals were dragged from their homes in the middle of the night and executed by an angry mob, which included members of the military.

Iranian students and mid-level government officials went to the streets and the rigid theocratic leaders were being subjected to the same treatment as was occurring in Damascus. While reforms were promised, the population's memory of their treatment over the past few years by these Mullahs and false Muslims had built to the point where there was no way that these despots could remain in power. Several unannounced flights left Tehran in the middle of the night over the next three days. Aboard these flights were the families and tyrants certain that their days were numbered if they continued their stay in Iran.

Damascus
Wednesday, October 19, 9:00 a.m.

Abu Bin Hadj was becoming more and more edgy as the early morning hours passed without any response to his call for immediate audience with the Patriarch. There were certain methods in place to circumvent the delays inherent in clandestine contact procedures. These diversions from normal must be held to absolute minimum, since using the direct approach could result in compromise and exposure at the top levels of the Movement.

Abu had pondered long and hard before deciding the situation merited this action. In the end, he was convinced that the necessity for information being exchanged on a hasty basis far outweighed the need for covertness. Certainly his elder leader would know that such a move would not be made by Abu if it were not under dire circumstances, didn't he? The area commander kept looking at the clock on his wall that was adding to his frustration. He had done so at least ten times over the past fifteen minutes with anticipation that his telephone would soon ring and the obligatory coded messages would be passed. He wanted to dispel the fears that were building up in the pit of his stomach and the only way that would happen was when the Patriarch could divulge some sort of meaning to the reports that were coming over the television.

He had been asleep when his wife came to the bedside and woke him in a nervous manner.

"Bu, come quickly and see what is happening!" she uttered in a voice he had learned over the years to understand to mean she was scared. He jumped out of his bed and instinctively followed his wife to the living room where the television's audio had been turned up several notches above what was the normal listening requirement.

" … United Nations Security Council is in session and the ambassador of Syria was being summoned to appear post-haste … documents … Alaska linked to al-Qaeda … Indonesia … complete listing of all agents of "The Movement" …"

Key elements were being divulged in the news commentary, and the announcer was making statements containing such terms as "imminent arrests here in Syria."

What could have gone wrong? Abu had planned his portion of the mission with complete professionalism that could never reveal the sources. Of course, the deaths of the bomb squad had been unfortunate. He could not be sure he had planned the timing of the cell to make their departure from the ship in a manner to keep them from being consumed by the force of the blast. He thought he had done so. Maybe the cell leader had failed to observe the timeline established to handle that aspect of the operation. Regardless, the entire crew had been blown to bits along with the ship and her crew. Indications were that the same fate had befallen the heroes in the Panama Canal also.

The problem inherent in covert operations was the inability to make assessments of their effectiveness first hand. The perpetrators had to rely on the information provided by the media. Naturally, the governments were reluctant to pass on any real tidbits of information, so the minutia details were sketchy at best. One thing, however, was coming through quite clear: There had been a complete breakdown of discipline when it came to keeping secrets once a member was captured. According to the reports coming out of Indonesia those people were singing like the birds. Abu had always suspected those non-Arabs to be inferior adherents to the faith. Apparently, he was correct in this assessment.

Had he been aware that his counterpart, Ahmed El Jamaal, the area commander for that part of the world, had been picked up in the massive sweep, he would have been even more concerned. Isolation of the various levels in the Movement had denied all but the most essential elements from the general membership. This was not the case at the area commander level. Effectiveness had demanded that the top leadership would be knowledgeable of the inner workings of the organization. Although Abu was unaware of the true identity of the Patriarch, he had long ago considered this matter and had narrowed it down to a handful of men. He was more knowledgeable of the chain of command below his position and there could be no doubt that each of his counterparts was blessed with the same acumen.

It took a full hour before the telephone had startled the terrorist from his musing and worries. So anxious was he to respond to the ringing summons that he had knocked the telephone off the table and had to retrieve it before speaking into the transmitter.

"Salaam," he greeted the caller in the customary Semitic manner.

If he had thought that contact with his beloved leader would salve his frayed nerves, he was sorely mistaken. The voice at the other end of the wire informed him that the Patriarch was unavailable and would remain so for the immediate future. Abu was admonished that he, also, should consider relocation and implement his own escape and evasion plan. The call had lasted for a brief few seconds before the caller had broken the connection. Abu had stood in silence for a few seconds before returning the receiver to its cradle. He felt the hair on the nape of his neck standing out and felt his color start to wane.

How quickly can fortunes change! Only a few hours ago Abu had been in a state of euphoria. He had succeeded in accomplishing one of the most horrific attacks upon the infidels since there had been the Movement. True, the saints who had sacrificed their lives in the process had a tragic end to their lives, but at this very moment they were in paradise and being rewarded beyond human capability to comprehend. Now, Abu's world was in complete free fall. He had always feared that this day might come, but his optimism had dispelled these feelings for the most part. This was something that "happened to other people, not him!"

Abu was strong enough to survive any hardships that might come from his forced exile, but he was sure that his wife did not have the same drive. He was going to have to collect her and very little of this world's treasures and make a hasty flight. He had made arrangements to provide funds that would last for some time, but there was not enough to maintain their present lifestyle. His "getaway" stash was complete with the necessary phony passports and documents to affect his departure. There was sufficient cash to obtain the necessary airline tickets and take care of the living accommodations until he reached his final destination.

How do you suddenly tell your wife, whom you have purposely kept in the dark concerning the double life you have been living, that she must leave immediately and forgo all her possessions? She would never again see her family members or any of the friends accumulated over a lifetime. There were no children resulting from their marriage, or the necessary arrangements would have been even more devastating. Well, that was all moot now.

He had moved with determination and practiced and disciplined procedures rehearsed many times mentally. In less than one hour the Bin Hadjes were in line at the ticket counter at Damascus International. Fortunately, the lines were short this morning and they would be aloft and on their way to a new life and identity. His training had put him on automatic pilot and anyone observing him would probably ignore him completely. That certainly was not the case when it came to his wife, though. She looked extremely nervous and distraught. Abu decided that if anyone should approach them he would tell them that his wife's sister had just died and they were en route to the funeral.

Just as he placed his bags on the scales and turned to the ticket agent, an airport policeman appeared out of nowhere. Without even looking at Mrs. Hadj, he told Abu, "Come with me." There was no rational reason for him to even protest and he turned immediately and left his wife standing in total awe as he was led away. Her wails continued to pierce his entire being as he was forcibly led to a small room common to every airport in the world.

"Papers, please," the policeman demanded with barely discernable politeness. Abu immediately recovered his facilities and went into the role he had practiced many times before.

"Certainly! Can you tell me why I am being detained? I don't want to miss my flight. My wife is very distraught at the death of her sister and we need to get on board in order to make it in time for the funeral."

"I see, my condolences to you and your family. This won't take long. I see you live in Damascus, Mr. Akmed. How long have you lived here?"

"Oh, we've been here for nearly five years now. It was one of the best decisions we ever made to move here. Do you come from here, too? The policeman didn't respond to the question and refused to be engaged in niceties that would allow his quarry to relax.

"Which mosque do you and your wife belong to?" the interrogator continued. After informing the man of the particular mosque he and his wife attended on a regular basis, the next question demanded to know the name of the mullah in charge of that particular congregation. When Abu was able to relate the name of the cleric, the policeman told him to remain seated and left the room.

In less than two minutes the door reopened and the policeman entered the room. He was not alone, though. Immediately behind him was the leader of the mosque he and his wife had been attending for years.

"Salaam, Abu, what is the meaning of all this?" the cleric stated in dismay. "This officer tells me that your name is Akmed; surely this is a mistake?" The smile that came over the face of the policeman was all the proof that Abu needed that his life had taken a drastic and downward plunge. The policeman thanked the mullah for his presence in the airport for the past twelve hours and dismissed him to return to his own life.

"Well, Akmed, you need to inform Abu Bin Hadj that he will soon find himself dangling at the end of a rope right out in the streets of Damascus. There is a new day dawning in Syria and Abu Bin Hadj will not see the dawn of it. The wife of that scoundrel will meet the same fate, too." The sarcasm in his voice could not hide the self-aggrandizement flowing through the mind of the policeman who was responsible for the capture of one of the most sought-after criminals in the entire world. Certainly, a promotion would be the least of honors he would soon be receiving.

— 6 —

Damascus Police Headquarters
Wednesday, October 19, 3:22 p.m.

Police stations in all third world countries are very similar in make-up and appearance. The dankness of the basement where the cells of the more violent criminals were placed could almost be felt on the skin. They must have gone to great lengths to find and import so many vermin as were present in the close confines of these dungeons. The mattress in Abu's cell was torn and most of the stuffing had long since been lost in the many years since it was new. His predecessors had figured out a way of moving the remaining padding to the top of the mattress in order to maintain some sort of a pillow. The room smelled vile and the stench of urine was only slightly quelled by the horrific odors emanating from what was purported to be the toilet in the corner. A faucet was jutting out from the wall and had been inverted to act as a drinking fountain and whatever other hygienic necessities would be forthcoming. All these inconveniences were the farthest thing from Abu's mind under the present circumstances.

He wondered what was going on with his wife. Hadad was not a very strong person. He had always prided himself for the selection of such a personality as his wife. People like that did not become inquisitive about the comings and goings of their husbands and were willing to put up with a lot of blank spaces created by the missions a soldier of Allah would be required to perform. But this timidity was now a source of great concern to him. She would completely unravel at the slightest interrogation. The bad part was that she possessed just enough information to destroy his cover completely. He didn't even know where all this was taking place, but knew beyond a doubt that it was. They would learn very quickly that she was completely innocent of any wrongdoing, but that would not be any salvation to her. She was a valuable asset to attack her husband's psyche and would be treated with intolerable and humiliating physical and emotional torture for the benefit of her husband. The bastards!

It was important to begin the interrogation of Abu as soon as possible after his arrest. He was vulnerable because interrogators throughout history have learned that people become talkative after a harrowing experience. Abu's training had made him acutely aware of this factor and yet there was no escaping this truth. He would try to withhold as much information as was possible, but if there was one thing he had learned over the years, anybody would talk under the right circumstances. His training was based upon his ability to withstand the torture for as long as possible in order to allow his allies to either change codes, plans, locations, or all the above. The longer he could hold out the better chances for his cohorts to escape.

Within twenty minutes of his deposit in the cell, a guard and escort had arrived and unceremoniously opened the metal door. "On your feet!" the more sadistic of the two had screamed, and added emphasis to his directive by placing an enormous boot into the groin area of the prone prisoner. The other member of the entourage reached down and assisted the injured man to his feet and began leading him to the cell doorway.

In the past, it had always been Abu who was the inflictor of punishment or interrogation of any subject worthy of such. He knew every trick in the book when it came to extracting information from a subject holding such knowledge. That was not going to be of much help to him in the present situation. In fact, it would be even more detrimental since he always knew what was coming next.

The interrogator did not disappoint him. The initial assault consisted of a full explanation of the fact that his wife was just down the hall and her welfare was completely in his own hands. They knew that he was too sophisticated to believe that she would escape final judgment, but the manner in which this would be meted out depended upon his cooperation with the interrogation team. They also knew that this approach would not gain them much outside the personal injury it would cause the man sitting in front of them. This guy would be fanatical in his beliefs and would not hesitate to sacrifice his own mother to the most unspeakable degradation in order to help his cause. Oh well, they had to go through the motions anyway.

Once it was clear that the niceties were out of the way the sadistic elements of treatment could begin. Once more, Abu's expectations were met in full force. Pain is a relative thing. The human brain has certain escape elements to allow separation of the pain from that part of the mind that causes severe reaction. Abu was not only aware of this but was a practitioner of this mode of defense. Severe beating had only entrenched his desire to withhold all information and when more sophisticated means of inflicting pain were put into effect he was able to hold out for a greater time period than was expected. The problem with torture is that the body knows when it has had enough and allows the victim to escape through unconsciousness. On two occasions the tormentor had to revive the prisoner to consciousness in order to continue the quest of excruciating pain. You also had to be able to detect the time when the victim was getting dangerously close to insanity. You could not revive such a person and all the information contained in the scrambled brain would be lost for all time.

It was nearly dawn when the first crack appeared in Abu's defense. It had come when they had brought his wife into the room and allowed Abu to see the bloody pulp her face had become. There was a large stain of blood just below the waist of her dress that said paragraphs as to the treatment she had received by her tormentors. That had been his undoing. The inquisitor had allowed himself to smile when Abu fell limp in his chair and began to sob hopelessly. From then on the information began to pour freely from a completely broken man. He even divulged the names of the four or five individuals he surmised contained the one of the Patriarch. Little did he know that his assessment had already been confirmed and the several members of the guilty parties were just down the hall from his present location. Abu even implicated men who were close to the president of Syria as sympathizers in the Movement. The two interrogators exchanged glances when this bit of information came out. It wasn't due to surprise, but more in anticipation that they just might have the opportunity to "question" his eminence.

Sarasota, Florida
Thursday, October 20, 7:18 a.m.

Mahmud El Bari was just finishing his breakfast and getting ready to leave for the taxi stand when a knock came on his apartment door. His flat still contained the aroma of the scented candles he preferred to ignite when he conducted his morning prayers in the true Islamic manner. He casually walked to the door, halfway expecting to be greeted by his irritating neighbor, who would accuse him of stealing his daily newspaper again. The guy was a complete jerk; even thought his accusations were completely true. Why buy a newspaper subscription when your stupid neighbor was too lazy to get out of bed and collect his early delivery?

This time, however, it was not the frumpy guy in his worn bathrobe and slippers. Instead, it was two gentlemen dressed in business suits and the undeniable appearance of all plainclothes cops. Both men, as if they were controlled by some hidden robotic device, had shown him their badges and FBI credentials almost simultaneously with a request to gain entry into Mahmud's home.

Instinctively, the Arab reached in his billfold and produced his green card and thrust it forward, hoping against all hope that these guys were checking up on his authorized presence in the United States. He had actually gone to the trouble of obtaining actual authorization from the INS some months earlier and even made sure that he continued to be a registered student at Florida State University. Actually, the classes had been interesting and fit in well with his scheduled hours at the taxi stand. His cover was well documented and would withstand close scrutiny. Unfortunately, that was not the reason the two agents were paying a call upon his residence.

"Mr. El Bari, we need you to come with us. We're doing a routine investigation of a completely different nature and, although you are not a suspect in any way, we feel that you could be of assistance in the matter."

Praise be to Allah! At first he thought that they might be on to him. It was silly of him to think so, since he prided himself as possessed of professionalism to the point of arrogance. No, they never would suspect a mere taxi driver of being the senior member of the Movement in the Western Hemisphere. He made a great show of cooperation as he got in the government sedan and allowed them to take him downtown to the typical grey building with the usual federal building plaque.

"We really appreciate your help, Mr. El Bari," one of the agents repeated for the umpteenth time since they had first met. They made entry through the front door. They were allowed to bypass the metal detectors when the agents showed their badges. That meant that they were "packin' heat," in the vernacular of the American television productions. They took the stairway rather than wait on the elevator and made three complete revolutions before arriving at the large metal door with the ceremonious "3" inscribed with the usual black enamel. From there it was a mere forty feet down the hallway. Mahmud had almost caught his breath once more when they entered the branch offices of the United States Federal Bureau of Investigation.

"Would you like some coffee?" the secretary offered with a big smile as she was closing the door to the outer office.

No, he didn't and it wouldn't have mattered what his response might have been because he caught the stern negative shaking of the head of the chief agent in the room.

"Mahmud El Bari, are you aware of your rights under the Constitution of the United States?" Without waiting for a response, the agent went on, "You have the right to remain silent; you have the right to representation from an attorney; if you cannot afford an attorney one will be provided you at no cost to you whatsoever. However, if you give up these rights, any statement you make may be used against you in a court of law—do you understand these rights?"

What ever happened to those two nice guys who had shown up at his door not more than half an hour ago? They were now gone and in their place were two agents in the same suits, but with completely different personalities.

"Due to the seriousness of the charges you now face, I am advising you to make no statements whatsoever without a lawyer present," the senior of the two stated. That could only mean one thing: they had him dead to rights and no matter what he said, or didn't say, they had him by the proverbial short hairs.

"You are charged with espionage and destruction of property under the Wars Act, which is a capital offense with punishment up to and including death." There was no emotion in the voice of the agent, but a strong hint of his despise for the man could not help but surface for the individual sitting right in front of him.

Unlike the interrogation methods practiced throughout much of the third world, the interview with Mahmud would be considerate and completely fair. Because of this the police officials in the United States were forced to do a much more thorough investigation of alleged infractions than would have been necessary elsewhere. The dossier on Mahmud El Bari was nearly two inches thick and would continue to grow exponentially in the next few weeks.

Not more than twenty seconds after the two agents and Mahmud had left his apartment, three FBI suburban vehicles had pulled up to the curb in front of the domicile. The team of agents from these vehicles, armed with all the appropriate search warrants, had swarmed upon the home and was still making a thorough examination of every nook and cranny of the apartment. There was another team doing the same thing at the mini-storage where Mahmud had rented a space under a fictitious name. The contents of this facility would be a treasure trove of evidence used in a future trial of Mr. El Bari.

Since there was no pressure to do so, the government agents decided to let Mahmud cool his heels in an isolation cell until the evidence that would be collected from his personal sources could be examined and allow them to question the subject armed with even more effectiveness. Regardless, this despot was toast. The information already on hand was his attendance at the meeting in Morocco, complete with itinerary from the time he flew out of Atlanta until his return to Miami International. His "tails" had been instrumental in getting fixes on other members of his organization who had attended the meeting. It was only the significance of that meeting that had eluded the agency until after the terrorist attacks. Too bad they couldn't turn this guy over to the allied Arabs, who had much better ways of dealing with scum like Mr. El Bari.

Discussions with neighbors of Mahmud was very enlightening. The bachelor living next door was more than willing to discuss all the shortcomings of "that camel jockey next door." He was a "thief and a liar and he constantly stank because he refused to take a bath. Did you smell that stench coming out of his apartment? Those guys who smoke "wackey tobaccky" always try to hide the smell by burning that stinkin' incense. I never did trust that S.O.B. Wha'd he do?"

The other neighbors were a little more objective in their responses and confirmed that the subject was always going off for trips that might last for a week or more. No, they didn't know where he went. When they would kid him about having a girlfriend that kept him on the move, he would never divulge any information on where he had been or what he had been doing. A couple of times several men had come to the home, but they never were loud and didn't seem to be drunk

"You know how those Muslims hate anything to do with liquor," one of the neighbors said.

In fact, Mahmud El Bari was the mastermind behind the assault on the Panama Canal. As area commander for Western Hemisphere operations, he had set up the entire operation from the beginning to the end. Even the decision to eliminate all the operational element involved in the actual destruction of the oil tanker had been his decision. The westerns had an old adage: "Dead men tell no tales." So high was the impact that the American government would never rest until they had arrested the culprits in such an attack. It was better to ensure that they could never have any closure to this episode, so Mahmud had made sure that the explosion was far more potent than what was needed. Further, he had sabotaged the charges by setting timed fuses that would detonate far before the saboteurs had an opportunity to escape before the explosion. Allah would have explained all that to them in satisfactory terms when they arrived in Paradise. They would thank him when they next met.

If you have occasion to visit any of the penal institutions in America you will soon discover the breeding ground for contempt. The inmates are already angry about their situation, so it doesn't take much coaxing to fuel that discontent. The Movement had been quick to recognize that these prisons hold a large population that can be exploited. A sympathetic ear to one of these malcontents goes a long way. All that was necessary was to convince the inmate that he, or she, had been the victim of a non-caring American who had exploited them and was the reason that they had justifiably taken up their life of crime. The indoctrination was designed to convince the inmate that he was truly a wonderful person and that he did not need to dignify the exploiters by living down to their expectations. From there, the target would be introduced to Allah, who understood how the satanic culture of the West had ruined their lives. Before long, the American inmate could adapt to the "true way of life" and would be ready to do whatever was necessary to destroy this evil society.

Mahmud had sought out some of the more militant converts for the special mission in Panama. They had eagerly agreed to strike a major blow for Allah against the evil influences of the infidel West.

The more difficult part of the mission had been the assembly of the munitions and getting them onboard the oil tanker. The Patriarch had come up with a stoke of genius when he had convinced the Movement that it would be wise to spend the necessary funds to become owners of their own ship. This had occurred several years ago and had been operating as a Liberian flagship since it became property of the Movement. The beauty was the fact that the same vessel had been flying the Liberian flag long before the acquisition. The ownership was so blindly hidden that it would be nearly impossible to ascertain the identity of its proprietor.

This vessel had been instrumental in several successful missions over the years and kept prying eyes from wondering about activities the ship was involved in. The fact that the ship had been employed in legitimate transport when not being needed had actually turned a profit that helped to fund some of the Movement's clandestine operations. The relocation of operative cargo was allowed to be moved freely to any port in the world. Several times it had been rumored that the vessel had moved high-grade uranium to places that would cause major concern in Western capitals. The ship had been quite active in the pre-positioning of the necessary items used in the recent attacks in all three remote locations. The leaders were so impressed with the import of the ship to the Movement that the captain, Augustus Numenoglu, a Turk by origin but a fine Muslim, was promoted to area commander. He had been in attendance at the Moroccan meeting as had all the other area commanders involved in the mission.

Still, it was necessary to exercise strict caution when assembling the various materials from which the explosives had been derived from. Then there was the difficulty in getting the explosive devices aboard the two vessels. It had posed very little challenges in making crew substitutions. Their friend in Kuwait had been very useful in eliminating the necessary crew members and replacing them with our own cell members. The ease with which the replacement members of the Panamanian effort had been almost as easy. It simply required that the new crew members be allowed to join the ship's crew in a manner of attrition which had been greatly assisted by timed disappearances of the original members.

The loading of the explosive devices was accomplished long before the crew members were installed. This effort had been done in several steps to avoid detection and from as many ports. Had the captains of these two ships realized the horrific bombs they had been riding upon for the past six months, they would have been candidates for mental institutions. All that was necessary for the Muslim crew members was to locate the items in the stowage compartments where they had been cached and make the appropriate assembly in the critical points. From there, all they had to do was activate the timers and jump ship. At least they thought they would get to jump ship.

Mahmud had not been in charge of the operations in Alaska, even though they occurred in his area of management. It was decided that the Indonesian Muslims could pass themselves off as Native Americans and be able to move freely about the state of Alaska in that guise. It had, apparently, worked since the papers had been full of stories about the "terrible tragedy" in Alaska.

And terrible tragedy it had been for the economy of the state of Alaska. A huge portion of the state's income had been derived from the pipeline and now that it was shut down, the pinch was really beginning to hurt. The cost of living in Alaska is one of the highest in the world. This fact had not been considered a major drawback to its citizens in the past because incomes were high enough to balance the equation. Now, with high unemployment resulting from the domino effect of the lost pipeline, the average citizen in the urban areas of the state were beginning to worry with just cause. Those people who lived in the more remote areas were less affected because many of them had learned long ago how to survive off the plentiful game in the wild.

It would not be long before many of the unemployed would be working under the lights of the Aurora Borealis in multiple shifts to get the pipeline back into operation. President Marshall had made it quite clear that all necessary steps to put every damaged element back to better than before status, and that this reconstruction would be done at a speed that would be talked about for many years to come. It would strain the budget to make it so but the alternative was not acceptable. The people were in full agreement and the Congress had better not forget that. They didn't.

For years now there had been an ongoing fight in the Congress over the Anwar Reserve. This land sat atop one of the largest oil fields in the known world. Its location was relatively close to the head of the Alaskan oil pipeline, but it had remained untapped due to the complaints of numerous "environmental" groups. Well, those days were coming to a swift end. There would be no more attempts to placate these obstructionists and tree huggers. The rapid development of this vast field would be explored and placed into production as fast as the drill rigs could reach the area and begin work.

— 7 —

Washington, D.C.
Friday, October 21 4:30 p.m.

It had been nine days since the terrible disasters had awakened the whole world up to a period when the nations of this earth were going to either solve the major problems facing it or fall back into a period paralleling those of the dark ages. For five decades the powers of the planet had turned a blind eye to the festering cancer in the Middle East. Most of them took the approach that since it didn't really affect them in any particular manner, it was OK to ignore it. Those people had been fighting with each other for over a thousand years and were unwilling to give an inch. Why should we trouble ourselves with them? Several presidents of the United States had tried to bring the parties together and all it got them was sorrow. Let them kill each other off once and for all and go in afterward and clean up the mess.

Todd Martin had been involved with the results of our neglect for only a few days when he realized that he was pretty much ignorant of the whole picture. He wasn't going to learn much sitting here in Washington and that was going to have to change. In his new capacity he only had to state what he wanted and it happened in an expeditious manner. He was getting used to that after only a couple of days on the job.

"Mrs. Johnson, I need to do some traveling out of the country," he told her after summoning her to his office. "Could you arrange for me to make some on-site visits to each of the disaster sites in the following order: Alaska,

Panama and then Egypt? I need to get on the road as soon as possible."

"Yes, sir, would that be next week; say, Monday?" she queried with pen poised over her note pad.

"No, ma'am. I mean right away—tonight, if you can handle it," he stated in more of a request than anything.

"Well … yes, sir, but what about Mrs. Martin? Should I notify her or will you be taking her along with you?" the matronly lady requested with a somewhat troubled look coming over her. She was like a mother hen and wanted to keep her boss out of any situation where he might become the victim of "those awful people over there."

"Let me take care of Cathy; you just see what you can do about getting one of those nice little jet planes over at Andrews ready for me," he said in a reassuring manner. "I think that the sooner I get a firsthand look at those sites before they get too far along in cleaning them up, the better I can do my job. Also, I may want to take a few side trips while I am running all over the globe. I really need to get down to Jakarta and thank those guys for the super job they did in breaking this case. I'll also want to pay a couple of visits to Damascus and Tehran while I'm in the neighborhood. Things are pretty shaky over there right now and it's about time that they quit being the cause of it. You'll have to take over here while I'm off partying," he said with a smirk.

Fifteen minutes later, Mrs. Johnson came back to his office and announced, "It's all set up, Mr. Martin. The guys will have an airplane ready for your disposal by 18:00 hours, whatever that means. By the way, while I was arranging for your trip, the people over at CIA and the FBI got wind of it and called to ask if they could send a couple of their people along with you. I told them I would get back to them after I talked to you. What should I tell them?"

"Please tell them that I would welcome the company but make sure they know that this trip may take a little time away from home. I want to keep off an itinerary and let the situation develop while it progresses. Maybe we should ask for a bigger plane … "

"I'm way ahead of you on that one, boss. The pilots requested that you take one of the larger aircraft since they have a much longer range and the sleeping accommodations are much better that way. I'll be getting back to those folks over at the bureau and the agency so they can get moving if it's OK with you, sir."

"Please do and thanks for the wonderful way you always are on top of everything. I don't know what I'd do without you—and that's the truth."

With that his secretary scurried out of his office and left him alone to make a phone call to Cathy.

"What?! You're going where? For how long?"

The usual and expected questions erupted from his wife as he was explaining to her that he needed to go and inspect the target sites. Cathy had always been the perfect wife for him. When he was a "shavetail" down at Fort Bragg she had gotten used to his short-notice departures as executive officer for a Green Beret detachment or the "A-Team" as they called it. He had been in Special Forces for three full years before he was selected to attend the career course down at Benning. She had been an absolute angel through all his absences and had taken over the household like a real trooper without once complaining.

When he was selected for General Croft's personal staff it meant that he would be working almost seven days each week with a little time off on Sunday afternoon to be a husband and father. His daily schedule caused him to leave before six in the morning and he rarely came home before the same time twelve hours later. He loved it and because of that, and her love for him, she had made the best of it. When he first approached her about getting out of the service and going to work for General Croft she did all she could do to keep from jumping up and down while clicking her heels. Now, he would be a civilian and they could live like real people! What a joke!

The call he was making to his wife right now was one of those times when he wondered how he ever got so lucky as to talk a gal like that into marrying him. After the initial shock her response was the same as always: "Well, honey, if you need to go then you should—but dammit, be careful. We need you, too."

"You know I always do, honey ... oh, damn, I haven't even called the president yet to tell him I'm leaving. I'll call you from the plane. Love ya, bye."

He hung up the telephone and immediately used the private number the chief of staff for the White House had given him. He had scarcely dialed the number before the COS answered.

"What's up Todd?"

He explained everything to the chief of staff and asked him to get the president's OK on it. Darn. What if he said no? But he didn't and even thought it was a great idea for Todd to get as involved as was necessary to do his job for the American people to the best of his ability. Todd made a mental note to never jump the gun like that again. He had always been a take-charge guy and now he needed to be more attentive to protocol if he was going to be working at this level. Nobody likes a "loose cannon."

Cathy had a bag packed for him when the courier had arrived at their home to pick it up. She never missed a thing and even took time to make him a couple of sandwiches to tide him over on the trip. He didn't need them since the VIP aircraft he had "commandeered" had a full galley and the personnel to provide gourmet meals. Of course, she would never learn about it if he could help it.

It was dark by the time he was transported to the door of the airplane by the limo. A guy could really get used to this VIP treatment if he didn't watch out. He ran up the stairway to the open door of the airplane and was greeted by the agency and bureau people as soon as he entered the door.

"Good evening, Mr. Martin," they chimed and, in turn, extended their hands for a firm handshake. It was obvious that they had been informed that Todd was in full charge of this trip and they would be taking their orders from him. He decided to let them continue to feel his authority until he could sort out how they would conduct themselves as the journey progressed. Without much chit-chat he left them and went to his assigned seat in the aircraft and strapped himself in for the takeoff.

Todd always enjoyed flying and tried not to look like some starry-eyed kid as he peered out the window of the aircraft. This was referred to as "fly over" country by most of the folks inside the beltway, but to him it represented the entire reason that the nation's capital existed. The tiny farms below represented all that was truly good about America. At the present time the farmers in those homes were thinking about an early retirement for the evening so they would be fresh when five o'clock came in the morning. The occasional city they would pass over was announced by the pilot with frequent anecdotes concerning various areas they, for the most part, could not really see due to the late hours. Nevertheless, it was truly a wonderful experience to fly across America during the hours of darkness with the distant lights of many cities and the numerous stars glowing in the sky.

By the time they reached Seattle, the glow of flying had started to wear just a little thin and Todd was grateful that they would be stopping at McCord Air Force Base just outside of Tacoma for refueling. The passengers were allowed to de-plane while the routine maintenance and refueling operation continued. The night air here in the Northwest was cool but comfortable even at this time of the year. During the approach the pilot had made it his plan to fly close enough to Mount Rainier so that its majesty could be observed even though the moon was only in half-phase. No wonder the people in this part of the country were so proud of the area.

After a short period of time had passed the "crew chief" (why did they call them that when they were truly flight attendants?) signaled them that it was time to re-board the aircraft once more. In less than five minutes they were climbing out over the Puget Sound, where numerous ferry boats were making their ways to their destinies only to repeat the circuit continuously year round. Just off the right wing of the airplane, Todd could see the entire city of Seattle. This was one of the most beautiful cities he had ever seen with its setting among the tall fir trees and clean air. No wonder they call it the "Emerald City." He and Cathy had chosen this place to begin their marriage and had never regretted it. The side trips to Vancouver, Canada, and over to Victoria over on Vancouver Island had been magnificent. One could stay in this area for years and never take in all the beauty of the San Juan Islands that dotted the inland waterways all the way up to Alaska.

Realizing that he would be having a rather hectic schedule in the immediate future, Todd reclined his seat fully and started to drift off to sleep when he received a slight nudge from the flight attendant.

"Would you prefer to lie down on a bed?" the airman inquired.

Oh, yes, they really did have them on board this VIP aircraft and Todd was beginning to really enjoy this pampered life. The drone of the turbine engines had a soothing effect and before long, Todd was in a world all his own in dreamless sleep.

"Excuse me, sir. We're beginning our descent into Fairbanks. Can I get you a cup of coffee?"

The attendant was already holding the steaming cup and it was obvious that they had taken note that he drank coffee with one packet of sweetener. Todd reached out and took the cup from her hand and nodded grateful appreciation. He had just enough time to finish the cup when he felt the slight bump that always accompanies the touchdown of the landing gear.

Scarcely had the wheel chalks been put in place when the door in the front of the plane opened and a smiling governor of the state of Alaska poked his head into the cabin and called, "Mr. Martin?" Governor Hansen had made it a point to clear his calendar so that he could join the entourage for the duration of the Fed's visit.

Although the temperatures in the Puget Sound area had been quite comfortable, the air coming in through the open door of the airplane was absolutely biting.

"Better put on these parkas, gentlemen," the governor said as he gestured to the pile of garments one of his aides was carrying. "It gets a little nippy up here at this time of the year." Nippy! What would it take for this guy to call it freezing?

Todd and his comrades donned the parkas with acknowledgments of undying gratitude and pulled the hoods up over their heads before venturing out into the night air.

"What time is it here?" one of the Washington group inquired as he gazed at his watch still set on Eastern Time.

"It's a little before midnight," was the response. Although the flight had taken much longer to make the crossing, they had been chasing the sun and had lost seven hours in the process. "We've taken the liberty to set up your accommodations for the evening over at the Hilton, since I gather that you boys could use a little shut-eye before we go out traipsing around the countryside tomorrow morning."

Thanks were extended and after the normal courtesies were accomplished during and after the five mile ride to downtown Fairbanks, each of the visitors had gone to their individual rooms to continue the interrupted sleep began aboard the airplane. Todd decided to shower before retiring as travel has a way of making you feel the need for personal hygiene. Half an hour after closing the door to his room, Todd was doing some serious snoring.

Although he had taken the time to request a wake-up call before retiring, Todd was awake for half an hour before the telephone jangled. He had been shaving and managed to cover the receiver with shaving foam when he answered it. He dressed hurriedly and decided to make a call home to Cathy and the kids since it would be well into their day on the East Coast. Luckily, he caught her just as she was getting ready to go out the front door and they exchanged their reassurance of love for a couple of minutes before Todd had to break off the call. Becky and little Hal were excited to talk to daddy on the telephone and told him they already missed him in the short conversation with each one of them.

By the time he got to the dining room of the hotel the rest of his group had already begun their breakfasts. Since they would be out in "the boondocks" for much of the day, the party had elected to eat a hearty morning meal and forego the continental breakfast that came with their rooms. There was no telling when they would be getting back to civilization once they started the tour.

The trip to the Air Force base was accomplished in short order and they found themselves boarding a Huey that would be their main source of travel throughout the day. Lift off went without a hitch and before long they were traveling over a twilight countryside which consisted of miles and miles of evergreen trees. The military pilot explained to them that although the forest was dense, it was quite different than "down below in the forty-eight." Due to the constant permafrost, the roots of the trees were unable to penetrate deeply into the soil and their growth was stunted to the extent that most trees never grew to a height of more than twenty feet tall. If you were standing next to one of them you would see a normal-sized trunk but the top was well within close proximity. Several times, the pilot pointed out wild game consisting of several contacts with moose, bear and the plentiful deer.

Before too long had passed they felt the aircraft bank steeply to the right and they had their first sight of the carnage at one of the blast sites. Wow! Below them was a huge pipeline that disappeared over the horizon in both direction, but their gaze was fixed upon the mayhem surrounding the blackened area of the forest below. The immediate area, which consisted of a circle approximately three hundred meters in diameter, was strewn with twisted pieces of metal that had once been part of the Alaska Pipeline. The area had an eerie sensation as there were many banks of high intensity lighting placed strategically around the blast site and there were not less than fifty workmen scurrying around the blast area. Heavy equipment had been positioned in the vicinity and was making the initial cuts to begin the massive cleanup effort that would take some time.

"You can see more from the chopper than if we put you on the ground and we can hover as close as you need to the points of interest," the pilot stated over the intercom. "Your call, sir," the aviator queried as he glanced to Todd. "If you get down there on that muck, I have a feeling you will wish you hadn't, though."

"Thanks, Chief," Todd replied to the chief warrant officer, who was their pilot in command. "I think this will do quite nicely. Can you take us over there to the right? I want to get a better look at the craters under the pipeline." The aircraft began a smooth movement to the right and maintained an attitude that would afford the best view for Todd and his people. They stayed on site just long enough to take in the full impact of the damage inflicted by the terrorists and then continued on their journey.

Before three o'clock that afternoon they had visited each of the disaster sites. It could have been done in less time, but the limitations on fuel for the birds required two separate returns to the Army base to take on more JP-4 in the fuel tanks. The passengers were grateful for the interruption, which allowed them to relieve themselves in the interim.

"You don't buy coffee; you rent it," one of the members of the party commented. The thoughts of the passengers went back to the breakfast table where they had each drank several refills of coffee in order to wake up. That would not happen in the future.

The anger that had been present in each of the Feds before the trip to Fairbanks was inflamed to the boiling point now that they had time to actually visit the sites.

"I'll want to get some report from our agents on the ground ASAP," the FBI guy had voiced when they were back on the ground in Fairbanks. "You'd be amazed to know the information we can pick up even in a mess like that. In short order we will know what types of explosives were used and even have a good handle on where they came from. Explosives have their own signature and there is a wide variety of each kind. We're gonna nail the bastards who did this!"

"From what I hear, we already have. Now all we need to do is police up their bosses and anyone else who had anything to do with this," Todd responded.

"Yeah, and I hear that the guys who caught up with them are not restrained like we are when it comes to meting out justice," the CIA guy blurted out. "Well, I guess that's what makes us *civilized*," he said with as much sarcasm as the comment deserved.

The next day was filled with meetings attended by both state and federal agencies, along with representation from civilians and the Army Corps of Engineers. The governor made an impressive speech to the group and thanked them, on behalf of all Alaskans, for the prompt attention this matter had gained. He stressed the importance of the pipeline to his state and how the residents of his state were grateful for any assistance rendered on their behalf.

On the way to the air field the driver of their vehicle said, "when you catch those sand niggers I hope you'll give them one for me, too. I've got some civilian friends up here that are really hurting over this and their kids will be missin' out on Christmas this year." Glances of embarrassment passed between the team of Feds in the vehicle since one of their team was a black man.

"Oh hell yeah," he stated with a big grin, "but I'm the only one who's supposed to use that "N" word." Due to the fatigue and sensitivity of the subject, there was a simultaneous burst of laughter in the vehicle.

"Sergeant, you might want to use more discretion in your choice of language in the future. Many of our Arabic citizens are as loyal as anyone in this sedan and we don't need to get into the habit of denouncing all of them based upon the action of a small minority, but just for the record, these guys are just what you called them," Todd said in a way to bring the topic to a close. Once more the occupants erupted into laughter.

"Guys, I want to stick to our general plan, so we will be flying down to Panama this evening. I don't know about you, but my bed on the plane was quite comfortable, so we should be able to get enough sleep to allow us to be functional by tomorrow morning when we arrive. I told the pilots to sleep in all day while we were running all over Alaska, so they should be well rested enough to keep us from flying into the Gulf of Mexico."

Todd mentioned as they were boarding the aircraft once more.

"Colonel McIntire tells me we will be making a refueling stop at Travis and then we will have plenty of fuel to get us to Panama City. By the way, I want to thank you fellas for your help on this trip. You've opened up some interesting aspects to this case and I think it's high time that we all got on a first name basis, if it's OK with you." Nods and smiles indicated that would be just fine.

None of the passengers woke up during the landing and takeoff from the California Air Force Base, as a tribute to the skill of their pilots. The sun shining through the port windows of the aircraft was a pleasant awakening as they began their decent into the canal zone. By the time that the jet arrived at the stopping point all the members of the team had dressed and completed their lavatory requirements to make the proper first impression on the greeting party.

Since Operation Just Cause had removed Noriega from power the relations between the Panamanians and Americans had grown even closer than before. That did not mean, however, that the Chinese government had not tried to make inroads in the country in an attempt to drive a wedge between U.S. and Panama leadership. It had failed and the Chicoms had made a quiet retreat back home. Now that this terrible tragedy had taken place, the Panamanians were glad to have the support that only the United States could give them.

Once more, the team was loaded onto the helicopter that had been assigned to ferry them to "the site," as it now had become known throughout the area. The aircraft had made several circles of the location at both high and low level so the entire impact of the situation could be ascertained. Once more the Americans were in stunned silence as they observed the terrible destruction caused by the explosion. The huge magnificence of the oil tanker lying at an obtuse angle and the knowledge that many lives had been lost in the surrounding area could not be described in mere words.

A few minutes later the helicopter landed at a designated pad and the members disembarked, still in silence. The first one to speak was their guide, who began describing the workings of the canal and how the functioning canal had operated before now. He pointed out the key elements that were destroyed and made an estimate as to how long it would take to bring the canal back on line. The sight of the locomotive lying on the exposed hull made the scene all that much more ominous.

The remainder of the day was filled with numerous assessments and damage control briefings so that by the time the sun was setting in the west, the team had formed a good idea of what they would need to accomplish in their respective areas. The CIA and FBI guys had long since abandoned any pretense of the normal turf war and were sharing information as it became known. The four men had broken away from the site for approximately two and one-half hours and had driven to the national police headquarters to discuss their areas of expertise with counterparts. All had agreed that the trip to town was well worth their while and had established rapport with "the right people" that would be useful in subsequent trips down here. Todd was glad he had followed his instincts to make this trip as it was going to be of much help when he was reporting to the president and taking the necessary future actions. He would be able to pick the brains of his compatriots on the final return to Washington to glean their valuable input.

As if a pattern was beginning to emerge, the Americans returned to the air field just after completing the obligatory diplomatic dinner with the local government people. The pilots, who would rather fly at night, were glad to do so while their "cargo" was catching some Z's. This time they would be flying directly east and the autopilot would allow them to relax as they made their way across the Atlantic. Just over a hundred miles out of the Azores the pilots disrupted the autopilot and took manual control of the plane. They were on the ground for not more than twenty-five minutes while the normal refueling requirements were accomplished.

Once they were again airborne and at the designated altitude, the command pilot had set a course that would take them directly over the Strait of Gibraltar and down the centerline of the Mediterranean. This time, however, the auto pilot was not engaged since the airplane would be traversing the North African coastline and there were known hostile people in those countries. That accounted for the two "Tomcats" from the Eisenhower that suddenly joined them on each wing. We were at DEFCON-3 due to the situation the world was now forced to deal with. You just could not deny the pride one feels when you have the professional military support that is the hallmark of our ongoing diplomatic arsenal.

By the time the airplane was passing over the toe of the boot of Italy, the entire passenger list was awake and enjoying another of the sumptuous meals that were constantly emerging from the galley.

"Was it acceptable to tip these folks?" the junior FBI agent queried as they were finishing the brunch. A discussion followed that resulted in the determination that it would be an insult to do so, but Todd was successful in obtaining the complete roster of all the air crew before the trip ended. They were going to get some great letters of commendation, signed by the president, to be placed in their service records.

The sudden southerly turn of the aircraft, followed by the beginning descent in altitude, was their notification that before long the airplane would be touching down at Cairo International. The pilots began their routine of the pre-landing checklist and the signs and countersigns so common in all the cockpits throughout the world progressed with the usual preciseness inherent in the occupation. They were passing through ten thousand feet when a violent action caused the aircraft to lurch to the port side and the attitude of the cabin to become tilted abnormally to the same side.

Instinctively, the members of the team tightened their individual seat belts and simultaneously turned their heads to see what had just happened to their airplane. From the left wing there was flame shooting out from a gaping hole just outboard of engine number one. The engine seemed to be functioning, but the loss of airfoil was causing the aircraft to pitch and roll at an increasing intensity.

The aircraft commander was a veteran of thousands of hours of flight with nearly four thousand hours of combat flight. He was the guy you wanted to be your pilot in the event of an emergency.

"Cairo tower, this is United States diplomatic flight 43, declaring an emergency," he stated as if he were reciting the latest weather report. "We have taken hostile fire from an unknown source and have sustained moderate damage to the aircraft. Request vector."

All the time he was reporting to the airport, the colonel was taking appropriate actions, one of which, to the delight of his passengers, was to extinguish the fire coming from the wing. He managed to bring the aircraft under a semblance of normalcy after adjusting the unaffected trim tabs on other air surfaces and, although there was a definite list of the airplane to the left, seemed to be maintaining flight without loss of altitude.

During the same period that all this was playing out the two fighter airplanes had rejoined the VIP bird and were providing escort to the injured aircraft as it continued to proceed toward the Egyptian capital. Suddenly, one of the escorts made a sharp bank and was joined by his wingman in a turning dive toward a point on the ground just aft of the lumbering American ship.

The military fighters, being equipped with the latest in defensive equipment, became aware of the second missile not long after it had left its tube. One of the fighters launched the first of two air-to-ground missiles directly at the launch site of the incoming rocket. There was a huge explosion less than a second later as the two high explosive heads detonated directly upon the firing enemy. The second aircraft engaged the missile that had been fired at the airliner and neutralized it a mere three hundred meters from its intended target. One of the jets resumed its defensive position alongside the wounded airplane while the other climbed to altitude and started into a holding pattern should any other enemy decide to go visit Allah.

The pilots resumed their pre-landing checklist as if nothing had happened and reached the item "landing gear down and locked." That was the indicator that not all was well.

"Landing gear *not* down and locked," the response came from the co-pilot. "Fuel on board sufficient for forty-five minutes flight time," the co-pilot added. In laymen's terms this meant that they would have sufficient time to rectify whatever was preventing the landing gear from locking into position.

The tower was informed of the newest situation and clearance was given to take whatever actions the pilot of the damaged aircraft needed to get the plane safely on the ground. Colonel McIntire came onto the cabin speakers and calmly announced, "Gentlemen, we seem to have had a welcoming party fire a one-gun salute to honor our arrival. We will be taking a few minutes to complete a few routine repairs so that we can get you all on the ground and not make you late for your lunch. We are not in any immediate danger, so you can best help by remaining in your seats and keeping your belts securely fastened. I guess this means that our in-flight movie will have to wait until our next flight. Thank you for flying the friendly skies of Arabia."

The co-pilot and one of the crew members came down the center aisle and removed a portion of the carpeting over a trap door in the floor. Both men disappeared down through the hole and moved to the place where manual operation of the wing landing gear could be effected. Before long, the two came back up into the cabin and the crew chief made the international sign of "its all right" by forming a circle with his thumb and index finger. A sigh of relief escaped the flight attendant at this piece of good news.

"Folks, Captain Hart tells me that we now have some legs to stand on, so we will be continuing our final approach into Cairo." Just after he turned off the cabin mike he stated to his co-pilot, "Why in the hell did I say 'final!'"

The airplane touched down with the smoothness that would have been the envy of any pilot in the world under normal conditions. Along the entire runway were numerous fire engines and equipment, which fortunately were not required.

"Ladies and gentlemen, this concludes your flight today. Sorry you won't be provided the usual steps to assist your decent to the ground, but we do have an exciting surprise for you; you get to ride on our giant slide. As soon as I can get myself unwrapped from my seat harness I will be back there to help you enjoy our special slide." Whether it was from the casual humor, or the delight to be safely on the ground, the passengers gave him a standing ovation as the aircraft commander entered the cabin from the cockpit.

Once inside the enclosure of the airport, the group of passengers was shuttled to a more secure area where a large group of Egyptian government people were waiting. Before they could speak, the airport manager stood up and told them that in all his years of aviation experience, he had never witnessed the absolute flying skill that had just occurred.

"Airplanes need both wings to fly—at least that's what they told us when I was in flight school. I don't know what resources Colonel McIntire called upon, but this was truly a miracle."

Once more, the room erupted into lengthy applause while the Air Force officer shrugged his shoulders and commented, "That's what they pay me for."

Then the Egyptian vice president rose and the mood changed from gaiety to somberness. "My dear American friends, I cannot express my sorrow for the fact that an attack of your airship came from our soils. I would like to tell you that the missiles were fired by foreign infiltrators, but I don't know that is true. But there is one thing that I know to be undeniable truth: We *will* hunt down these vermin and cause them to regret that they have been born. Were any of you injured as a cause of this attack?"

Once he had been reassured that only the emotions had been damaged, and possibly some laundry challenges incurred, he continued on with the matter at hand.

A repetition of the previous itineraries at the other impact sites occurred with no less shock at the ability of man to inflict hurt upon his fellow beings. But that was not uppermost in the mind of Todd Martin. He managed to get the Egyptian leader alone just long enough to whisper in his ear, "Mr. Vice President, can we talk in private?"

An almost imperceptible nod indicated the Egyptian leader's willingness to acquiesce. Todd understood that this meeting would occur in a covert manner, which is exactly what he had hoped for. After completion of the visit to the canal site, the entourage once more re-boarded the helicopter and made the short flight to Cairo.

When the party was ready to move by ground transport to the presidential palace, the Egyptian vice president casually stated, "Mr. Martin, why don't you and I ride together in my personal limousine on our way back so we can discuss another matter?"

Right on cue, Todd jumped at the bait and the two men climbed into the back seat of the automobile. They allowed the rest of the convoy to leave first and followed at some distance. At the right time, the VP told his driver, "Turn right at the next corner and I will give you directions from there." The vehicle continued on in the directives given from the Egyptian dignitary and before long, they had left the urban setting and were in the country.

When they reached a spot satisfactory to the Egyptian vice president he directed the driver to stop the vehicle. He then ordered the driver to get out of the automobile and walk fifty meters to the front, leaving the two men alone in the limousine.

"What can I do for you, Mr. Martin?"

Todd began by telling him, "Sir, thank you for this opportunity to talk to you in private. I want to give you my assurances that whatever is said from this point forward will be kept a matter of the closest confidence between you and me. Is that agreeable?" After gaining the affirmative response, Todd continued. "Mr. Akbar, I have studied you in admiration for a number of years now, and I am absolutely convinced that you are a man of honor. Because of this fact, I feel compelled to be open and frank with you. Also, I think that after this morning's incident, you will accept my comments in the light of those events.

"The sovereign government of the United States has been directly confronted in still another act of war. This time the attack originated within the borders of one our most trusted allies. Sir, there are several governments here in the Middle East that are the best of our friends, who have many of their citizens who wish to do us harm. Unfortunately, Egypt is one of those countries. While the government of this great nation strives to be good neighbors and honorable people, there are those who do everything possible to disrupt the peace process.

"It would be wonderful if the governments of those good countries could come down hard upon the dissidents supporting terrorism, but the size of these bodies makes it nearly impossible to quell them in the manner both you and I would like. An example of this occurred when that wonderful patriot, Anwar Sadat, was cut down in the prime of his honorable life. Should you cross the line of open warfare with these individuals, the outcome would be in similar doubt.

"With that in mind, I would like to suggest that you allow the United States to be "the bad guy" with these guys. They already hate us, so we would not have much to lose by building upon that hatred. This could all be done while the Egyptian government makes feeble attempts to stop us and thereby maintain the status quo with these elements of terror.

"What I am proposing is that we be allowed to infiltrate these organizations inside Egypt with members of our intelligence community. You would be aware of these infiltrators, but their personal identity would be withheld so you can honestly claim plausible unawareness. I realize that what I am suggesting is highly irregular and requires that you accept our honorable intent toward the sovereign nation of Egypt. I am not going to lie to you and say that we have no agents operating in your country at the present time; however, I will tell you that at no time have any of our operatives ever taken any action that would be questionable with regard to the trust and friendship we have enjoyed for many years now. If, however, we are to be effective in this effort to completely rid your country of these terrorist groups, it will require a larger expenditure of our intelligence resources. Any information gained that does not pertain to this single target would be immediately passed to you for whatever action you deem necessary.

"I want to assure you that I have the full blessing of my president to make this approach and that the only person other than yourself who even knows that it is being made is President Marshall. If you decline this overture, it will never be discussed again and no actions pro or con will result from your acceptance or declination other than what I have just stated. I don't know how to put it any plainer than that, Mr. Vice President."

The vice president tried his best to maintain a poker face, but he had not ever been approached with such pure honesty during his diplomatic life. He genuinely liked this American and knew beyond any doubt that Mr. Martin was not capable of deceptive action. He was just too open and aboveboard to lie. Further, Todd had just put his entire career in the hands of a foreign leader and this was going to be one he could absolutely trust.

"You realize that I will have to obtain the consent of my president before I can commit to a matter of this importance?" the VP said after a full twenty seconds of silence. "In my country, were I to act independently would surely result in the most extreme of consequences. I really want to watch my grandchildren grow up in a world that is safe. If I am to proceed in this matter I will need your authorization to bring one more individual into our confidence. I believe I can convince him that it will be in the interests of Egypt to favorably act upon your suggestion. Is that acceptable to you?"

"Of course, sir. We would have it no other way, but I would caution that our agreement should not become known outside this immediate circle of trust. This information could do grave harm to both our countries."

Todd felt quite sure that the necessary authorization would be coming forth in a matter of hours. While the concept had been discussed and authorized by President Marshall aboard the airplane even before the refueling stop in the Azores, the fact that the attack had occurred over Egyptian territory made it doubly certain that the Egyptians would cooperate. This was quite a coupe and it had been accomplished by a relative newcomer to the upper echelons of diplomacy. President Marshall would not forget Todd's accomplishment.

— 8 —

Cairo, Egypt
Wednesday, October 26, 4:00 p.m.

"Hey, Todd, what's this I hear about you wrecking one of our airplanes?" the president kidded in a good natured manner to let Todd know he was keeping close tabs on his trip. "Man, I can't believe the gall of those guys, thinking they could pull off something like that!" Todd filled his president in on all the details that might have been missing from the Washington dweebs. President Marshall waited until Todd was finished and asked him how the Egyptians were taking the information.

"Well, sir, they were really caught off guard on this one, I'm positive. They have been falling all over themselves to roll out the red carpet for us since we landed. By the way, Mr. President, whatever you can do to show appreciation to Colonel McIntire would be greatly appreciated."

"What do you mean, Colonel McIntire? My boy don't you know how to address a brigadier general? Todd, the colonel was already on the list for promotion, so I pulled a few strings and pushed it to the front of the line. From what I hear, that guy did something that was nearly impossible in getting the bird on the ground safely. He gets another award of the Distinguished Flying Cross to put on his blues." Todd thanked him and then quickly changed the subject.

"Sir, do you remember that little chat we had about our assets? As you will recall I was going to try for the Saudis first and you suggested the Egyptians.

Well, I owe you five bucks. I decided to go for broke and used the incident of the enemy firing on our bird to gain some leverage and Mr. Akbar was more than happy to go along with us under the provisions you and I talked about. Maybe I shouldn't say this, Mr. President, but since we all survived it, I'm sorta glad that it happened if it will cause our success in the Middle East."

"I know where you're coming from, Todd, but we will never discuss this matter again except in person once all this is over. The boys over on the hill would have both our butts dangling from the top of the Washington Monument if they knew we'd pulled this one off without their blessing. Keep up the good work. Oh, incidentally, Todd, I called your lovely wife last night to tell her how much I appreciate what you're doing. You are one lucky guy to have such a support as that lady is for you. I see your son is named 'Hal.' I bet I know where that came from … "

"Mr. President, I would expect that you will be getting a call from the president of Egypt regarding the matter we will not be talking about, so I'm going to back off at this point and let you negotiate whatever comes from these talks. Do you still want me to talk to the Saudis about this or should I back off on that?"

Maybe it was asking too much to make this much headway for the guys over at the agency in one fell swoop. Oh well, that's why President Marshall made the big bucks, Todd mused to himself.

"What do you think about that, Todd?" the chief executive asked.

"Well, sir, maybe you could arrange for someone to take a pot shot at us when we get over their territory and put some huge guilt on their backs," Todd mused.

"Not a bad idea there, Todd. I did such a good job of it on your way into Cairo," the president shot back at him. Tell you what, Mr. Martin; I trust your judgment on this. If it seems like a good idea, then you have my support. Just remember, I get the top bunk when we go to jail."

Todd went on to discuss the high points of the trip thus far and was delighted to be able to report what both men thought to be some real progress. They talked for a short time and then the connection was broken. Before hanging up the President told him that another airplane was on its way to their location and the shuttle crew would be handing over the aircraft to General McIntire and his crew before returning to the States by way of Germany. Both men had felt it best to keep the same crew in place for security purposes. "You better not be breaking *this* bird, 'cause it's an upgraded version of the last one you had," President Marshall chided before the line went dead.

Over the past few days Todd had made lengthy briefings over the secure lines to the Oval Office to keep the President informed of each facet of the encounters with foreign and domestic bureaucrats and his assessment, backed by his team, of what the situation was at each location. These SITREPs were detailed but conformed to the military style of organization of information so the guys back at the Pentagon, or wherever, would be able to digest them without having to sort out the facts.

That afternoon, just as promised by the President, another official government airplane landed at the Cairo International Airport. Whoever had come up with the color scheme of these planes really had an eye for beauty. The familiar mixtures of blue and white on the fuselage with the distinctive seal of the United States of America were unmistakable. Of course, those features had nearly caused Todd and his cohorts to be brought back to Andrews under flag-draped caskets a couple days ago. Todd had been asked to meet the aircraft when it arrived and was ready and waiting when the ship taxied up to the VIP tarmac and the engines were silenced.

As the pilot and his crew disembarked a courier rushed over to where Todd was stationed and hurriedly handed him a brown sealed envelope.

"The White House chief of staff told me to personally give this to you, Mr. Martin."

Todd thanked him and the unnamed man rejoined the airplane's crew on the far side of the airplane. The pilot in charge was conversing with General McIntire and from the gestures and glances toward the airplane, it was obvious that the latter was being briefed upon the intricacies of this particular bird. There was ample evidence that the two aircraft commanders were old friends and congratulations were being offered concerning the skill with which the pilot of the damaged aircraft had demonstrated. Salutes were exchanged and the shuttle team boarded a mini-bus and departed toward Flight Ops. Todd found himself missing the camaraderie of the military community as he watched the friendly brotherhood being unfolded in front of him.

When the various elements had accomplished whatever it was their responsibility to do, the remainder of them re-entered their modes of transportation and returned to the hotel in downtown Cairo. By now, the American ambassador had made it his priority to accompany Todd wherever it was that Mr. Martin would be traveling. He had been fully briefed on who the "new guy" was and was prepared to assist in any manner requested.

When the two State Department men were in the ambassador's limousine, the ambassador mentioned, "You probably should open that envelope from President Marshall." Todd studied the diplomat for a couple of seconds in an attempt to discover the motivation for the comment and soon decided that the ambassador was probably aware of the contents and was anxious for Todd to become equally cognizant of the materials.

Carefully, and in order to not damage any pages of the contents, Todd slid his forefinger into the flap of the envelope and managed to open it without tearing the container. The folder was approximately half an inch thick and had a cover sheet denoting that the information was "Top Secret" classification. A small notepaper held in place at the top of the booklet contained a hand written message stating, "OK for your eyes only." He turned the page and began reading while the statesman shifted his gaze toward the window on his side of the vehicle.

After years of military and civilian service to his government, Todd was not easily shocked. Had anyone noticed his reaction to what he was reading they would have observed that Todd's mouth was literally hanging open and his face was turning paler with each paragraph he was reading.

Two years earlier, the United Nations had installed the new secretary general amid the usual hype that such events produce. For the first time the world body was to be led by a member of the Middle East. The Lebanese diplomat had been touted as a real statesman who brought a fresh breath of air to the office that had become rather stuffy due to the self-aggrandizement of the incumbents. Mr. Tomalas was a man with impeccable credentials, but gained the favor of the entire body due to his self-effacing and modest character and his wonderful sense of humor. It was only due to appreciation of his tremendously affable personality that waning support for the UN had been gaining throughout the United States.

But what Todd Martin was reading right now presented a completely different picture of Daniele Tomalas. His activities over the past ten months were well-documented in the dossier. He had been making alliances with such entities as North Korea, Cuba, Syria, Sudan and a host of other nations considered by the United States to be the worst of governments in the world today. For a long time now the intelligence communities of the United Kingdom and the United States had been aware of an off-shoot group from al-Qaeda with unthinkable evil ambitions. This group was simply called "The Movement." It was headed up by a super-secretive hierarchy and their leader, whom they had begun to call the "Patriarch." That individual was none other than the current secretary general of the United Nations!

Once Todd had finished reading the manuscript, he re-read it once more. He had been so absorbed with the intense concentration which he had developed over his adult life that he failed to observe that the limousine in which he was riding had been stopped in the courtyard of the American embassy compound for several minutes. The American ambassador had not interrupted this concentration in order to allow Todd to gain the full impact of what he had just read.

"That sonofabitch!" Todd uttered, first in a whisper, and then several more times in an ever-increasing pitch of irritability as he sat with the open folder on his lap while Todd seemed to be glaring off at some unseen fixation that neither existed nor at the same time lacked substance.

"How did we ever let this happen?" Todd continued, speaking to no one. His dismay had now evolved to full-blown anger. The top secret document had listed, by name, those known collaborators in the Movement and the roster contained numerous names of various high-level government officials in a "laundry list" of nationalities. Fortunately, Mr. Akbar's name was not included on the list. His President, however, was named under the category of "Probables." That fact made it imperative that he get to Mr. Akbar before he had the chance to make contact with the Egyptian president. Fortunately, Mr. Akbar had been filling in for his chief of state, who was out of the country and would not be returning before tomorrow night. Todd just prayed that this information was too important to be delivered by telephone and he could put a lid on it before it came up.

The next hurdle was to come up with a way to broach the topic with Mr. Akbar. You just don't walk up to the vice president of a country and simply say, "By the way, Akbar, your boss is a criminal." Well, he had managed to accomplish much so far by just being honest. He would inform the Egyptian VP in a diplomatic manner, but would leave no doubt that there was a strong possibility that the president of the oldest nation in the Middle East was a murderer and terrorist.

In order to substantiate this to the satisfaction of Mr. Akbar it would be necessary to allow him to read the manuscript in Todd's possession. Before he could do that, however, he would need to have the concurrence of the president of the United States. He felt that his boss would go along with it, but he needed to act fast.

"Mr. Ambassador, may I have access to your secure communications capability to contact the president?" Todd inquired. The positive reply was quick to come and Todd was ushered into the communications room of the embassy by the ambassador to Egypt. The connection occurred much quicker than Todd expected and he was a little surprised when he heard the voice of the president.

"I take it you got my little note," the president quickly said as soon as Todd identified himself.

"You bet your ass I did!" Todd blurted and then turned beet red as he remembered who he was talking to. "Yes, Mr. President, I read the entire document and please forgive my outburst. It's just that this information is earthshaking and I was not prepared to expect that we could have been blind sided like this."

"Well, Todd, we weren't taken quite that easily. We had some forewarning that this guy might be up to mischief even before he took office up in New York. We haven't been exactly sitting on our hands either. I'm afraid Mr. Tomalas will be receiving some surprises before too long. "

"Sir, one of the reasons I called at this ungodly hour is because of the situation as regards our friend over here in Egypt. I still believe our best friend in that government is the vice president. Since his boss is probably in the enemy camp it would not be a good idea to bring the Egyptian president into the loop regarding our intelligence plans for this country. I'm ninety-nine percent sure that Mr. Akbar has not discussed the matter with his president at this point. I don't think there is any way to prevent this from happening if we do not lay our cards on the table before that time. I know I'm asking a lot, Mr. President, but I'd like your permission to show Mr. Akbar the documents I hold in my possession. He needs to see firsthand such serious charges against his sovereign leader."

"Well, Todd, this is highly irregular. You do realize that by showing him this document that some of our collection methods will be exposed and then there are the field agents' lives and safety to be considered."

"Yes, Mr. President, I have already considered these facts and I still think the situation demands that we take my recommended action. After all, if Akbar cannot be trusted we need to re-evaluate all our thinking in this part of the world, anyway. Maybe we should kill 'em all and let God separate the good from the bad. You and your predecessors have given your all to gain peace in this part of the earth and we have little to show for it. The old saying, 'If it ain't broke, don't fix it' implies that if it is then we should get busy right away and make all the necessary repairs and we should do it before some other administration has to deal with it all over again."

"You know, Todd, you would have made a great senator. You have a way of cutting to the chase and making it all clear. You go ahead and show that paper to Mr. Akbar and if he's all you believe him to be we will have made one of the best moves in the past generation to begin a real peace process. If he turns out to be another bum, then I expect you to just whack him," the president said in a tongue-in-cheek manner.

Cairo, Egypt
Thursday, October 27, midnight

You wouldn't believe what access a person could gain as a representative of the leader of the Free World when it became known who you are speaking for. Todd halfway expected to be firmly rebuffed when he asked to speak to the Egyptian vice president at this time of night.

"Yes, Mr. Martin, the vice president would be happy to receive you. We will be expecting your arrival within the next half hour if that would be suitable to you," which meant, "Give the poor guy time to get out of bed and have a cup of coffee so he can wake up enough to engage in whatever diplomatic topic that could be so important to invade his sleeping hours."

"Will you be coming alone or do we need to plan on others attending as well?" the polite buffer to the Egyptian leader queried. He was just dying to ask, "What the heck is this all about?"

"Actually, sir, I realize that the hour is late so please give my apologies to His Excellency and tell him he need not get dressed. Although this is a personal call, I can assure you it cannot wait until morning," Todd explained, hoping to avoid the formality inherent in dressing up for the visit.

"I'm sure he will appreciate that, Mr. Martin, but the vice president might feel it an insult to greet the representative of the United States in such a casual manner, but I'll make your comments known to him." With that the line went dead and Todd notified the driver assigned to him by the ambassador that he would be leaving the premises shortly.

The living quarters of the Egyptian vice president would satisfy the greatest of Pashas. The long driveway was lined with towering palm trees and the gardens were exquisite. When the driver had gained entry from the guard, who was anticipating the arrival as the lights all along the drive had been lit as a means of welcome. The driver brought the vehicle to a halt and almost made it to the passenger door to open it before Todd had extricate himself from the car and was heading toward the huge entryway of the mansion.

Once inside, Todd was ushered immediately to a large room adjacent to the entryway and invited to have a seat on one of the sumptuous couches scattered throughout the room. In less than fifteen seconds the doors opened again and he was greeted by a smiling Egyptian vice president, who projected great pleasure at having his sleep interrupted at this hour.

"It's so nice to see you again, Todd!" The Egyptian had apparently felt their rapport such that a first name basis was appropriate. "What can I do for you this evening?"

Although Todd had begun to really like this guy and would have liked to exchange niceties, his mission was too important to waste time exchanging pictures of their children. "Mr. Vice President, I'm afraid I have some rather unpleasant news to bring to you and it just wouldn't wait until tomorrow morning. I have been authorized by my president to pass on to you extremely disturbing news I received just a short while ago. Obviously, we must take you into our full trust to relate this internal document and we hope that you will honor that trust by keeping this information completely secret between the president, our ambassador, myself, and you. Once you have seen the contents you will fully understand why this is absolutely imperative."

With that, Todd handed the entire packet, complete with the protective envelope, cover note and "Top Secret" cover sheet. He then leaned back in his chair and waited for the VP to read the entire document.

In his total disarming shock, similar to that of Todd's when he first read the document, Mr. Akbar read the packet. Several times while reading he had quickly skipped back a few pages to review previously read pages. When he had finished, he was visibly shaken. All attempts to maintain a diplomatic decorum were now gone and the exhausted man turned to Todd and tried to speak, but the words would not come out. He was experiencing shock, anger, disappointment and fear all at the same time. Instinctively, and for no apparent reason other than compassion, Todd reached out to the man, put his arms around him, and gave the vice president of Egypt a firm and healthy hug.

"All my life I have been a strong believer in the tenets of Islam. I never miss my obligations and have tried to live my life in a manner that would be pleasing to Allah. I have studied the Koran daily for as long as I can remember and have tried to be an example to the non-believing Western world in the hope that someday they would fully understand the plan of Allah. Never did I believe that these ignorant people from my own religion would gain a foothold in our society. Now I must admit that there are worse things than non-believers; there are those pretenders to our faith who would shame the name of Allah throughout the world. I now declare my personal war against these sub-humans," the kindly man stated with the reverence uncommon to his craft.

"My dear brother from the West, I can only offer my most sincere and heartfelt apologies for your sufferings caused by these despots. I am ashamed that it has been you who has had to waken me from my self-induced sleep. You can be sure that the people of the United States have gained an ally in the struggle for the peace of Allah."

With that, the Egyptian reached out and gave Todd and equally heartfelt hug. Never had Todd been so filled with love and emotion outside the barriers of his own family. Mr. Akbar had gained a friendship that would only grow from this day forward.

The hour was late and any plans to address the matter further would have been useless until each member of the new fraternity had opportunity to mull over all possible avenues of approach. Todd offered his thanks one more time and promised to get back to the vice president the following day in order to develop a strategy for addressing this latest situation. Before he left, though, Mr. Akbar put his arm around Todd's shoulders and squeezed. Todd was sure that he witnessed moistness in the Egyptian's eyes.

— 9 —

The flagship of the United Nations taxied up to the VIP parking pad for the first time in history. The U.S. Army band was in full dress uniforms and the contingent from the "Third Herd," the Third United States Infantry Battalion, was decked out in their finest to await the arrival of the secretary general of the United Nations. As the doors of the jumbo jet opened and the secretary general stepped out onto the platform of the mobile stairs unit, the band broke out with the hymn of the world body. Most present had no idea what was being played by the band, but it sounded officious so they assumed a modified position of attention. The color guard conducted its ritual duties and once the music ended there was a brief pause before the band began playing our national anthem. This was an intentional breach of the normal etiquette, done solely for the purpose of letting the UN representative know, in no uncertain terms, that he was a guest of the greatest nation on earth and he better not forget it.

The secretary general waved to the crowd and then began his decent to the tarmac, where a red carpet had been placed to honor his office. Once he stepped onto the carpet, the members of the honor guard popped to attention and rendered the presentation of arms usually reserved for heads of state. The president of the Free World and his vice president were on hand, as were the chairman, and joint chiefs of staff of the uniformed services.

They might as well let the guy know right from the start what he was up against.

The secretary general was quite impressed with all this and took it to be an underscoring of the esteem in which the government of the United States of America held him. He put on his most friendly smile and made a point to wave to the crowd assembled outside the chain link fence of the VIP compound. On cue, the crowd responded with cheers.

Just keep right on smiling, you rotten bastard, were the thoughts of those in the know.

Daniele Tomalas was never one to miss an opportunity to speak into a microphone and was delighted that he would be given an opportunity to address the assembly. It pleased him to see that a huge contingent of the world's press had made it a point to cover this event.

"My fellow citizens of the planet earth," he began in his usual gifted manner of speaking. "We are here today to begin a historic chapter in the processes to benefit all mankind. I felt that it was important to meet you here in the capitol of the United States of America in order to honor the tremendous sacrifices your nation has made to support the United Nations throughout its lifetime."

"Bullshit," one of the senior members of the State Department whispered. "You're here because we told you to get your bony butt down here and face the music."

The secretary general went on a few more minutes and left the podium to a rousing wave of applause from an unknowing public. The news media made it a point to aim their cameras at those most appreciative of the international leader.

The dispersal of the parade occurred with practiced precision and fifteen minutes later there would be little evidence that anything out of the ordinary had occurred at this part of Andrews Air Force Base. Departure areas, established in accordance with rank of those attending, had been vacated as the "beltway gang" made their separate ways to wherever it was that they earned their government pay. The Presidential motorcade was among that group.

In the ensuing minutes the motorcade drove to downtown Washington and on to Pennsylvania Avenue. The occupants of the main limousine continued to wave at the bystanders as the bulletproof conveyances made their way. The usual banter between the two leaders was abandoned since both were well aware of why the secretary general was here. At least one of the passengers knew the real reason for this summons and he was wearing the American flag on his lapel.

The normal greetings took place once more when they arrived at the White House, but this time there was a large contingent of anti-UN demonstrators present on Pennsylvania Avenue immediately to the front of the presidential mansion. The President frowned, but inwardly wished he could join them after learning the full knowledge of not only the organization's ineffectiveness, but the corruption that extended to the very top. Well, they were about to get the surprise of their life.

The House Chambers
Friday, October 28, 10:00 a.m.,

All morning long the secretary general had been polishing his speech to be given before the entire Congress of the United States. As was customary, all the various embassies around the city had been invited to attend as well. In fact, the entire gallery and the entire floor space down in the well was filled with extra chairs to accommodate the Cabinet, the joint chiefs, and the Supreme Court Justices. Anybody who was anybody was present for this momentous day.

When the doorman came to the front of the aisle way and announced, "Mr. Speaker, the President and Mrs. Marshall," the room erupted into standing ovation that lasted for a full five minutes while the presidential party made its way to the front of the chamber. No sooner had the president and first lady found their seats when the doorman came forward once more to announce, "Mr. Speaker, the Secretary General of the United Nations, His Eminence, Mr. Daniele Tomalas."

Due to the mixed feelings regarding the UN, the applause rendered from the upper levels of the room were not as cordial as those coming from the main level. These diplomats knew that it was required behavior to act like they adored the secretary general.

It had been decided that the president of the United States would be the one to make the introduction of the UN chief. President Marshall waited for the audience to become quiet and then approached the podium in the front of the chamber. The room became quiet.

"Mr. Speaker, members of the United States Congress, Chief Justices, Chairman and members of the Joint Chiefs of Staff, and my fellow Americans, this will be one day that will live forever in the history of this great and honorable nation. Today, we have with us the secretary general of the United Nations. This man represents all those tenets of that body which has found its home within our borders. We have always welcomed members of that organization and have supported the decisions made there with our hospitality and our finances more than any other member nation.

"Now, I would like to provide you with a list of benefits we have received in return for our continuous support.

"First of all, there have been many times when we have championed those activities that have provided relief for the weary, medicine for the sick, food for the starving, protection from villains, supplies for areas of disasters, and numerous expenditures of American forces when it was called for.

"Many members of that body do not share our concern in these areas and have taken every opportunity to thwart our efforts to be a good neighbor in the community of mankind. We have always taken the high road and tried to work within that system for the good of all. This has not always been easily accomplished, but in the end the charitable nature of this nation's citizens have prevailed.

"Americans delighted when the current secretary general came to office. His openness and personable spirit were a welcomed transition into what had become a somewhat stuffy body of people more concerned with parliamentary procedures and diplomatic acumen. Not much was being done to alleviate the deplorable conditions throughout the world, but we were dignified.

"A new birth of appreciation began in this nation of people who had started becoming disillusioned with the turn of events over several decades. It was becoming unpopular for candidates for elective office to badmouth the UN in order to garner votes from the discontented.

"That is why it pains me deeply to expose to you and the entire world irrefutable proof that our faith in that body has been for naught."

A simultaneous gasp escaped from the mouths of most people in the room and could be heard throughout the chamber.

"You probably have been wondering why I requested Secretary General Tomalas to stand before you instead of taking my message to the Assembly of the United Nations. There is no doubt that every member of that body is watching the events occurring in this room right now. My main purpose was to place this man in front of the major support he has been the recipient of during his entire tenure.

"Mr. Secretary General, you are a terrorist. You are the head of a worldwide network of terrorists calling themselves "The Movement. Your title among those evil people is "The Patriarch." You are the individual who planned, obtained the materials for, and sent your thugs out to do your dirty work and cost many of them their own lives. You have caused the economies of the major industrial nations to suffer one of the greatest losses in history.

"Right now, while we are all in this chamber, documented proof of your activities is being distributed to all member nations of the United Nations. In addition, copies are being delivered to the United Nations headquarters in New York. This investigation has been conducted over a period of many months by several independent sources from as many nations.

"There can be no doubt of the accuracy of this evidence that is supported by documents, personal accounts and the signatures you left behind while you were accomplishing your dastardly mischief. Yes, Mr. Tomalas, the proof is irrefutable.

"So, where do we go from here? First of all, you are free to leave and go wherever you may choose. While you have brought great dishonor to the office which you have held, we will not damage it further by taking the justified punitive measures to do likewise. However, I would caution you against several places you might be considering for your exile. It would be unwise to return to the United Nations building. The assistant secretary general is meeting with the staff as we speak and has requested that the property of the UN be returned. The airplane that brought you here has probably already landed in New York and the control of the proper agencies of that forum. There is a strong desire to gain control of your person by the enforcement arm of that body as well.

"You should be warned that certain governments in the Middle East are clamoring for your hide. The Egyptians are anxious to have you explain to them why you blew up their canal. The Panamanians and Central America are having the same feelings in regard to their canal, also. I guess I needn't tell you how we Americans have taken umbrage at your treatment of our oil pipeline. Due to the impact upon the Pacific Rim nations, I would suggest you give them a wide berth. In fact, Mr. *Former* Secretary General, I really cannot think of any place where you would be welcomed right now. I certainly would not be recommending Indonesia since there is quite a lot of anger that has not been completely controlled by their police forces. Those people are quite creative when it comes to seeking revenge.

"Those places where you might have found comfort in the past, such as Syria, Iran, or other sympathetic locations are undergoing their own purges at the moment and some of their leaders will be competing with you for places of asylum. No, Mr. Tomalas, I would say there is no place that you can hide and that will be your punishment for the terrible things you have done."

It is doubtful that there has ever been a more eventful gathering since there have been world governments than what had just happened in this chamber. News anchors, usually at no loss of words, were sitting in stunned silence. Many radio stations were experiencing the most dreaded bane of all—a dead microphone. The faces of our most prolific public prognosticators of television stations were blank stares.

"I can hardly believe my eyes and ears," the commentator at *Fox News* was saying to members of the panel gathered to cover what was to be the speech of the secretary general.

"One thing I think we can all agree upon is that the president would not have dared to take this unprecedented action if there was any doubt of its authenticity. Not only that, but he would have to be able to prove his statements beyond any shadow of a doubt and in a manner that would convince the entire world that he has the goods on our Mr. Tomalas. Did you notice the look on Tomalas's face during the comments of President Marshall, Alice? If ever I saw the look of guilt written all over a person's face, we surely witnessed it this day." The panel continued to comment upon the historic event and, regardless of which station you turned to, the statements were the same.

When the president had concluded his remarks to the man whose life had just been destroyed, he began to address those other people in the audience.

"My fellow citizens of the United States of America and those of you listening all around the world, today you have witnessed one of the more tragic events to befall us in many centuries. So many of our countries and their peoples have worked so long and hard to provide a forum for all nations to benefit the weak and the mighty. When I first learned of the treachery being inflicted upon the moral and decent people who make up the large majority of mankind, I struggled hard to convince myself that there had to be some mistake. This just couldn't happen. After having independent and thorough investigations by several different sources, we learned that our worst fears had really been confirmed.

"My next conflict was what to do about it. Were I to present the facts before the UN General Assembly, it would have resulted in a lengthy fight that would have destroyed whatever credibility the United Nations still possesses. If I were to take it to the nations, which ones would be the appropriate ones to inform, or not? After careful considerations, I decided that the only way to bring closure to the matter was to take the actions I have today. You can see that I would never be able to bring such charges against a man so powerful and admired as Mr. Tomalas without conclusive evidence. In the next few days you are going to have opportunity to examine the evidence yourself. This will occur because a complete transcript of all the compelling evidence will be circulated to the media, all governments, and those charged with examining such matters. There will be complete agreement at that time.

"Throughout the world there has been a massive manhunt to capture all the members of this outlaw group. All nations who have been the victims of this terrible and atrocious behavior have banded together and, with the help of God, or Allah, or Jehovah—you choose the name that best fits your understanding of the Almighty—we have been successful beyond all expectations.

"There are nations that have been called, "rogue," "evil empires," and a host of other descriptions by this and other governments over the past decades. I am announcing today that we will no longer be calling names and using hostile verbiage against our fellow world citizens. The internal actions of these former enemies have resulted in a cleansing and return to basic goodness that knows no national boundaries.

"Mr. Tomalas will be provided protective custody from this moment and until we can deposit him at a departure point where he will be expelled from this sovereign nation. Where he elects to go is completely up to him. We have learned that his organization is in possession of an oceangoing vessel. Perhaps that is the just exile for this disgraceful man. Now, if the sergeant-at-arms will get this despicable man out of our sight it will be greatly appreciated."

As the sergeant-at-arms collected the limp body of the thoroughly broken man from his slumped position and stood him on his feet, the people in the chamber rose as a single body and began hissing and booing the former world-body leader as he was dragged from the room. As the doors to the House closed behind the departing duo, the crowd turned back to the podium where the president was standing and simultaneous applause broke out. Cheers and whoops could be heard all the way to Pennsylvania Avenue as the folks in the room, regardless of political affiliation or country of origin, in the case of the Diplomatic Corps, showed their affection and pride in the man standing before them.

"We just won the next election!" the Majority Whip commented to the person standing next to him.

"Forget the damn elections; the whole world just won the only one that really counts!" the man retorted.

Over the next few hours, the White House was flooded with telegrams and e-mails coming from a wide spectrum of sources. National leaders from most of the countries on earth had sent their strong endorsement of the actions taken by the United States and its leader. The mail coming in from the domestic population was running in excess of ninety-eight percent in approval of what they had just witnessed. The ALCU, of course, took the opposite side and verbally scourged the president for "his violation of all rules by punishing the perpetrator without the benefit of a normal trial."

The chief of staff made the comment, "I hope they continue to send us their comments. It will save us a lot of toilet paper."

The president was spending most of the remainder of the day on the telephone. Incoming calls kept him busy, but he wanted to make a few of his own. The first one he accomplished was to the assistant secretary general of the United Nations.

"I want you to know, Mr. Secretary General, that we in the United States of America will continue to support the United Nations and offer our assistance in any way you may find helpful in the immediate future. We have before us a chance to repair the damages and create an even stronger world leadership if we have the courage to seize the moment. I understand that you folks up there had quite an eventful meeting this afternoon. If it was as positive as the one we had down here in Washington then we are well on the way to recovery."

The new secretary general, who had been proclaimed by acclamation during the day, provided the President an in-depth accounting of the recent developments. He thanked the president for his statesmanship, but informed that Mr. Tomalas would not be the recipient of so gracious handling if he ever showed up in the UN precincts. "I hear he may be taking a lot of seasick pills for the rest of his miserable life," the secretary general commented mirthfully.

During the conversation, the president received an invitation to come up and address the full general assembly at some date in the near future. "I think you will find that your popularity up here will allow you comfort," Secretary General Salinas, of Chile, reassured. President Marshall stated that he would be delighted to come up and asked the secretary general to have his staff work out a convenient time with his own.

The events of this day were overshadowed by the effects of the terrorist acts, but the stock market reflected a gain for the first time in three weeks. There was a lot of work to be accomplished at every level and there would be no chance to relax for months to come.

— 10 —

Panama
Tuesday, October 25, 7:30 a.m.

"Keep that line tight," the foreman of the construction crew yelled to the men holding the ropes on the two ends of the huge I-beam dangling from the overhead crane. Teams of workers were milling about the construction site like an active ant hill as each one was determined to keep pace with the schedule posted on the community bulletin board. Safety was not being ignored, but the level of action was set at a higher level due to the need to get the canal back in operation as soon as possible.

The plan of attack was to build a solid platform on each side of the canal that would support the heavy machinery that would be needed to clear out the channel. Before that could be accomplished it would be necessary to build up the banks and make them solid enough to support the platforms. An endless line of trucks had been going and coming to the canal from both sides for two days taking out the existing landfill so they could bring in the large boulders that would form the base of the canal walls. The last Euclid truck had made its deposit of rock just before daybreak and now the platforms could be constructed.

The large steel plates were stacked in position so when the steel girders were put in place they could be situated on top of them and locked into position. That should happen before the third shift went home in the morning.

The site manager was pleased to note that the platforms had actually been completed on schedule and today would begin the movement of the large cranes that would be needed to lift the locomotive out of the channel so that work could begin on the extrication of the super tanker.

It took nearly four hours to bring the two cranes to each side of the canal and anchor them in place to ensure stability. Once that was accomplished the lines were extended to make the slings that would be wrapped around the locomotive. The cables needed for this were too heavy to be manipulated by men, so ropes were put in place to be used to drag the heavy cables that would replace the ropes. This was done in less than an hour and now the two cranes were hovering over the wreckage like two giant praying mantises.

With the expertise that could only be developed over years of experience, the two operators of the cranes worked in tandem to lift the many tons of locomotive from the side of the ship. The groaning of the winches gave evidence to the strain being required to make the lift possible. The remaining water that had collected in various parts of the machine reluctantly gave up and fell back into the chasm of the canal. Once the locomotive was suspended high above the carnage the two operators of the cranes expertly moved the engine to the selected side of the canal and deposited it on the pad that was to be its home for the next few days.

A sigh of relief went up from every member of the construction team when the lines were retrieved from the locomotive and the next task could begin. The removal of the locomotive was to be child's play in comparison with the removal of the ship. It had been determined that the only way to proceed was to cut up the ship into manageable sections that could be removed in the same manner as was the case of the locomotive. Before that could be done, there would be a need to secure the ship so it did not roll as the elements of its carcass were disassembled. This task would require a minimum of three shifts. As it turned out, it took five.

The next two weeks saw the dismantling and removal of the vessel and the hauling away of the metal to a scrap yard that had been set up for that purpose. The locomotive found its way to the same "bone yard" toward the end of the first week. It now seemed dwarfed by the huge pile of steel that was growing by the hour. By the end of the second week, though, the canal was completely empty of the ill-fated debris. Work could now begin in earnest to make the repairs that would be required before the world's trade ships could resume their constant flow through the wonder that had been constructed almost a century before.

The walls of the canal were the first to be rebuilt. Massive frameworks of re-bar and fittings were constructed on the sides of the chasm and then put into place by the two cranes. Seeing the numerous construction workers clamoring all over these structures with their continuous arcs of blue-white light emanating from their acetylene torches was reminiscent of worker bees constructing a monstrous bee hive.

It always amazed the onlookers that these mesh-works of tangled metal could be placed exactly where they were needed to reinforce the concrete that would be poured when complete. Anyone who doubts the scientific minds of these construction workers should have the opportunity to witness what was going on down in this remote part of the world.

The enormous cost of this enterprise would have exhausted most of the world's nations before the project was complete. Normally, the world would stand by and allow the United States to pick up the tab for the project, but the mood in America was such that the entire European and Asian governments who could afford to do so volunteered their financial support before it was even requested. Based upon their actions during the Iraq War, France and Germany were the first to bring the matter to the European Common Market.

Suez Canal
Tuesday, October 25, 9:00 a.m.

At the very same time as the huge repair job was being initiated in the Panama Canal, a team of equivalent proportions was making progress to restore the Suez Canal. Using the same logic as would be so effective halfway around the world, the decision was that it would be necessary to shore up the immediate area around the disaster site before any real efforts could be initiated toward restoration.

Unlike the conditions in Panama, however, was the need to isolate the problem of erosion that had exacerbated the damage to the canal. Once more teams of welders and construction workers had constructed the spider works of metal that would be the retaining walls for the canal. This would form the basis of a barrier between the desert and the waterway. The fact that platforms were not feasible made the pouring of cement much more difficult and necessitated the use of many long tubes used for shooting the concrete into place. These long arms, situated at intervals along the construction site, took on the appearance of IVs being administered to a patient. Actually, that's exactly what they were.

Due to the set-up time for the curing of the new concrete walls, a hiatus lasting two weeks would be required before the backfilling necessary to continue the project could begin. In the meantime, all the necessary equipment and preparations were being put into place so that when the work could resume there would be no delays caused by waiting for materials to be delivered.

Engineers decided that it would be dangerous to begin removing the dirt in preparation for the solid fill materials until the walls of the canal were sufficiently hardened. This was one process that could not be hurried, so the frustrated engineers simply had to set back and wait. Such idle time usually causes unsettled nerves and this was no exception. Several times the supervisors of the different crews had to break up fights among the men. That, plus the fact that Muslim law forbids the use of alcoholic beverages, was a condition these hardened construction workers felt to be a violation of their basic human rights now that they found their host government would not tolerate deviance of this tenet.

"Next, they'll be tellin' us we can't smoke, either," one of the crew members voiced one evening as they were sitting around the table, playing their umpteenth game of pinochle.

The hostilities, for the most part, were diverted to anger against those persons responsible for their being here. Management didn't mind this diversion and nurtured it whenever possible. At least that should keep them from killing one another, was the prevalent mindset of those in charge.

On the morning when the supervisors came into the tents of the workers and announced, "OK, you lazy bastards, its time to quit layin' around on your butts. Git back to work!" the men sprung from their cots enthusiastically and rushed to get dressed. Some of them actually shaved for the first time in weeks. The mood around the camp was such that the guys were telling each other their stale jokes and the listeners even laughed. The cooks, in anticipation of the long work day, had prepared twice the normal amount of breakfast food. They had even managed to smuggle in some bacon, sausage and ham for the men, who were cautioned not to mention the fact that they had consumed pork in this Islamic state.

Trucks were waiting in endless lines on the sides of the canal; both the North and South. Scoop loaders and shovels were in place and before two hours had passed, the surrounding area had drastically changed its appearance. The removal of the earth around the enterprise didn't take long once the process began. It was going to take more of the earth away than was originally anticipated, but nothing could dampen the spirits of the workers once they had begun the task.

Some seepage was starting to occur at the ends of the excavation sites and had to be dealt with on an expedited basis, but the skills of the engineers in charge rectified the damage quickly and efficiently. After the excavation had been accomplished the fill began without any interruption. Fortunately, the construction companies had the foresight to bring in the boulders while the lapse in work had occurred. The source of these building materials had to be brought in from some distance and would have caused delays while the trucks were making their turnaround trips to the quarries. Filling of the backfills required five full days, even with the close proximity of the materials.

When the last truck had dumped its load of fill, the cranes, which had already been strategically placed, lumbered forward to a point where the canal-side pads could be constructed in the same manner that had occurred down in Panama. The exchange of information being passed from each canal construction base camps had proven invaluable and precluded glitches that might have otherwise happened.

The pads took a full three days to put in place, but the turning point had been reached. It was now time to begin removal of the ship blocking the canal. Taking the lessons learned by their counterparts down in Panama, the ship was being dissected like some huge bug and the scrap metal was taken to a mirror image of the bone yard down in Panama. The local economies would be favorably impacted by the windfall of steel for their building trades. Smelters would be constructed and the quality raw materials would last for quite some time before the supply was exhausted.

A major setback did occur that would cause two additional weeks of delay in the progress. Unlike the situation in the Panama Canal, there was no means of adequately anchoring the oil tanker to keep it in place during dissection. Late one afternoon in the second week the grinding of metal was the only notice the work crew had before the huge vessel slipped back into the trench and, in the process, killed several of the workers who had the misfortune of being in the wrong place at the right time. Fortunately, the ship had done only minor damage to the new walls of the canal, but still, the loss of life is always a demoralizing factor that faces every construction crew around the world. Even with the strictest attention to safety, these instances were a part of the life of every crewman of the trade.

With renewed caution, the work continued until during the fourth week the last scrap of the former oil tanker was lifted out of the trench accompanied by a celebratory yell by all those who had worked so long to make it so. That didn't mean that their work was over, but it sure marked a milestone in the progress. It would take several more weeks to replace or repair the damaged canal and, in the process, begin a refurbishing of the long ribbon of water that had suffered some maintenance deterioration over the decades of neglect.

Reports that the Panama Canal was nearing completion caused the workers on the Suez to work with renewed vigor. There was an unspoken competition between the two camps to see which water way would be able to pass the first ship.

— 11 —

Alaska Pipeline Repair Camp #3
Monday, October 24, 7: 15 p.m.

It was now night time. The only way to discern this was the fact that the clock in the mess hall stated that it was. There was little to indicate that there was any daylight left in the earth's voyage around the sun during this time of year. The seeming perpetual darkness seemed to take its toll on the spirits of the men who had now been on-site for well into the second week.

One bright spot in what was otherwise a dismal existence was the food that was being prepared for the working men in all the camps along the stricken pipeline.

"I'm getting a little tired of steak for every meal," one of the construction workers joked to his compatriots.

"Hey, that's not so," joined in another. "Don't forget we had lobster and crab the night before last." It seems that the government of the United States wanted their laborers to enjoy the very best of food while they continued to work at a feverish pace on the pipeline. While the other living accommodations were somewhat Spartan, the chow was not to be an area of complaint.

"I hear those guys down at number two are having to fight off the bears while they work," another man seated at the table joined in. "Some of those grizzlies can be real mean. I sure wouldn't want to tangle with one of 'em," he continued.

"Hell, I married one of their sisters," another chimed in and caused a certain amount of laughter. A discussion of every encounter, real and imagined, for the sake of the conversation, continued until the last man decided to go back to his bunk house and retire for the evening.

The crews had been divided into three shifts so as to provide continuity to the repair effort. The work was filthy and the lingering crude oil seemed to fill every pore of your body. Showering helped some, but one never really felt clean. It got into your hair and every man in camp took on the look of some shady car dealer with the slicked down hair that was unavoidable.

The cooks had been plagued with requests for lemons once the workers found out that you could clean your fingernails by cutting one in half and vigorously rubbing the open fruit over them. Maybe the rest of their bodies were bearing evidence of the filthy oil, but the appearance of their hands during meal time would have done justice to a dentist.

Daily interchange of information was occurring because somebody had the foresight to publish a daily bulletin for all the campsites. The remoteness of the four camps, along with the perpetual night time, were somehow easier to take in the knowledge that there were others engaged in the same endeavors as those in your camp. The air drops of newspapers out of Fairbanks and Anchorage further helped to dispel the gloom of isolation. Bechtel had provided movies for the men and had obtained some of the more recent ones to give relief to the boredom created by off-duty hours. All in all, the government and the companies were doing their best to keep the workers happy.

The removal of the dumped crude oil required some special handling. Dump trucks needed to have a plastic liner placed in the beds before the oil could be placed in them. It just wouldn't do to have the trucks driving to the disposal sight, dripping oil all the way. The "tree huggers" would go nuts over that one. When the dump truck pulled up to the loading site a team of four would quickly unroll the heavy black plastic and place the sheet in the bed for another load. It was doubtful that any one of these guys would ever want to make a bed again after they went home.

Once the top level of crude was removed and the craters emptied of the spilled oil, bulldozers came to the site to remove the contaminated soil to a satisfactory depth and, finally, after countless hours of cleaning, there was no evidence that there had been an oil spill within twenty miles of the four sites.

The task of horizontal construction could then begin. Fill materials were dumped into the crater sites and the entire area contoured to provide a smooth landscape for the next phase. The first consideration was the restoration of the pillars upon which the pipeline would rest. Exacting specifications were demanded to ensure that the passageway under the pipeline would allow for game to move uninhibited from one side to the other. Also, the pillars must be able to allow expansion and contraction of the pipeline during the extreme operations that would occur.

The strength of these pillars must be efficient to handle the tremendous weights they would support without sinking into the Alaskan countryside.

The skills of the construction crews ensured that each of the aforementioned criteria would be accomplished in standards which allowed for a buffer zone. The next task would be the installation of the new pipeline. The connection points had already been prepped for this action, so all that was required was to make the connections per the blueprints. Each of the four sites had different lengths of pipeline, so double checks were accomplished prior to delivery of the sections to each of them It just wouldn't do to try and make the connection only to find out that the pipe you were trying to match was one that should have been at a different work site. The whole process took on the same requirement for precision as was necessary in the docking of two separate space craft.

All this activity required a matter of several weeks and then, when the pipeline was ready to begin operation, there were the required pressure tests to be performed and certification by the inspection team. But like all such endeavors, one day the management announced to the world, "The Alaska oil pipeline is repaired and the first transport of crude in months has now been completed." The ceremonies accompanying this tremendous effort and accomplishment would last for several days as the nation and, certainly the state of Alaska, sang the praises of the men who had sacrificed so much to make it a reality. Such celebration was not just limited to domestic populations. The impact of this milestone was to be welcomed in Tokyo with as much enthusiasm as was forthcoming from the Western world.

President Marshall used the enthusiasm to generate the needed support for the Anwar oil field. Constituents across the country had sharply criticized politicians who, heretofore, had blocked the exploration and drilling that would have provided reserves to avoid the recent shortfall. The measure had passed the House and Senate by wide margins. Demonstrations had erupted in San Francisco, Portland and Berkley. Things must be getting back to normal.

The flow of oil down the Alaska corridor and the imminent re-opening of the two international canals signaled a renewed attitude of cooperation between most countries throughout the world. Those few countries where dictatorial governments were in place began to feel the intense pressure from their neighbors to reform. Fidel Castro, Kim Jong Il and several others who had long been talking tough became subdued and were putting out feelers to see if they could re-enter the mainstream of mankind. As a gesture of "good faith" the communist dictator in Cuba had recently pardoned some of the political prisoners he had been tormenting for a number of years. This "humane act" did not dissuade the opposition in Miami and only served to inflame their desire to oust the Cuban government and install one based upon democratic principals.

The Syrian president had been taking some steps to appease the growing opposition in that nation, but the real power had always come from the army generals and they weren't ready to budge one inch. So long as the chief of state remained in their favor, they were willing to prop up his government. Now they were beginning to recognize that he just might be ready to jump ship and join a popular revolution that would deny their hold upon the country. Several clandestine meetings were called by these military leaders to assess the best manner to deal with this renegade. Decisive actions were called for.

On the morning of October 28, the limousine carrying the three children of the Syrian president made its way out of the presidential palace to their last day of school for the week. The children were engaged in a game that always took place during this ride, which entailed the number of times the driver would take his eyes off the road to observe them as they took turns reaching out and touching his hair on the back of his head.

The limousine made the final turn onto Straight Street and would travel nearly half a mile before coming to a stop at the state school operated for the benefit of the elite in society. One block later the driver noticed that the normally busy sidewalks seemed to be empty. He had scarcely a second to reflect upon the matter before the impact of the shoulder fired anti-tank missile struck the automobile with an explosion that lifted the rear of the limousine vertically to a height nearly fifteen feet off the pavement. The entire automobile was full of an intense inferno that extinguished the lives of each occupant instantly.

It took nearly a full two minutes before any rescue or firefighting equipment arrived on the scene and by then the once beautiful limousine with its beautiful cargo was nothing but charred ashes and twisted metal. The engine of the vehicle had been blown nearly a hundred meters beyond the front of what was once a motorized vehicle.

News of the violence quickly reached the office of the president and he did not even wait for his body guards to prepare, but commandeered the closest sedan and drove at high speed to the location of the attack. He might just as well have waited for his support group because there was nothing he could do but stand in complete disbelief and stare at what had once been most of his reason for living. His body guards quickly took control and forced him into the bulletproof limousine reserved for him. Obviously, bulletproof vehicles were no deterrent to a determined enemy.

"Why not me?" the completely distraught president sobbed in the back seat of the car. There was no attempt to even try and console the defeated man. "Why would they kill little children?" he continued, but there was no doubt as to why and everyone in the limousine knew it.

The armored limousine returned to the palace and deposited a broken leader in the courtyard where he quickly moved to enter the safety of the home. The grief of the man was such that no one dared to even approach him, for his directives regarding the tragic event. He went directly to his private part of the mansion and fell across his bed and cried for half an hour.

Forty-five minutes later he emerged from his bedroom, but the eyes of the man had changed from a whimpering and defeated person to one with total hatred that could almost be physically felt by everyone in the presidential palace. No longer were tears streaming down his face, but the scowl that replaced it was enough to turn the observer to resume the flow of tears.

"Get General Aziz in my office immediately!" the enraged president stated with enough fury to cause his aides to jump as if stabbed by the words. General Aziz is the commandant of all military forces in Syria and was known to be the main power behind the president.

"Sir, the general is making an inspection of the honor guard this morning. Should we wait for his return?" the aide questioned in perplexity of the moment.

"I don't care if you have to shoot him in order to get him in my office. You get him here right now! I'm the president and he will do as he is told unless he wants to face a firing squad," came the quick reply. With that the military aide left the room, scurrying toward the vehicle assigned for his personal use. There are times in life when one recognizes the need for immediate and strict compliance. This certainly was one of them.

When the presidential aide brought his vehicle to a stop at the honor guard barracks he quickly rushed to where the general was being led among the troops. Without explaining why, he called to the general and received a quick rebuff from the senior officer. How dare this young lieutenant colonel interrupt his inspection tour! His outrage could not be withheld as he responded to the subordinate.

"Have you lost your mind?! What would possess you to dare come to me in this manner? I should have you shot!" the commander of all Syrian forces demanded.

In embarrassment, the presidential aide explained what had just taken place back in Damascus and informed the general that the president was demanding his personal presence immediately. The general did not seem to be surprised at hearing the terrible news about the first family and didn't seem all that anxious to obey the summons given him by the aide.

"I'll be along directly when I complete my duties here," the general stated with a note of finality that should have repulsed this arrogant lieutenant colonel he would deal with later. The general turned his back and began to move away from his subordinate.

"General!" the presidential aide stated in a firmness of voice that came out at a much higher pitch than the lower ranked officer would have liked. When the irritated general turned back toward the colonel, he was shocked to see that the officer had drawn his pistol and was aiming it directly toward the commander of all forces in Syria. "You cannot know how distressed I am to be the one doing this, but our president had ordered me to bring you to his office right now, and I intend to do exactly that by any means possible."

The general was visibly shaken to see one of his own pointing a weapon at him in such a manner. The fact that this trusted officer was doing so right in front of the elite forces under his command was even more galling. The general looked around and sized up the situation and remembering that he had personally directed that the reviewing body not have any ammunition in their weapons for his own personal security, suddenly realized that the only one with the ability to enforce rules was the mutinous soldier standing not more that five meters away with a clear shot should he desire to fire his weapon.

"My dear Colonel," the subdued general stated in as diplomatic a voice as he could muster, "Certainly, my desire is to immediately obey our president. I simply misunderstood the importance of your comments. Come quickly. Let us return to our nation's leader. I'll follow you back to the compound." The ingratiating senior officer stated this in a voice to be heard by the military group in the immediate vicinity.

The presidential aide, smelling a rat, decided that there was no longer any reason for pretenses, stated with as much authority as he could muster that the general would ride back to Damascus with him and told the local commander that no vehicles were to follow in pursuit for the sake of the general's continued safety. With that, the aide reached out and grasped the elbow of the general and guided him to the aide's transportation.

Once the vehicle was under way, the general regained some of his accustomed arrogance and told the army officer that his career in the military was over and he would be extremely fortunate if he only had to spend the rest of his days in a military prison. The presidential aide did not react to the threats and became more and more convinced that the man sitting right next to him was the person responsible for killing the children of their president. He kept his pistol in his hand all the way back to the palace and occasionally glanced at it just for the benefit of his irate passenger. If the general gave him any excuse to do so, he would gladly carry out the just punitive measures so richly deserved by this pompous bag of wind.

When the vehicle came to a stop in the courtyard of the presidential palace, the general quickly disembarked and began hurrying toward the main entry of the mansion. He'd show not only this upstart and insubordinate a thing or two, but also the weak excuse of a president, who could not last a week without the support of himself. He stormed into the foyer of the home and began to bellow his outrage, when the president walked directly up to him, put a gun to the general's forehead, and pulled the trigger.

"Colonel," the president calmly stated, "do you think you can manage the leadership of the military might of this nation?"

"Yes, my president, I can and will do whatever it is that you require of me and for the good of our country," the officer replied in appropriate humility.

"Good! Then General Hamad, you are the commander of all Syrian forces at this very moment. Together, you and I are going to take charge of this country and bring it into the current century. Are you ready to get started?"

The sudden change in events had left the former lieutenant colonel in a near state of shock. Since this morning the family of the president had been murdered. He had taken a four-star general prisoner and watched from a distance of not more than two meters the execution of the Syrian chief of armed forces. As if that were not enough, the president had just promoted him to four-star general and commandant of all the Syrian army. And, it wasn't even lunchtime yet!

"General Hamad, I want you to be ready to address the nation with me within two hours. We are going to announce sweeping reforms that will require your firm directives to the military. We are going to make a public proclamation to all Syrians in a manner that will gain their support. After that, no revolt by the military will dare to come off. I think that the results of such mutiny have been forcibly demonstrated by that traitor, Aziz, lying there on the floor. What do you think?"

"Well, my president, I can tell you that I've never been as proud of you as I am right now. Your kindness in the past has been misinterpreted by treacherous individuals, but I have seen the resolve you can show when it is necessary. I share your sorrow for the terrible hurt you have been afflicted with and I promise that any member of the armed forces who had any part in this murder will be dealt with in a manner fitting."

Two hours later, a shocked Syrian nation heard directly from the president all the events of the day. With a firmness heretofore not observed by the citizens of that country, President Hakim began to lay out the reforms that were to be affected immediately. No mention of the Parliament even entered into the speech, so the people recognized that a type of martial law had been imposed by their leader. They rejoiced at all the changes being introduced and realized that for the first time in many decades that Syria was truly a democracy. Things would never be the same in that country.

One of the first directives given the new army commander was that he was to take whatever forces he needed and go into the Bekka Valley in Lebanon and disarm and remove the terrorist elements in that area. In an unprecedented move, President Hakim contacted the Prime Minister of Israel and informed him that the Syrian armed forces would be moving into the Bekka Valley to eliminate all terrorist enclaves located there. Should the Israeli Defense Forces desire to do so it might be wise to place a blocking force along their border to ensure that none of the terrorists might escape to the south during this sweep. The prime minister of Israel nearly had a coronary when he heard the words of his arch enemy to the northeast capitulate in an unprecedented gesture of peace.

Could this possibly be true? Israeli intelligence sources had forewarned their government that something of major importance was about to occur in Syria, but this was beyond their wildest of dreams. Prime Minister Goldstein immediately contacted the key members of the Knesset and related the conversation he had just ended with the Syrian president. They shared his unbelief, but saw no reason not to take it at face value. After all, the Syrian had invited the Israeli Army to move troops into the area. He would have hardly made this invitation if he intended treachery. It was better to be on the safe side and accept the offer to reposition friendly forces in order to be prepared for any event. The alert notification went out to military commanders within the hour.

General Hamad wanted to minimize the casualties, so he ordered a complete blackout of radio communications until the actual hostilities began. The plan was to move Syrian armor and mechanized units during the night and have them in position to attack at 06:00 hours the next morning. Even if some of the Hamas units observed the Syrian mobile units it was hardly likely that it would cause concern, since the Syrian armed forces were supposedly allied with the extremists in the valley. It would be dismissed as routine patrolling by any observer. By the time that the true intent was discovered it would be too late for counter measures. The entire valley should be in General Hamad's control by noon of that day.

The only area for concern would be the reliability of the Syrian army. President Hakim had made a stirring speech to the nation and, from all appearances, had been an overwhelming success in the eyes of his countrymen. There was always a danger, though, that forces loyal to the late General Aziz would rise up and attempt a coup d'etat. The longer they delayed this move, the less chance for any success, but the incursion into the Bekka Valley could provide the means of affecting such a move. General Hamad contacted key individuals known to him to be loyal to the president and himself and laid the groundwork to stave off any attempt to thwart the will of the people. The rest, he would just have to trust Allah to control.

The Syrian army had been well trained by the former Soviet Union in the art of mechanized warfare. The Russians had once conducted such an operation in the Czech Republic several years back. The entire Republic had been infiltrated by five Russian armored divisions without a single radio contact. The Syrians had studied this tactic and were capable of duplicating it.

The following morning, CNN and FOX's lead story was the coverage of the surprise invasion of Lebanon by Syrian forces with the full cooperation of the Israeli Defense Group. Had the date been April first, the whole matter would have been dismissed as an April Fools' joke, but the story had been confirmed by unimpeachable sources. The whole world stood by in dismay.

Due to the time difference, by the time the story broke in the Western Hemisphere, the battle had already ended with very little bloodshed. Apparently, the terrorists had been caught completely by surprise. The news media showed long lines of captured enemy sitting on the ground in disbelief. Large stockpiles of munitions and explosives were made a part of the public record when Syrian military leaders escorted media to the sites. In a side story, the Syrian government announced that several army leaders had tried to sabotage the operation and were summarily executed by their own troops.

— 12 —

New York
Wednesday, October 30, 9:00 a.m.

Secretary General Salinas called the members of the current Security Council into session to review the actions in the Middle East. The present confused state of international conditions demanded that a close watch be maintained in the several hot spots around the world. Although it appeared that no action would be required by the UN, it seemed that to ignore the major activities around the world at this time would be improper to say the least. The Security Council should be on top of the situation and be ready to step in should the need arise.

As a permanent member of the United Nations Security Council, the Americans were able to provide much in the way of intelligence to the body. Satellite surveillance had been directed toward the Middle East when the Israeli prime minister made a hasty call to the president of the United States not more than ten minutes after receiving the call from the Syrian president. Every intelligence asset was honed in on the area of concern and the United States intelligence community had a front row seat of the entire operation conducted by the Syrians and Israelis from start to finish.

Direct contact had been established between Syria and the United States and both presidents had talked for over half an hour regarding the personal loss of the president's children, the "change of command ceremony," and all aspects of the current situation. President Marshall pledged US support for all his efforts to restore common decency in the Syrian nation. The United

States ambassador to the UN gave a detailed briefing to the council and was followed by the Syrian ambassador, who was not currently a member of the security council, but had been invited to sit in on the talks. The bottom line was that there was no need to do anything but remain alert and monitor the fluid situation over there.

The Syrian population seized upon the moment and went to the streets in massive demonstrations designed to reinforce the position of their president and to lay siege to some of the former adherents to the late General Aziz. It seems that every senior military official was trying to outdo each other in decrying the former commandant and to show where they had been a friend to the administration. President Hakim declared amnesty for any individual willing to renounce terrorism and swear allegiance to their government. Many of the officers stepped forward not, as they claimed, to receive amnesty, but to show their support. General Hamad had taken firm control of the armed forces and established a new set of rules of conduct designed to ensure that the military would remain subject to civilian rule rather than what had been the case previously. A state of euphoria was sweeping across the country.

If the mood of Syria was one of ecstasy, then so was the inhabitants of the United Nations headquarters in New York. People would stop each other in the corridors to share upbeat stories coming from their respective countries and the sound of laughter could be heard coming from many areas

That, of course, was not always the case. Those nations under the government of dictators and some of the more corrupt leaders were "very concerned about this whole silly mess." They couldn't wait until people returned to the sanity that had always prevailed in the past and the United Nations could begin to "make sense" again. You could readily discern who these people were by the large frowns that they had in common.

Several of the worst offenders of human rights from the African continent threatened to pull out of the UN altogether. This almost backfired when many of the more civilized nations were ready to joyfully accept their termination.

"Just think about how much we would save if we didn't always have to foot the bill for their ineffective leadership at home," one prominent delegate had voiced when the threat was made in his presence.

"Let 'em leave; what have they ever contributed to make this world a better place?" another said. In the end, all those who had used this ploy decided "to give the United Nations another chance to do the right thing."

Secretary General Salinas suggested that every member nation take some time to peruse the original documents that caused the UN to come into being. Instead of using the United Nations as a vehicle to cause nations to behave in an acceptable manner, it had deteriorated into several camps that were forever jockeying to establish separate bases of power. If the organization was going to survive then every member was going to have to become a good neighbor to the rest of the world.

Much to the delight of most members and the chagrin of others, the secretary general heaped heavy praise upon the people of the United States of America, who had once again come forth to help the entire world by making the repairs of the destruction caused by the terrorists. He went on to tell all who would listen that the Americans had probably saved the entire organization by having the courage to expose the cancer that had almost succeeded.

Backdoor meetings had been conducted between the members you would expect from the free world as how to best reform in a manner that would deny the trouble makers a forum to spew forth their venom during future activities. There seemed to be unanimity within that community that no longer were some of these small dictatorships who relied upon their numbers rather than the number of citizens represented. It was recommended that voting weight would also factor in the monetary support being provided by the individual nations.

Atlantic Ocean, off the African coast
Thursday, November 3, 7:00 Zulu

The *Eastern Star* was sailing at half her available speed as the ship maintained a heading of 165 degrees. Not that the heading meant anything special since the vessel had been wandering about this quiet area of the Atlantic Ocean for a period in excess of a week now. Captain Numenoglu had been spending much of his time at the bridge even though his presence was, for the most part, contributing to the progress of the ship. His mind was focused upon an area well over a thousand miles away.

Back in Ankara his wife would be returning from the market, where she would have purchased the fresh produce and one of the nude chicken carcasses that were hung near the front of the store for the patrons to select. The one she would choose would be selected on the basis of having the least amount of houseflies swarming over it. She would try her best to be inconspicuous as the news broadcasts had made much about the infamy of her husband. How could Augustus have ever allowed himself to become embroiled in the terrible things they were accusing him of? They had shared a good life and he never seemed to be a crusader, even though he was a devout Muslim. Was it ambition or conviction, or even both that had made him join up with those evil men? The bottom line was that he would never be able to return back to Turkey and the loving wife whose loneliness was becoming more and more intolerable with each passing day.

Aboard his ship Augustus was having similar thoughts as he began to analyze the steps that had led him to form an alliance with the likes of leaders of the Movement. The governments of the world had affected an unwritten rule that the *Eastern Star* would be allowed free passage in its endless roaming of the seas. Any contacts with any port would be for the purpose of refueling and replenishing the food supplies and drinking water. During the period when the ship was at portside, no person would be allowed to disembark from the ship, which was under heavy security for that reason. As soon as the stores were completed the ship's captain was directed to get underway and leave for another series of weeks on the sea. This was to be the punishment for those allowed to live. Captain Numenoglu was beginning to ponder whether those left alive were the fortunate ones. This exile would be absolute hell!

Down below decks, another individual was lying upon his cot. The accommodations of his domicile were much better than most of the crew aboard the vessel, but that was not a point that would give him much consolation. A month ago, every citizen of the world had looked at him with the utmost respect and admiration. Presidents and prime ministers were at his beck and call. Now he was the pariah of the same world. He dare not show his face in any part of the world, regardless of how remote that place might be. As the Patriarch, he was elevated to a near-Godlike level by his subordinates, most of which had now gone to join Allah.

Daniele Tomalas had tried to convince himself that Allah was merely testing him by the terrible collapse of his world. The hated Jews had a story in their Torah about a man named Job that seemed to parallel the present conditions Daniele was being forced to exist under. Maybe Allah would step in at any moment and elevate him to an even higher position than before, if he just kept the faith. No, they wouldn't beat him! He was correct in his convictions and would never abandon his crusade to unite the entire world under Islam and rid it of the infidels who had opposed him. A smile came over his face at the divine revelation just revealed to him by his God. Allah be praised!

The ship's crew was comprised of zealots to the cause espoused by their leader. Even though all seemed to be lost, their faith in the Patriarch had never faltered. If anything, their reliance upon him had grown significantly during this trying time. It was truly inspirational to watch them in their prayer times out on the decks of the ship. The crew had been selected on a criterion of un-attachment. None of the men were married and few had any relatives to miss them before and now.

Captain Numenoglu had determined that this particular area of the ocean had the least amount of traffic and he was anxious to avoid contact as much as possible. There was no telling if some ardent archrival might take it upon himself to take revenge on the high seas and he didn't want them to have the opportunity to approach the *Eastern Star* undetected. Maybe, on the other hand, that would not be such a bad thing, he reflected further.

As a man of the sea, Augustus had always longed to return to it when periods of shore living had occurred. He had always loved his vocation and the challenge of sailing his ship in any conditions that Neptune could bring about. Now, though, when he was forced to remain at sea with no hope of ever returning to land, the romanticism had started to fade with each passing day. His orders to the crew had become more and more terse due to his low spirits and they were beginning to avoid him whenever possible. He had even taken to having his meals in his cabin in order to avoid hearing the repeated tirades against the usual target of conversation. A plan began to formulate in his mind that, had the crew recognized it, would have led to immediate mutiny.

During the previous travels, which included deliveries of contraband to various ports, the *Eastern Star* had transported some of the most volatile cargos ever to be moved at sea. Once, several months earlier, the ship's captain had discovered that one of the pallets to be delivered had been overlooked and was located in a part of the hold that rarely was frequented. Inspection of the pallet had revealed that it contained huge quantities of plastic explosives. Rather than admit that he had failed in his responsibility to deliver the material to the intended recipient, Captain Numenoglu had remained silent and had intended to add it to the shipment of some future destination. That had never occurred.

He waited until the middle of the night and went to the location where the explosive materials were stored and began removing blocks of the high explosive to a strategic point in the ship's lower compartment. The task required many trips between the points and had to be accomplished covertly. This resulted in Augustus spending many sleepless nights as he performed the necessary relocation.

By the end of the third week he now had achieved his goal of placing the charge and then consulted one of the manuals for improvised explosives he had obtained from one of the crew members on the pretext that he was bored and needed some new material to read. The manual provided a wealth of information, in language he was able to understand. He had made several visits to the engine room and other machine shops around the vessel where he accumulated the equipment required to provide the necessary fuse for the bomb.

After he finished the preparations at 2 a.m. on the last night, he returned to his cabin and began a long prayer session that included a complete confession of what he now knew were sins that only Allah could forgive. After he finished the long session of prayer, he returned to the bomb site and triggered the device that would send the *Eastern Star* to its watery grave. The only recognition of the sinking ship came from a passing vessel some fifteen miles away when the night was lit up by a large fiery blast noted on the horizon. An appropriate entry was made in the passing ship's log. The stricken vessel had not given any distress signal, so the witness had not made any guesses as to where the ship had originated or its identity. Without even being aware of it, the world had just become a much better place. Events elsewhere were occurring that would underscore this statement in a more evident manner.

The fall of the Indonesian element of the Movement had provided a veritable "Who's Who" of the terrorist organizations, which included both the Movement and al-Qaeda. When this list of unsavory individuals became widespread in the international community, there was very few places where members who had been placed on that list could hide. Governmental agencies with the mission to capture them had carefully analyzed where these places might be and had taken strong measures to deny them entry to such a haven.

Teams comprised of international flavor had been placed in various "hot spots" around the globe in an attempt to intercept fleeing terrorists should they try to gain entry to these places. So far, the net had managed to take down several major criminals from both al-Qaeda and the Movement when they had arrived on these sites. When the leaders were captured, the rank and file of the terrorist organization lacked the ability to make good choices and were falling into the hands of authority as well.

It is doubtful that there would ever be an end to those dedicated to the vicious attacks that mankind could inflict upon their brothers, but the terrible blow to the evil organizations would cause them to be completely ineffective for a long time to come. In the meantime it was up to those individuals who subscribed to the principles of brotherhood to build upon the huge successes that had been accomplished in a relative short period of time.

Washington, D.C.
Sunday, November 6, 9:00 a.m.

It had been several weeks since Todd had spent in any of what some would call "quality time" with his family. In fact, he had spent no time and it was beginning to cause some frayed feelings in each member of his brood. Cathy had tried to keep up the dutiful wife roll, but there is only so much a woman can endure and still maintain her devotion. Both Becky and little Hal were beginning to miss their daddy to the point of fighting with each other and crying at the drop of a hat. Well, today he would try to make up for that.

"C'mon, you sleepy heads," he chortled as he threw back the covers on Becky's bed and watched as her sleepy eyes opened just enough to look at him with barely a nod. Little Hal turned over in his bed and stuck a foot out from under the covers just enough to show his Scooby-Doo pajamas.

Always ready to jump right into anything, he sat up and demanded, "Are we going to do something fun this morning?"

"You bet your sweet buns we are, so you guys get up and get dressed while I go and see if I can roust your mother out of bed and make us some breakfast." This was the daddy they had become used to before all that bad stuff had happened and they were not about to waste one precious moment of it. Before Todd left the room both of his children were scurrying around to find their clothes and get them on before this beautiful dream ended.

Todd came to his wife's side of the bed with her first cup of coffee of the day. He didn't have to wake her because their children were squealing and laughing up and down the hallway.

"What's all this about?" his wife said with a slight smile beginning to gain a foothold on her face.

"Well, why don't you just get your beautiful tail out of that bed and get ready for a fun day with the rest of this family," Todd responded and took the time to reach out and give her butt a playful swat.

"Does this mean that you're actually going to stay home with us today for

131

a change?" his wife inquired with a ray of hope that had begun to grow now that she was finally awake enough to take a few sips of the steaming coffee in her favorite cup. Her eyes were almost pleading and unsure that she was reading the whole situation correctly.

"Well, why don't you just get up and come along with Becky, Hal and I and find out?" he said as he rose and began walking toward the door of their bedroom. How had he ever become so lucky as to have such a wonderful brood? Well, today he was not going to even question that, but he would do everything in his power to devote the entire day to them and be the "daddy" they all deserved.

Cathy came downstairs in her bathrobe and trudged to the kitchen and began doing the magic only she could perform in that room. Todd heard the water running in the kitchen sink and pots and pans rattling as she moved about the kitchen in robotic fashion, making a feast she had done so many times before that she could do it on autopilot. Before long the entire family was sitting at their breakfast table enjoying a hearty breakfast.

"What's on the agenda?" Cathy finally inquired as she finished the last swallow from her coffee cup.

Todd winked and nodded his head toward the kids and commented, "Well, why don't you just wait until I can surprise all of you? By the way, it might be better if you got out of that bathrobe and put on some comfortable clothes, unless you want to really be the center of attraction."

"OK, OK; just let me get this mess cleaned up and I'll get started," she said, returning the previous swat on his butt as they all rose from their chairs.

"No way!" Todd stated emphatically. "You just let me take care of all this and you go up and get dressed. Time's a-wastin'." Not waiting for her response, he began clearing the table and getting ready to do the dishes.

"Are you sure you don't want to come up and help me get out of this bathrobe?" Cathy said in a playful manner that made him stop and consider that idea for a fraction of a second.

"You just get goin' and if you're real good today I'll help you get ready for bed tonight," Todd said with his most persuasive voice. Within half an hour Todd had his family safely secured in their seatbelts in their SUV and was backing out of the driveway.

The traffic was light this morning so they were able to drive out of town without the normal delays and blaring horns. Within a few minutes they were crossing the beltway and making a certain amount of progress toward their destination. The weather was cool, but there wasn't a single cloud in the sky.

This was going to be a perfect day.

"Perfect days" in the eyes of children did not include being cooped up in the back seat of a car for any lengthy periods, so Todd was pleased that the drive from Suitland, where they lived, to Northern Virginia passed before the first, "Are we there yet?" came from the back seat.

"Why are we stopping here?" Cathy questioned as Todd brought the vehicle to a stop at Mount Vernon and near the long drive leading up to the home of our first president. The two of them had been here several times in the past, but the fact that Todd had made it the first stop on this day could not be discerned. Without answering, Todd opened his door and each of the three remaining occupants did the same.

As they walked toward the mansion, Todd pointed out the large trees that were alongside the long circular drive and told the children that George Washington had actually planted these trees many years ago. That brought about a history lesson for the benefit of the children about the birth of our country and the major role this man had played in making everything we now enjoy a possibility. The kids seemed impressed, but Todd was sure that most of their feigned interest was for his benefit alone.

As the family procession proceeded down toward the waterfront and the crypt containing President Washington. The children had run along ahead, leaving their parents to trail along holding hands.

"Why here ... today?" once more his wife inquired.

"You know, honey, during the past month I have had a front row seat to observe evil forces trying to take away our freedom and everything good we stand for. I just needed to come and refresh myself and draw from the strength of a place like this in order to re-charge my batteries and get ready for whatever else might be needed to get rid of the last traces of these evil men. I couldn't think of a better place to do that than here."

Thirty minutes later they were back in the car and leaving Mount Vernon.

"Anybody here want to go to the zoo?" Todd inquired in an upbeat voice for the benefit of the passengers in the back seat.

"Yeah!" was all the response Todd needed from the simultaneous yell in the backseat to realize he had picked a winner. Both parents glanced at each other with a smile and Cathy placed her hand on the top of her husband's and patted it gently. The return trip to Washington seemed to pass much faster than the trip south had required and before long the Martin family was rushing toward the entry to the zoo once they had located a parking space that met their needs.

The next two hours were spent in following the gleeful children as they traveled from one group of animal enclosures to the next. Many "oohs" and "ahs" were all the barometers Todd needed to hear to bolster his confidence that he had selected properly. A clown came by and each of the children had bought a helium-filled balloon that would meet the same fate as they always did. True to form, Hal had lost his grip and began to cry when he watched his balloon lazily climb up into the atmosphere. Cathy had managed to turn the whole thing around by getting her son to see how high his balloon would go and they watched it until it became a fading speck in the clear sky.

Right on schedule at noon, Little Hal announced, "Hey, I'm hungry!" This ensued into a discussion between he and his mother in which she was trying to convince him that cotton candy is not among the three major food groups. In the end, compromise was affected when Hal agreed that he would first eat something healthy, like a hotdog, before he had the desired desert.

"Oh, great!" Todd thought as he pictured sticky little fingers moving about the back seat of his car on the rest of the trip.

Once the family had replenished the required nourishment it was time to leave the zoo and get on with the next adventure. Todd had not failed there, either. There was a new animated cartoon movie out that every child in America "just had" to see. When Todd announced this wonderful surprise to the children he could never again do anything that would ever diminish the fact that he was a true hero.

After leaving the theater in the knowledge that Nemo was once more safely with his daddy, the family had become weary after the eventful day. There were no protests when Todd turned the car toward home as his children in the back seat were engaging in "whale talk" to each other for the duration of the trip. As a treat to his wife he decided to stop on the way and they went to a restaurant in order to keep Cathy from having to prepare the evening meal. Like Todd had promised, this had been the perfect day.

The exhausted family members sat around the living room of the home for the remainder of the evening and passed much of the time playing a rousing game of Uno, in which the rest of his family had united to make sure Daddy would bear the brunt of such adverse cards as "skip you," "reverse" and "draw four." The squeals of playful delight each time one of the children were able to lay one of these cards in front of his pile and his feigned agony at being the loser were the source of much laughter. He was only too happy to see one of them win the game and come away as the champion Uno player of the world.

The evening ended early and the four members retreated to their respective bedrooms. Todd was the recipient of much love that evening while down the hallway two children were immersed in dreams that included giant whales, sea turtles and a little red fish with an impaired fin. All was at peace in the Martin household.

— 13 —

Baltimore
Sunday November 6, 9:00 a.m.

At precisely the same time that the Martin household had been involved in eating their breakfast and preparing to spend a leisure day relaxing and doing what so many others had either been doing, or should have, Abdul Al-Khalifa was making some preparations of his own. While the Martins would be involved in their creation of happiness, Abdul was involved in his own creative thinking of some activities that would bring him joy as well.

Rahman had been successful in accomplishing his task so vital to the plan and was sitting across the dingy apartment rented only a week before by Rahman's sister. Rahman knew better than to interrupt Abdul when he was engaged in the intricacies with which he was now laboring over. The table Abdul was seated at was covered in materials strewn in a manner that caused Rahman to wonder how anyone could keep track of the various elements that would be required for the device. There was no reason to be concerned, however, since Abdul had accomplished the same task so many times in the past that his major concern had to be that he would become complacent enough to make a single and catastrophic error that would create a vacancy in the bomb unit.

Rahman was more involved in recapitulating his own contribution to the plan. When you steal a van there is going to be a much greater risk of being observed while doing so than the mere procedure of taking an automobile.

Further, the vehicle being stolen would usually be missed quicker than one left on the street while the owner is sleeping. If you were going to steal a van it would need to be from a large pool of trucks where its absence might not be discovered for a matter of days. Finally, the vehicle should be one that could travel freely and not cause any alarm at being in high traffic areas. For this project, Rahman had selected the ultimate vehicle to meet all this criteria. He had slipped into the major hub of the United Parcel Service shortly after midnight and had driven the vehicle out of the yard with no challenge whatsoever. In fact, the gate guard had waved at him in a friendly gesture and commiserated with the driver at the thought that both of them were working the "graveyard shift." Sometimes it was just too easy.

Nobody ever really notices a UPS truck traveling in either a housing area or any of the business districts in the community. Rahman had driven the van to a pre-designated garage capable of housing the vehicle and far enough away from the busy areas where it could be found during the next forty-eight hours when it would serve its purpose.

Abdul finished his work and threw up his hands in triumph as he conducted a final visual inspection of the device on the table in front of him. His skill was evident and several harmless test runs had been completed before the actual fuse and C4 had been put in place. He had created a detonating fuse that would be the primer for the much larger explosion that would result once placed in its proper position.

Abdul carefully placed the entire assembly into a large container box with an address indicating it was nothing more than a typical parcel to be delivered to some destination that would never see it happen.

He and Rahman spent the next few hours transporting similar packages to the docking point where the UPS truck would arrive and load them at the proper time. There were sufficient "packages" to completely fill the van when they were loaded on the unobtrusive vehicle. The two men worked in broad daylight. Long ago it had been learned that the best way to ensure that discovery would not occur was to be completely obvious. People never paid attention when you acted in a completely open manner.

Both Abdul and Rahman were in possession of green cards that identified them to anyone interested in checking as students at George Washington University. They had applied for their student visas several years earlier and, as far as they knew, the inept INS had never checked them to ensure that they were engaged in academics. In truth, neither of them had attended a single class during the past year once they discovered that nobody ever checked.

This allowed them to fade into the mainstream population and do whatever it was the Movement had desired them to become involved with. In fact, they had not been contacted to do anything and both the men had been considering going back to class to alleviate the sheer boredom of sitting around doing nothing. That is, until last month.

Not much news had been available once the complete collapse of the organization they had dedicated themselves to began to occur. Of course, this was normal. When a high state of activities was in the offing, it was important to completely isolate the cells from one another in order to maintain freedom to operate. This had not stopped the two men from receiving marching orders that led to the current spate of activity. Both were glad to have the long period of inactivity come to an end and were overjoyed when the full scope of their mission was made plain to them. They were to conduct a plan that would be a joy to Allah and give acknowledgments of pride to their families back home.

Washington, D.C.
Tuesday, November 8, 10:32 a.m.

"Hear ye, here ye, hear ye; all persons desiring justice come forward and be heard," the clerk of the Supreme Court of the United States of America called out as the nine members of that August body entered from the side entry and took their places at the bench. Every person in the chamber was standing at a rigid attention in the inescapable awe that always accompanied the convening of this court of last resort.

The justices took their respective seats and, without any signal to do so, the remaining individuals in the room did likewise. There was a complete hush of silence for nearly fifteen seconds as each member of the high court opened and scanned the portfolios placed in their appointed position. There was no need for them to have done so since every member had been dealing with the cases they would handle today for months now and there was scarcely any aspects of the cases to be presented that they had not had their law clerks research thoroughly.

The first case was one that had been initiated the previous afternoon and was continued over until this morning. The main attorneys arguing the case had long before the arrival of the justices been sitting at their respective tables, pouring over the notes they would be offering this morning. The first to begin the timed presentation before the panel was the petitioner who had not completed his appeal before the close of business the preceding afternoon. He stepped forward and opened his folder, pulling his half-frame glasses down on his nose in order to complete his demeanor of scholastic acumen.

The attorney looked up from his notes and peered over the top of his glasses. "May it please the court ..."

Five minutes earlier the second UPS delivery vehicle of the day had pulled up to the delivery point adjacent to the courtroom and the driver had walked to the side entry with a clipboard that would list the numerous packages he would be delivering. This was not uncommon when the court was in session as any appellant would be required to submit supporting documents in multi-copies for whatever use the court deemed necessary. Nobody paid much attention as the driver had changed direction once inside the building and walked directly to the entry way on the far side of the building and went outside.

If anybody had been near or in the delivery vehicle exactly seven minutes later they might have heard the click of a contact between two electrical circuits closing. One thousandth of a second later there was a gigantic blast that completely disintegrated the UPS truck and created a crater nearly thirty feet deep and fifty feet across. The fireball that enveloped the area was approximately one hundred feet in diameter and was accompanied by the sound of three tons of high grade C-4 as it detonated with a force that could actually be seen in the air as it continued to expand at greater than the speed of sound.

The breach in the side wall of the Supreme Court was cluttered with the remains of the columns that had surrounded the building. Those same walls had instantaneously become fragments that had the same deadly effect of shrapnel in a conventional bomb and had completely destroyed the Supreme Court chamber and every occupant therein. Not one of them had even had the chance to know of the force that had sent them into eternity before their fate had already been sealed. Very few occupants anywhere else in the structure had not been killed outright or would die in a matter of seconds after the blast had occurred. In a matter of less than a second, the third branch of government had ceased to exist.

Washington, D.C.
Tuesday, November 8, 11:02 a.m.

Todd Martin was in his own car and fighting the usual traffic coming in from Baltimore when his cell phone rang. Instinctively, and without even bothering to take his eyes off the road, he reached down and flipped the audio switch to the on position and answered. The conversation that ensued over the next two miles was one that no American ever wanted to take place.

Ignoring any posted speed limit and driving like a wild man, Todd drove directly to the White House and pulled his vehicle to the space that had now been designated as his. He got out of the car and raced to the side entry and was ushered into the Oval Office, where several other cabinet members were filing in.

"I guess by now that all of you are aware of the terrible act of war that has once more struck our country," the president began in as somber tones as the situation warranted. "I really thought we had seen the last of this with all the recent arrests that have occurred all over the world, but as you can see, we may be in this for the long haul. I want to commit to every person in this room that I will never give up my fight against these bastards, so long as there is a breath in my body."

The chief executive continued on for five more minutes, stating exactly what was on the heart of every person in the room. Tears were flowing down several of the faces, one of which was the president and another was Todd Martin.

"As of this moment, the apprehending of whoever did this or even supported it in any way will occupy priority in this administration. Nobody will do this to our country and escape justice. I want every nation on earth to be made aware that the United States of America will respect no sovereign border of any country even suspected of harboring elements that have taken this cowardly act of war against this fair nation." He then turned toward the secretary of defense and stated, "As of this very minute I am declaring DEFCON 4 and may God help us all."

A few minutes later, those who needed to return to their respective cabinet posts were allowed to leave the White House, but those not absolutely required to do so were told to remain. The anger and frustration in the room could be cut with a knife. If any enemy could have observed the mood of the room, there would never be an attack on any United States facility in the future. There's an old saying, "You don't kick a sleeping lion in the ass." This lion was enraged and had a hunger for blood that could not be satiated until the last remnants of any terrorist group or individual in the entire world was laid to rest.

"Todd, you remain in full charge here and I want every government agency to provide him with whatever assets he needs to do his job. I will support you in any action you take to achieve our common goal. You act, Todd, but be assured I will assume full responsibility for those actions."

"Mr. President, I intend to be the most aggressive S.O.B. ever to fulfill all our wishes, but rest assured, I will do nothing to bring shame upon you or this country we all love so dearly while I am doing it. It looks like you're going to be getting some more television time, Mr. President. I would suggest that this is a matter that cannot wait until prime time this evening."

The president turned toward his press secretary and directed her to make the necessary preparations for a presidential address to the nation in not more than an hour from now. Next, he turned toward the chief of staff and told him to set up an emergency session with the Congress so he could brief them and seek their required approval to do some of the direct actions he was formulating in his mind.

"I want to be in the House chamber this very night," he told the departing COS.

The secret service, augmented by every law enforcement agency in the District of Columbia, was in the process of locking down every possible route away from town. For the first time since the disaster of 9/11, the Washington airport was closed to all outgoing traffic. In addition, the director of the Immigration and Naturalization Service was being severely raked over the coals to provide a list of every foreign national in the country. The fact that this government bureaucracy had egg all over its collective face for allowing lax enforcement of the rules prior to this time was about to jump up and bite them in the butt.

"Get the governors of the states bordering our borders on the line and tell them … rather, ask them, to activate the National Guard of their states and get them on our borders as soon as they can get them there. Tell them that the Feds will pick up the tab on the mobilization and let me know if any one of them drags their feet, OK?" President Marshall stated to his military liaison.

"Mr. President, I have the directors of Homeland Security and Immigration and Naturalization Service on the line for you. Which one do you want first?" his secretary stated.

"Put 'em both on together, I want to make sure that they are working hand in glove on this one," the president responded and walked over to his desk and picked up the telephone. The first one to speak was the chief of INS.

"Mr. President, we really need to be careful how we ... "

The face of the president went red and he was in no mood to deal with this guy with kid gloves. "You listen to me right now, Bob, I want you to move your zipper around to the front and start being a man! The time for political correctness bull shit is gone. That's exactly what it is, both politics and bull shit. We have a sworn duty to protect the people of America and that's going to be the driving force in this administration from this day on until we overcome this terrible time. As far as that goes, I don't give a darn who doesn't like it; profiling is to be implemented and enforced. We'll worry about hurt feelings later. That doesn't mean that we start rounding up our good Americans of Arabic descent and hauling them off to interment camps, but I want dignified questioning of any individual who might remotely have an axe to grind against the United States. Those who are true patriots and worthy of the name American will not resent it and if they do, tough!"

"You just answered all my questions, Mr. President," the director of homeland security stated in satisfaction and then excused himself so the president could salve the feelings of his counterpart over at INS.

"Bob," President Marshall began, "you inherited a mess over there at INS. Many of the staff members in that organization are so far to the left that they have become a detriment to the safety of our country. I know it's impossible to root all of them out in one fell swoop, but I want you to become very unpopular among the rank and file of that department. They have made a joke out of the responsibilities they are supposed to be fulfilling and that day is over as of now. Call a general meeting or whatever it takes and lay it on the line with every member of your service and make it clear that they are to do their job as indicated in their job description. Since we are in a wartime situation, their dereliction of duty could result in criminal prosecution if they fail to take appropriate action. I really mean this, Bob. I am prepared to do whatever is necessary to secure our borders and ensure the safety of this nation's citizens. I want you to know that I have complete faith in you to turn this organization around and make it effective. If ever there was a man who could do it, it's you, my dear friend. Don't despair."

It was during the period just after the fateful day of September 11, 2001, that a new beginning was started in these United States of America. During the aftermath of that dark day the people of the United States had begun to take on an attitude similar to what must have motivated the original founders of this great nation. Oh, it didn't happen as a spontaneous combustion, but the flame of patriotism had been rekindled and the constant fanning by those who continued to inspire us built that small blaze into a fire of dedication that could never again be quenched. Now that we had just taken a mighty blow that struck at the very heart of our form of government, the people of this nation were prepared to do whatever necessary to let this peal of liberty come forward as never before heard.

The president and Congress were quick to respond to the vacuum left when the judicial third of the government was needed to fill out the triangle of Jeffersonian Democracy within the republic. A lengthy session similar to that of selection of the Pope was conferred with the result that nine new members of the Supreme Court were confirmed within ten days after their predecessors had been brutally murdered. Construction workers from all over the United States had swarmed into Washington with equipment and the clean up was completed in record time. The people of America were anxious to rebuild the United States courthouse in an expeditious manner to show the world that no evil organization could defeat this nation for long.

With the mandate given by President Marshall, Todd wasted no time in redoubling his efforts to reaching an early conclusion of the huge task in front of him. He called a meeting of the secretaries of defense, homeland security, attorney general, and directors of the FBI, CIA and INS. He informed them that he would be working as a member of their team and promised them full backing as long as they broke no federal or state laws. They were to turn over every rock and seek out each nook and cranny where a possible enemy or terrorist thought they could hide. If borders had to be violated to make this so, so be it. Any nation who tried to invoke its sovereignty to prevent this diligent search would find itself in dire trouble with this super power. The gloves had suddenly been taken off and survival was at stake.

Already there were invitations pouring into the White House that would allow complete freedom of movement in their countries along with police cooperation from the host countries. It seems that the nations of the world were clamoring to be the first to provide assistance to "their good American friends." In several belligerent nations there were hastily called meetings to discuss how to approach the Americans without complete capitulation. It really didn't matter if they decided to cooperate or not, because regardless of their intent, they would in the end anyway. For once the element of fear was in those who normally tried to impress it upon the peace-loving nations. It felt good.

The president of North Korea called the president of the United States by way of the Chinese embassy and requested that they converse as soon as possible to discuss how they could be of assistance. The President mentioned that he needed Communist North Korea's help as much as Custer needed more Indians at the Little Big Horn. He thanked the people of North Korea and stated that he would take them up on their gracious offer when the need arose. In a similar manner, the Cuban dictator made an offer of assistance from the peace-loving people of Cuba.

"I wonder what he'd do if I took him up on the offer," the president mused.

The Central Intelligence Agency had been given the green light to move and they took complete advantage of it. For the past couple of decades the CIA had been restrained from doing their job by naïve administrations and a weak congress who were averse to playing the game in the only way to do so successfully. When you're looking for the baser elements in the world community, you can't send in Boy Scouts to do the job. Throughout the history of the CIA they have had to deal with some pretty shady characters in order to penetrate the world of espionage. It simply was a fact that this was the only way to effectively build an intelligence collection organization. It was about fifteen years ago that some members of Congress and the incumbent president got all hot and bothered about this aspect and directed the CIA to cease working with any but upstanding individuals. In effect, they were saying, "Destroy your complete network of spies and come on home."

When the results of this information vacuum began to be felt, the same people who had gutted the system were angry at the CIA for not giving advance warning to several incidents that had caught the United States by surprise. They formed Congressional and Senate sub-committees to investigate the inefficiency of the CIA and were demanding that the head of the agency resign immediately. Morale in the agency went in the toilet and a lot of their best people left. With this invigorating return to effective leadership some of the old pros were returning and with them would come the networks of field operatives and clandestine resources loyal to them in the past.

When the Shah was in charge in Iran the CIA was given pretty much a free hand in that nation. The assets of that nation were abandoned when Jimmy Carter had pulled back the resources of this nation, leaving the network in the country to fend for themselves. Those that were not caught up in the Ayatollah's purges had become so angry at the abandonment that they turned to the anti-American movement. Some of these folks still remained faithful, though, and were ready to pick up where they left off two decades ago.

Field agents were back on the ground and were in the process of rebuilding their networks in order to penetrate to the core of the terrorist movement. It was going to take some time to repair all the damage that had been building over the last decade and a half, but Todd Martin was determined to push as hard as he could to regain the advantage lost. For this he was given the homage due a saint over at Langley. Although the work level had escalated many folds over the past month, the morale of the agency was at an all-time high.

While the CIA was feeling the crunch to produce on the international level, the Federal Bureau of Investigation was getting the same kind of pressure on the domestic front. Much of their work was involved in interface with the INS and Homeland Security, with the preponderance being directed toward the former. Over at INS the people were working at a fever pitch to update records and locate both green card holders and illegal aliens. The guys at the FBI were doing their best to assist their sister department and gain access to the records being updated. The atmosphere of cooperation was a breath of fresh air on the federal level, since previously the turf of each agency was guarded with extreme jealousy. Todd Martin had made it clear that we were all Americans and any petty games would result in extreme corrective action. No longer did you hear comments like, " … those pukes over at such-and-such department." Instead, some interagency personal relationships were developing and that could not mean anything but good for the American people.

Out in California there was a great deal of resentment building now that the illegal aliens were not being given carte blanche to every program being paid for by the taxpayer. The FBI, armed, with a court order that had been challenged by the ninth circuit court and overturned the same day by the newly formed Supreme Court, had walked into the Department of Motor Vehicles in Sacramento and seized the driver's license records for the state. Some months earlier the left wing assembly had passed legislation giving illegal aliens legal driver's licenses. The Feds had now secured the names and addresses of these illegal immigrants and were moving quickly to round them up. The American Civil Liberties Union was having apoplexies and were busying themselves with numerous filings of lawsuits while the usual crowds were out in the streets chanting anti-US slogans and burning flags. Once more, the more macho types were going out and confronting the demonstrators and inflicting numerous black eyes and broken noses.

The directive from the president and Todd Martin to the enforcement agencies was that no detainee was to be treated with anything but the respect deserved by fellow human beings. On the other hand, though, each illegal alien was to be taken to the border and released. Before being released, however, each of them was photographed and fingerprinted. When they were released they were told that should they be found in the United States at any future date without proper entry documents they would be incarcerated for not less than two years or more than five. This should stem the repeat offenders.

Illegal aliens found to be in the United States from countries not adjoining our borders were transported to holding areas to be investigated and then, if found to be innocent of any crimes against the country, deported to the nation of origin. There would be no exceptions. People who had gone through the proper procedures for entry into this nation were not going to be made to look like fools anymore. We would still welcome immigrants into our society, but it would be done the right way or not at all. Many of the career politicians rattled their disapproval of these actions to satisfy the various ethnicities in their constituencies, but in the end they were silenced by threats of recall by the vast majority of the voting bloc.

Todd was just leaving the State Department when his cell phone began to vibrate in his trousers pocket. He almost didn't feel the sensation and cursed at himself for not turning the sound alert back on when he had left the meeting a few minutes before. A heavy drizzle of rain had begun to fall, so he made a dash for the overhead protection of a door awning before he ventured to talk to the party on the other end. Based upon the seemingly endless chain of calls he was receiving both day and night, his telephone etiquette had begun to suffer.

"Yeah," he grunted into the small receptacle designed to pick up his acknowledgment. From the other end of the airwave he heard the voice of the White House chief of staff respond in a tenor that seemed to be questioning.

"Did I get the wrong number?" asked the familiar voice. "Todd?"

"Oh, I'm sorry, sir. I've been meeting myself coming and going and I'll have to brush up on my telephone procedure. What's up?"

"I hope you have kept a suitcase packed 'cause you're gonna need it. We just had a contact with your old friend Akbar over in Egypt. He contacted the president a few minutes ago and stated that it would be best for you to come to his location ASAP. From the sound of his voice, that meant sooner rather than later. President Marshall wants you to get on over there and see what's up. Do you think you can leave this afternoon so you'll be there when he gets out of bed tomorrow morning, his time?"

"Did he give any indication of the subject matter?" Todd asked, already knowing the answer.

"No, but he did say that it was imperative that you talk to only him when you got there and he left an address and special telephone number for you to contact him as soon as you arrive. It must be pretty important and I can only guess what it's about ... " the chief of staff's voice trailed off.

"Come on by the White House before you leave. The president is going to use you as a courier for this trip." Then the telephone went dead. The "chirp" just after the line faded indicated to Todd that the entire call had been scrambled by the White House communications department.

Todd was not used to the VIP treatment he was now getting and automatically looked around to find his blue SUV before he realized that his beefed-up SUV, with its professional driver, was parked up against the curb not more than twenty feet from where he was standing. Hoping that the driver had not spied his confusion in the matter, he raced to the back door where the driver stood with the open door ready to receive him. He leapt into the vehicle and before he even got his seat belt secured, the driver was back behind the steering wheel.

"Where to, sir?"

Todd arrived at the now familiar White House without fanfare and took only a few seconds before he was standing in the doorway of the office of the chief of staff.

"What took you so long?" the chief said with as much humor as his position allowed. "Let me see if the boss is ready for you."

Three minutes later Todd was standing in front of the desk in the Oval Office while the president was walking back and forth with his telephone receiver up to his ear. The chief executive motioned for Todd to have a seat and nodded in approval of the latter's quick response to his page. The conversation took less than a couple of minutes while Todd gazed around the room, taking in the history of the honored place he was viewing. It still sent chills up and down Todd's spine to think that this old country boy was sitting in the office of the most powerful man on earth.

"Todd, I want to thank you for coming so quickly. How're things progressing over at State? I hear you got some people hopping over there and a few other places. Good!" the president asked and stated.

"Well, sir, we've got some really talented people over there and now that they have a complete understanding that you are the boss and not them, we're getting some very important work done. The secretary of state must have really laid down the law 'cause I didn't hear one time the worn out cliché, 'We've always done it this way.' Todd's brief, in appreciative terms, was a back door compliment to his president.

"Mr. President, the chief of staff sounded like we need to do some things in an expeditious manner. I contacted my wife on the way over here and told her to pack me a suitcase so the courier could swing by and pick it up. I guess you want me to get my tail back over to Cairo. I hope they have a better reception for me this time. I get a little nervous when someone tries to blow my airplane out of the sky," Todd said with the appropriate humor.

"Todd, you have made some very strong inroads with the vice president of Egypt and he trusts you more than even me. He seemed to be in quite a hurry to talk to you in private without his government knowing that you are even there. I'm sending you by commercial airlines so your arrival and meeting will remain our little secret. You're booked on Egyptian Airways all the way through, so you're sure to lose all your baggage. The chief told me you're ready to go, so we sorta expedited your booking."

Todd left the Oval Office and just as he was getting ready to open the door, the president called to him. Todd turned around and the president said, "Todd, be careful. I'm getting pretty used to counting upon you."

By the time Todd reached the office of the chief of staff he was handed two packets. One contained his air accommodations, round trip, and the other was a large manila envelope that was clearly stamped "For Your Eyes Only" and a handwritten message, "For Todd Martin" written in black felt-tipped pen. His SUV had pulled up to the receiving point and the driver was holding an umbrella when he stepped outside the White House side entrance. Both men walked briskly to the SUV with the motor idling in anticipation of a quick departure.

"Do we have my luggage?" Todd inquired of his driver.

"No, sir, but they tell me that it will marry up with us once we get to Washington International. Did they give you any tickets?" the driver asked his passenger.

"Yes, Henry, these guys keep me pointed in the right direction and take care of me like I am some sort of baby. At least they haven't started pinning notes to my shirt yet." Both men laughed as the vehicle sped on its way under the expertise of his talented driver. Before Todd had completed reading the information in the envelope that the chief had handed him, they were sitting in front of the "Departures" sign at the terminal.

Todd arrived nearly half an hour before his flight would be departing and he had managed to rate first-class tickets, so he was being pampered in the executive lounge found at every airport to accommodate the snobbery of our society. He wanted to pull out the envelope and continue to read, but rejected the idea in case some prying eyes were around to read over his shoulder. "My God, I'm getting paranoid," he thought to himself, but reflection upon the recent events indicated that maybe he should be.

A few minutes later Todd was seated in seat 2-A, which meant he would be gawking out the window for as long as there was any light to allow visibility this evening. The rain was continuing, so the aircraft would soon be above the clouds and the only sight he would be able to take in would be the endless cloud cover below him and the full moon just off the wingtip. Better yet, he thought, I'd better take advantage of this chance to get some shut-eye. No telling how long it would be before he would get into the sheets, nor even how long this trip would last.

"I wonder what's on Akbar's mind," Todd considered as he laid his head back in the reclined comfort of the leather-stuffed seat and before long he was in a state of a long and sound sleep for the first time in several days.

The rest of the trip was fairly uneventful and the flight attendants had the good sense to not disrupt his sleep in order to provide him crackers and peanuts. By the time Egyptian Airways began making its decent into Cairo, Todd had shaved, washed the sleep out of his eyes, and had taken an extra long time to brush his teeth. He actually looked presentable by the time the smoke announced contact with the landing gear on runway 2-6. He managed to extricate himself from the aircraft and showed his diplomatic credentials to the satisfaction of the "customs sheriff" at the gate before he was free to move into the terminal. He managed to find a bank of telephones in an out-of-the-way hallway and took out the small piece of paper where he had written down the secretive number provided by Mr. Akbar. He felt like James Bond as he managed to dial the telephone all by himself. It was just 6:30 in the morning, local time, when Todd heard the voice of his new friend on the other end.

"Mr. Martin?" the voice inquired

A brief greeting was followed by the announcement that a certain sedan would be waiting for him outside the arrival area. The driver would know him by sight and all that was necessary for Todd to do was to get himself to the appointed place out front with his luggage in tow.

This was the kind of things that happened in the movies, Todd thought to himself and wondered even more what this meeting would uncover for him.

Sure enough, Todd had scarcely set his bag down on the curb when a friendly voice called from one of the sedans at the curb, "Mr. Martin!" Todd immediately picked up his bag and stepped toward the waiting vehicle. The driver made great pains to relieve him of his bag and placed it into the trunk of the car and then rushed to the right rear door and opened it with a flair. Todd got in and sat down. The driver re-entered the driver's compartment and, with a honk of the horn, pulled out into the busy street.

The automobile sped along the streets for some time and then left the urban area to a more open roadway. The morning sun was bright as the vehicle moved in a southeasterly direction that allowed the warmth of the sun to penetrate the automobile from the left front. The sedan proceeded for a period of almost half an hour once it had left Cairo behind. Todd estimated that they had driven about twenty-five miles when the driver turned into the palm-shaded lane of a large villa. The vehicle pulled up to the water fountain that centered a circular drive in front of the house and came to a smooth halt. "We're here!" the driver announced with a smile that could not hide his several missing teeth that gave him an even, friendly appearance.

Well, nothing left to do but go on in and see what had brought him halfway around the world once more in a short period of time. He made it to the last step of the entryway when the doors flew open and standing in the middle was Mahamed Akbar, vice president of Egypt.

"Come on in, my friend! It's so good to see you once more," the VP stated in a voice that could not deny the pleasure that accompanied this meeting. "How was your trip? I hope you are rested after such a long journey," the man said with genuine concern. "We have much to talk about."

Todd exchanged niceties with his host and managed to stretch his arms and legs when the vice president left the room for a few seconds to alert staff to perform various welcoming procedures involving his honored guest. The room reflected tasteful accoutrements, but also indicated that the owner of such a mansion was a person used to the nicer things in life. Well, it couldn't happen to a nicer guy, Todd reflected just as his host returned to the room.

"I took the liberty of preparing an American-style breakfast for you, Todd," the diplomat in Akbar stated as he gently guided Todd toward what turned out to be an open lanai with a sumptuous layout of this "American breakfast." The table was covered with an impeccably starched tablecloth and folded napkins. All the utensils, with the exception of the fine chinaware, was polished silver and the water glasses in front of the two place settings glistened with the ice water that suddenly seemed something Todd could not live without. The two men took their appropriate seats at the table.

In politeness, the vice president did not engage in any serious table talk, but limited his conversation to the topic of Todd's family and his background. He gave a synopsis of his own life up to this point and the two were on a first name basis before Todd took the final bite of his chilled melon from the plate. Without any signal, the two men rose from the table and the Egyptian leader began to guide him out to the exquisite rose garden with manicured walkways through a series of hedges that reached a height of not more than two feet. Only then did the conversation turn toward the reason for the hasty summons to the only American the vice president felt he could trust implicitly.

"My dear friend, I want you to know that I have developed a strong feeling of trust toward you in the short time we have been friends. What I am about to tell you has not been uttered to any person but you. Further, what I intend to relate to you would result in the death of me and the dishonoring of my family forever were it to fall into the wrong hands.

"It grieves me deeply to tell you that my president has been a close ally with the despicable former secretary general of the United Nations. Daniele Tomalas and President Ruel Nadad have been in a conspiracy to gain power beyond comprehension for the past decade. President Nadad has formed a coalition of terrorists right here in our beloved land and has allowed them to build their ranks and train right here under our noses. This highly secretive organization has reached the stages of development that few would have thought possible over the past three years. It is these people who were responsible for the destruction of your halls of justice in Washington!"

Todd felt his knees go weak as the two men were standing in front of one of the beautiful statues located at various points in the garden. He was unable to speak, so the host continued.

"I have conducted my own investigation into this matter and have successfully discovered the entire list of names of all these traitors to Egypt and am prepared to take whatever action is appropriate. This is where you come in, my friend. I am prepared to hand over this list of thugs to you, but only if you are willing to come into my country and cleanse us of this cancer that reaches to the very top. I'm not even sure how this can be accomplished, but I do have faith that there are those in your country who have expertise in such matters.

"Certainly there is risk on your part as well. If I were a person desiring to humiliate and cause severe damage to the United States of America, there could be no better scheme than what I am proposing to you to make this happen. By now, I hope that you have learned that I am a person you can trust as much as I have learned to trust you and your government.

"Unfortunately, I am in no position to take on this tremendous task myself since my president has seen fit to portray me as a power hungry politician who would use such a ploy to gain control of our government. I must rely upon an outside source to accomplish what must be done if this world is to retain any sanity. Now, as you Americans say, I'll shut up and listen to your sage advice."

What? Am I King Solomon? Wow! Todd thought. There must be some appropriate thing to state at this time, but Todd was too stunned to evaluate just what that would be. His only reaction was to reach out and grasp this dear man in an embrace that lasted nearly half a minute before they separated and Todd was able to comment.

"I have been a government employee in the service of my country for all of my adult life, Mr. President. I have encountered some of the most bizarre developments any human should have to face during that time. However, my dear friend, what you have just related to me tops anything I have ever come face to face with. Were I to make a hasty decision and blurt out some response at this moment could possibly be exactly the opposite of what, together, you and I are going to do with the full assistance of my government.

"I would think that I should immediately return to my president and get him involved in the proper solution to this explosive information you have just given me. My concern, however, is for your immediate safety. Do I dare leave you here in a hostile territory when so much is at stake? When this is all over all of us will want you at the helm of leadership in this vital link in the Middle East. Maybe you should find a reason to come back with me, just in case."

"No, my place is here with my people and my country more than ever right now. What kind of leader would I be if I were to tuck tail and run for cover when so much is at stake? I'm sure that I have managed to keep my name out of the center of the investigation I have conducted. In fact, I made it look like it was your CIA operatives meddling in our internal affairs should it come to light—forgive me ... "

The two men managed to laugh at that one. It was just plausible enough to be true with the current situation and the announced policies of Todd's government.

"How about the driver who brought me here? Do you want me to execute him after he drops me off at the airport?" Todd stated with a wink to his host. Actually, Todd wished he had been allowed to drive himself here now that he had heard the full story.

"No, Todd. This man has been my personal driver for nearly five years now and I chose him rather than have him seek me out for the position. I am certain that his loyalties are with me and these loyalties have been tested and retested during all those years. He has no idea why you are here and believes that I am trying to obtain sizable loans from your country to rebuild the Suez Canal. I'll be just fine, but I'll feel much better once your government makes its move in this matter."

Less than half an hour later Todd had rejoined the vice president's driver and was taken back to the Cairo Airport for a quick turnaround flight back to the United States.

"Damn! I sure wish I had access to the White House scrambler right now," Todd thought for the umpteenth time in the last hour.

Five-hundred-eighty knots may seem fast if you're driving an automobile on the ground, but the Egyptian Airways jet seemed to hang in space for the longest time as Todd made his trip homeward. He wanted to get into the president's office as soon as possible with the information he was carrying. The packet he had been provided prior to his departure was a detailed study into the life of vice president Akbar. Todd didn't need to consult this dossier any further. He was certain that his information about the man was more accurate and important than any he had been able to glean from the report. Not that it had been incorrect in any detail. His own study of the man revealed the quality of homework of whoever had put the packet together, but there was no way to get inside the head to the extent that Todd Martin had accomplished during the past month.

There are times when the body demands rest that you are unable to comply. Todd realized that he was the only person in the world outside of Egypt who knew for certain who had murdered the entire bench of the Supreme Court. Then there was the fact that a list of all the individuals involved in terrorism from the whole of Egypt was tucked into his briefcase ready to be handed to the CIA and all the other agencies the president might select to prosecute the war on terrorism. Right now, Todd Martin was probably the most important individual in the whole world. This was a dubious honor he hoped to rectify as soon as he could hand the information over to his president. That would be in approximately five hours from right now. Sleep! Are you kidding?

— 14 —

FBI Headquarters , Washington
Thursday, November 10, 7:22 p.m.

"Abdul Al-Khalifa? Hey, that's the guy I was interrogating about an hour ago," the FBI agent stated in surprise. His coworkers had been going over the list that Martin had brought back from his trip and when the mention of Abdul's full name was read aloud the interest of the interrogator had suddenly piqued.

"What about him?" the agent asked as he rose to his feet and went around the desk to his co-worker's station to look at the list being examined.

"What about him!" the reader stated with alarm. "This is the asshole that blew up the entire Supreme Court!" the administrative agent exclaimed. "You mean we actually have this guy in custody right here in this building?" the excited man said in astonishment.

"You bet your ass," the interrogator stated emphatically as he rushed toward the doors that led to the basement elevator. Two other agents joined him as he ran to the elevator and pushed the down button. Deciding that it was taking too long, the agent ran to the stairwell and charged through the door in a headlong dash for the lower levels of the building. He managed to cover the four flights of stairs in what was probably the record time for the building and burst through the double doors that led to the holding cells.

"Please, oh please, God, don't let him have been released yet," the panting agent breathed as he tore though the hallway to the front desk of the holding area.

"Do you guys still have that guy, Abdul, in the tank?" the agent queried.

"Yeah, we were ready to release the bastard a few minutes ago when he decided to spit in the guard's face. We hauled his butt back to the cell to let him stew for a while longer. What do you need him for?"

When the desk clerk heard the story of just who Abdul really is, his jaw dropped wide open and he rose to his feet quickly while he reached for the keys that would allow entry into the cells. Within five minutes the three agents who had raced down the stairwell had taken control of the terrorist and had placed him in restraints of both ankles, his wrists, and placed a black bag over his head. "Now lets see you spit, you bastard!" one of the guards said as the team led the master criminal out of the holding cell area and brought him to the interrogation room once more.

This was too important a development to handle through normal procedures and the agent in charge decided to call his supervisors to announce the discovery. The flurry of activity that occurred after the revelation reached top brass in a rapid and decisive manner.

"Call Todd Martin and let him know that we have this guy in custody. I'll bet a month's pay he will call the president as soon as he hears the good news," the assistant FBI director stated. He went to another telephone to call his boss.

Abdul's entire background and his complete itinerary for the preceding month were determined within twenty-four hours by a team of investigators that must have numbered in the hundreds. If he had stopped to pee, they had the time and place and probably his protein count from the specimen. One of the aspects of the case unfolded when another name from the list appeared in his list of contacts. There was this guy Rahman who was probably involved in the terrorism as well. They'd have to put out a net to haul this guy in too.

Friday, November 11, 5:00 p.m.

"My fellow Americans and those watching from around the world, we have been the recipient of a great blessing in the midst of our sorrow. As you are aware, evil forces attacked the third branch of our government and murdered the justices of our Supreme Court just three short days ago.

"Earlier yesterday afternoon I received a packet from our close friend and ally in this war against terrorism. The packet contained a list including the names and addresses of every terrorist in the country of Egypt. Included in that list were the names and addresses of the two men responsible for blowing up the Supreme Court of the United States. These despicable men had been right here in the United States and enjoying the freedoms we all love and they were attempting to destroy. Those two are sitting in custody right here in the nation's capital, awaiting the sure justice that they deserve.

"The wonderful news I bring to you is that our dear friend, President Ruel Nadad of Egypt, was the person who provided this list of terrorists from his own country. As I am speaking to you, members of that great nation and ours are in the process of rounding up these villains and bringing them to justice. This nation and the world owe a great debt of gratitude to this courageous leader."

The newscast continued for several minutes and then clips of those being arrested here and abroad were televised to add emphasis to the president's report to the nation. Of course, the remaining elements of terrorists from around the world were watching, too. That traitor over in Egypt would never dare to show his face in public ever again! Every assassin would be ready to make the ultimate sacrifice in order to extract the last measure of vengeance on Ruel Nadad.

Another person who had been watching the American president was the president of Egypt. "What?!" he exclaimed when he heard his name broadcast all around the world as the source of that terrible list exposing him and his brothers. How did they get that list and who was the traitor in their midst that would name Ruel Nadad, who had been completely loyal to the organization from the day he joined and up to now. He must do something immediately to clear his name.

The Egyptian arm of the Movement had access to some of the finest audio/visual equipment to be had. Right here in his presidential mansion were all the facilities necessary to produce television-ready video tapes when the need arose. He would make use of this equipment to reach out to his brothers and assure them that this was all just another CIA plot to attack the Movement. Twenty minutes later Ruel Nadad was seated behind his desk, wearing his best suit and his head cover to show his devoutness to his comrades.

"Salaam, my brothers in the struggle for Allah. By the time you see this video you will have seen the horrible lies that the great Satan, the United States of America, has been telling all over the world. This is just another lie by their hated Central Intelligence Agency designed to discredit me and all I have done to support our jihad.

"Was it not I who first broached the idea of destruction of both the Panama and Suez Canals, one in my own country? Was it not I who provided billions in funding of support for the attacks upon the evil countries of the West? You all know how I worked so hard behind the scenes to bring our brother, Daniele Tomalas, to the very leadership of the world government. I have served the cause well and never once did I do anything to bring discredit to our cause. I swear by all that is holy that I was not the one who gave that dreadful list containing the names of my brothers to the hated infidels!"

This tape would be given wide dissemination among the members of the Movement and Ruel Nadad would clear his name once and for all.

There was one thing that Ruel Nadad did not know, however. The man behind the camera was an agent of the United States government. The entire broadcast was forever locked on video tape and would be routed to a completely different audience than it had been intended for. That very morning, in Cairo, and the rest of the Middle East, people would turn on their televisions and be greeted by the Egyptian president making full confession of his role in the false Islamic jihad that had brought so much pain to them and the rest of the world.

Immediately following the broadcast of the damning tape, the vice president of Egypt came on the screen to explain the complete and full explanation of the activities of his former traitorous Egyptian president. Vice President Akbar was, at the moment, being declared the new president by the entire Egyptian house of government. All across that nation many international police forces (American and Egyptian) were in the process of rounding up every dissident terrorist who had been holding the world hostage by their evil deeds for much too long.

For much of the remainder of the day there were spontaneous parades and crowds gathered to pledge their support to the new president and his government. Leaders of the military, eager to show their support for President Akbar, were conducting musters of their troops and reading proclamations of loyal support to their new leader so richly deserving of it.

Unfortunately, Ruel Nadad had missed the airing of the broadcast to the world. Unlike the jails in the United States, Egyptian inmates are not provided televisions to watch. Instead, Ruel was sitting on a dilapidated cot in a dark cell wondering what had happened. Just ten minutes after he had completed the video tape, members of the secret police had burst into his home and had dragged him out into the street and into a van used for hauling common criminals away. He thought he had spied his vice president standing across the street during the commotion, but he was not sure.

The vehicle carried the president and sped through the streets of his capital and directly to the prison where so many of his enemies had been dispatched in the past. His shock at what was occurring left little time to reflect on its cause. Could this be happening to him? Hadn't the president of the United States claimed him as a hero only a few hours ago?

Ruel was not given any clues as to the reason for his incarceration. He was told to be silent when he made his initial protestations and one of the captors had dared to slap him very hard right in the face. Had the whole world gone crazy?!

Once in his cell he had a visitor. At first, he was elated when Vice President Akbar had appeared through the bars of his cell. Surely now things would change and he would be able to take his revenge against those who had treated their president so rudely. But that was not to be the case. Mahamed Akbar had stood in front of his cell, looking at him through eyes of pity and shaking his head in shame. In the brief minutes that followed Mr. Akbar related to his former president that his days of terrorism were over. There wasn't even anger as he recapped the acts of terror inflicted by this man and his band of hoodlums. Only when he brought up the Suez Canal did Ruel see a trace of anger, but it was quickly replaced by the same sadness as before.

"You have disgraced your office, your nation, Islam and even the Great Allah by your evil war against all that is taught in the Holy Koran," Mahamed stated in a matter-of-fact voice that could not be denied. "Your place in history will be among the worst of leaders of this great nation, but you could never bring it down. As long as there are Pyramids towering over our land there will always be an Egypt. Many have tried to destroy this country and their bones are out among the sands. I have a feeling that yours, too, will soon find their way to these same sands where, in time, even you will no longer even be a memory. For that I am deeply saddened. May Allah forgive you because your nation cannot." With that, the new leader of the nation slowly turned his back and walked away.

Ruel Nadad had managed to escape the vengeance of an irate membership of the Movement only to create his own inescapable snare that would accomplish the same result. His trial would be a public spectacle that would make him the laughing stock of the whole world. The video tape would be played over and over again along with the captions addressing the fact that the person filming the entire confession was smirking during the whole taping session. He could stand failure, but being humiliated in front of the whole world was more than he could stand. The Americans had been quick to humiliate the spokesman in Iraq and had even made up an insulting name of

"Baghdad Bob" for the man when his reports became unbelievable. Ruel could not stand the thought that he would become "Cairo Comic."

The following morning the changing of the guard caused them to walk to the cell where Ruel Nadad was incarcerated. It took only a second to make the observation that would be the subject of widespread news that day. The dangling feet of the former ruler were suspended approximately a foot from the floor. The shirt which Ruel had been wearing the night before had been torn into strips and woven to make a rope. The rope had been secured to one of the cross members of the ceiling pipes traversing the cell and the other had been used to create a noose that would serve to end the life of its victim. Ruel had managed to stand on the rail of the cot in his cell and then swing free in his final act of defiance.

The only reaction of the discovering guards was a shrug of the shoulders and a certain relief at the thought of not having to constantly feed and care for the inmate during the rest of the day. The body was cut down and allowed to slump into an unceremonious position on the floor while the guards removed the last remnants of the makeshift rope from the overhead pipes. They then grabbed his heels and dragged the lifeless body out of the cell and loaded it on a gurney for transport to wherever their superiors would direct.

Washington, D.C.
Monday, November 14, 7:31 a.m.

Todd Martin, now a regular at the president's morning briefing, was making notes as "The Boss," as the inner circle were used to calling him, made his observations based upon the situation reports coming in from the normal sources. The recent disaster at the Supreme Court was still on all their minds, but there seemed to be a feeling of recovery with the final stages being completed on the Alaska Pipeline and the progress down in Panama and Suez. The country had been put though the worst time of disaster since Pearl Harbor and the World Trade Center and we were still in there pitching. It said a lot about the spirit of the nation.

Todd had given a lengthy briefing on each situation entailed in his verbal job description and, in spite of the incidents of recent days, his report had reflected a very positive reflection on all areas. The monetary contributions he had been successful in amassing from the various governments in Europe and Asia had been a Godsend with the financial burdens caused by the three first attacks. His progress reports on the key areas in the Middle East were such that he cautioned against being too optimistic because of the events in the past two weeks. Could it be possible that the hostile relations between Syria and Iran were not only thawing, but becoming downright friendly? Indications here and coming in from longtime allies of the United States were euphoric about the reports coming from their resources.

The situation in Egypt seemed to have cooled down and President Akbar was making reforms for the betterment of the Egyptian people in an unprecedented manner. Countries such as Yemen and Morocco were remaining silent and watching to see which side to come down on once the dust settled. North Korea was beside herself and had turned to China to rekindle favorable relations that had been strained in recent years by the belligerence of the pipsqueak dictator in North Korea. China was not about to be so forgiving and was using the situation to extract concessions that were sure to rile the Communist regime on the Korean peninsula. It would have been humorous were it not for the seriousness of the matter. The Korean leader was just too dangerous to be backed into a corner by anyone.

The reforms begun in Syria continued, but now that the pinch was beginning to be felt by some of the more affluent families in the country, the enthusiasm of the first days was beginning to wear thin. The military operation into the Bekka Valley had missed a lot of the major targets and was beginning to come home to roost in Damascus. Just two days ago a car bomb had exploded in front of the main police station in the heart of town and members of the Movement had been quick to claim responsibility for it. The casualties had been few, but never before had the pain of suicide bombers been felt by residents of Syria rather than the hated Jews.

Todd announced that it was time for him to make the trip to Syria and try to prop up the regime of the president before things got too far out of hand. The president and national security advisor joined the secretary of state in endorsing the idea and offered any assistance to Mr. Martin should he need it.

That afternoon Todd returned to his home and broke the news to Cathy and the kids that once more he would be leaving their home for a few days. This was not good news to his wife. She was becoming more and more concerned for his safety now that he was making frequent trips to places they kept hearing about on the news each day. The news from these precincts was not all that good. The odds of something terrible happening to their husband and daddy were going up in a manner that was getting to be alarming.

Todd assured his wife that he was in places far enough away from any possible violence that the guys down at the office were calling his trips "the milk run." With that she dropped her objections but told him to stay safe anyway. Todd had never told his wife about the near fatal crash of his airplane when he made his first trip over to Egypt. No sense in getting her all worried about situations that he had no control over in the first place.

Andrews Air Force Base
Tuesday, November 15, 6:00 a.m.

The VIP jet was just moving into takeoff position at the end of the runway and Todd was feeling refreshed after getting to bed early the night before in anticipation of this early start. He had risen two hours earlier and had a quick breakfast of coffee and orange juice before the familiar SUV and his driver pulled into the driveway next to his Suitland home. Todd gulped down the last of his cup of coffee and kissed his wife before leaving home for the car.

He had managed to read most of *The Washington Post* on the trip to Andrews and had inadvertently left the paper in the car. Too late to go back and get it now, so he leaned back in his seat and felt the acceleration of the powerful airplane as it gained speed sufficient to make it airborne. The rain had stopped long enough so that he could see quite clearly the local urban sprawl between the clouds as the aircraft climbed and began its long journey. He even managed to locate his own home as they were passing just to the south.

Arrival at Damascus International Airport was a welcomed sight after the long trip across the Atlantic and down the length of the Mediterranean once more. This was really getting to be a drag and Todd was beginning to look back with nostalgia to those days when he was just another face putting in an honest days work for the taxpayer. He thought that the Customs agent even recognized him as he presented his diplomatic identification and smiled at the man.

Outside was the expected embassy vehicle ready to whisk him off to the embassy and the in-country ambassador. Scarcely a word passed between Todd and his driver as they made their way through the now familiar streets of Damascus. He should have been impressed, since the city is one of the oldest continually occupied towns in the entire world. Even the street he was now traversing is clearly mentioned in the Holy Bible and had been traveled by the Apostle Paul.

Maybe he was just fatigued from the travel.

The ambassador was on hand to greet him as he alighted from the bulletproof SUV in the inner compound of the sovereign property of the United States in Damascus. His departure from Andrews at 6 a.m. this morning only meant that he would be having a short day as he sped into the direction of the oncoming sun. He had managed to arrive in the late night and he made a point to make better decisions regarding travel in the future. Although he was wide awake, his hosts were showing signs of being up for too long. He took that into consideration when he begged off the offered nightcap from the ambassador, who looked relieved at the declination.

The following morning Todd spent quite a bit of time with the American consulate before venturing out to the city. The ambassador confirmed Todd's suspicions that the Syrian president's popularity had been suffering due to the small acts of terrorism that seemed to be emanating from the same old hot spot over in the Bekka Valley. Unless they were able to take complete control of this fortress of the terrorists and soon, the momentum would be lost and there was no telling how long it would be before the Middle East was back in the quagmire that had held a firm grip for many years. The more they discussed the matter the more Todd began to formulate a plan to take decisive action.

Back on Smoke Bomb Hill at Fort Bragg, many years before, when Todd was an active member of the United States Army Special Forces and, specifically, the 7th Special Forces Group (Airborne), there had been ample training designed specifically for the situation they were now facing in Syria. An enemy force was occupying a country (used to be called "Pineland") and was living off the forced contributions of the indigenous people in the area. A Special Forces mission would be to infiltrate into the heart of the fictitious country and begin to build resistance and then to recruit and train the local populace as militia. The local residents were given those items necessary to have a better life by the infiltrators. Medical treatment would be provided to the families so long in need of such. Everything possible to earn the respect and trust of the people of the area would be exercised. Along with this would be certain acts of warfare against the occupying army. The key was to make sure that any attacks by the Special Forces were highly successful so that the locals would see that the A-Teams were just that.

Once the popularity of the infiltrated Special Forces was a fact they could begin to recruit and train small elements to assist in the interdiction of enemy positions. This would continue and before long the guerrilla forces would secure a foothold and the enemy would be put on the defensive. Critical to the success of the Special Forces' mission would be the ability to meet the needs of the people in a manner that no opposing force could. The goal was to work yourself out of a job. When the local element was strong enough to impose their own government and drive the occupying forces out, what would remain was a country friendly to the United States. All the elements for this type an operation were present in Lebanon.

The first order of business was to isolate the terrorist groups in Lebanon so that they could not gain resupply from the outside. The Syrian Army was capable of fulfilling this element of the plan. Next would be to convince the Congress to allow such an operation. A plethora of quality "Sneaky Pete" forces were ready and well-trained to accomplish the mission. The various Special Forces groups were trained with specific areas of the globe in mind. The detachments were language qualified in the appropriate local dialects and there was no doubt that these super soldiers would perform at optimum professionalism to make the outcome almost unfairly tilted in their favor.

Before he went off half-cocked, Todd placed a telephone call on the secure line to MacDill Air Force Base, and specifically to his old friend, General Harry Thompson. When Todd bounced the idea off the general he got an enthusiastic whistle for his response.

"Hell yes, we can do it and I'm surprised someone upstairs hasn't come up with this idea before now. You have my full backing if you can talk those guys up on the hill to turn us loose. Let me know if you need my horsepower. I'll get cracking on this end to see what we can shake loose from here and you just get us the authorization. Its time that someone showed those thugs how a real army operates."

Todd ended the call and then began to conduct a thorough examination of the order of battle for the enemy camps in the valley. Although the list of units and personnel were somewhat sketchy, the new information collected in recent days made the accuracy of the list pretty impressive. He knew also that just over the hill in Jerusalem was a collection of information that would significantly add to that roster. Based on his current plan there was no doubt that Israel would gladly hand over that information in a heartbeat.

After four hours of intensive study and planning, Todd made the call back to the White House. A detailed report on all that had transpired in Damascus, supported by his findings, and his knowledge of Special Warfare Operations, enabled Todd to proffer a very impressive OPLAN for consideration by his cohorts back in the Oval Office.

After a few questions for clarification, the President was the first to speak.

"Todd, this is just radical enough that it will probably work. How do you think the Syrians will react to the idea?"

"Well, Mr. President, based upon the recent developments here in Damascus and the need to shore up his government, I believe that President Hakim will jump on it. It's not him that gives me concern; I'm not sure how the boys over on Capitol Hill will respond to this action," Todd voiced for the benefit of everyone in the room.

"Why don't you leave that one up to me?" the president stated with a wink of his eye toward his chief of staff. "These days there are not too many folks over there who are not clamoring to look very patriotic based upon the recent developments. If you don't hear otherwise from me, in the meantime I want you to get cracking on this matter. I assume you've already done some preliminary work with the guys down at MacDill?" the president queried.

Todd told him of his conversation with the four-star general down in Florida and that seemed to satisfy all the questions for that morning. There being no further business, Todd hung up the scrambler phone and left the communications "shack" in the embassy.

When Todd told President Hakim that the United States was contemplating a complete sweep of the Bekka Valley, the president's eyes lit up with anticipation. He would support any move to clear out that nest of rats.

He mentioned to Todd, "You may not be aware of this, but my popularity has begun to drop because the people are not sure that I am up to the task of removing the terrorists from my nation. If you were able to assist me in this dilemma, I'm sure it would go a long way in restoring their faith. Yes, you have my endorsement on your plan and may Allah go with you."

There was no need to prolong the trip to Damascus any longer, but Todd wanted to make one more stop on his way home. Once aboard the aircraft Todd directed the pilot to set a course for Lod Field in Israel.

— 15 —

Israel
Thursday, November 17, 9:00 a.m.

Todd always liked to come to Israel. As far as he was concerned this land was the absolute cradle of anything spiritual throughout the world. Three major religions could trace their heritage back to a small town called Hebron located in the hill country southwest of Jerusalem. Unfortunately, the same could be said of most of the wars mankind has inflicted upon itself as well. Everywhere you turned there were places and sights that carried huge amounts of historic value to the point that he felt compelled to watch where he stepped lest he desecrate some holy ground.

But his purpose for being here right now was not to be a tourist. He needed to make some momentous decisions and the manner in which they would be carried out depended upon the talks he would engage in over the next few hours. He felt confident that Israel would respond favorably, but that he should avoid taking anything for granted.

Todd had arranged for a meeting with the top government officials and had been vague in his description of the reason why. He had played his trump card once more when he said he was on a mission for the president of the United States. The hierarchy were more than happy to meet once they heard that key phrase. The meeting was laid on for the first thing after lunch, so Todd had plenty of time to get over to Jerusalem and even do a little shopping for some trinkets to take home to Cathy and the kids.

After a leisurely lunch Todd had made his way to the office building where the meeting would transpire and found his hosts waiting for him when he was ushered into the room.

"Mr. Martin, it's always a pleasure to welcome you to Israel," the self-defense group secretary stated as he grasped Todd's hand in a vicelike grip that sent chills up to his elbow. This guy must have been as strong as a horse in his early years and he certainly was no slouch even now, Todd observed, trying not to wince from the pain of a mere handshake.

As was his usual manner, Todd laid out his plan in entirety for the assembled group, complete with his manner of insertion and general battle plan. The whole presentation lasted for not more than forty-five minutes and when he was finished the SDG looked over toward him and asked, "What will be our role in this operation, Mr. Martin?"

Good, Todd thought to himself. Obviously they think this is a good idea and are willing to support it.

"General Eban, we are not asking you to get involved just yet, but we would never do anything right here in your back yard without your approval and full knowledge. We have developed a pretty good order of battle portfolio on the terrorist group and I want to share that with you. We should compare our notes to make sure we both have a good handle on all their units and people while I'm here, don't you think?"

There, he had laid out his reason for being here and had even sounded diplomatic in the process. The members of the self-defense group took the bait and were eager to see what new information they might glean from their greatest ally. The next hour was spent with members of the Israeli intelligence weenies gong over the U.S. report and putting in entries where they needed to be entered on both the list that would be going back to the United States as well as their own. During the update procedure the intell guys were very excited at discovery of several key positions that had escaped them for years. Several times one or more of the analysts let out a whoop when they made such a discovery. This was one of their greatest coups in the intelligence field. When Todd disclosed that the entire list had come directly from the Syrian president, emotions overflowed. There was a new day dawning and it promised to be a glorious one for the people of Israel.

When Todd got back on his airplane he was armed with a nearly complete listing of every unit and its membership in the whole Bekka Valley, as well as their general areas of operation. The boys down at MacDill would be ecstatic. Now the real work could begin. He was torn between diverting his arrival to Tampa, but his personal loneliness for the warmth of his family won out and he would be spending the next day with them to make up for the long absences that had been a part of their lives. It appeared it would be continuing at the same pace for some time to come.

Cathy and the kids had been given the time of his arrival at the air base and were standing by waiting for him when his aircraft taxied up to the parking area. His driver had taken the liberty of stopping by the Martin residence and brought them with him to the airport. He had just made a career move that would keep him in good stead as far as Todd was concerned. The trip back to their home was one of excitement and happiness as the children could not give their daddy enough hugs and kisses to satisfy their need. Mommy was in there somewhere, too. Todd's driver kept his eyes on the road, but a slight smile was emanating from his face as he tried to be inconspicuous.

"Should I pick you up in the morning?" the driver inquired when the Martin family had disembarked from the vehicle.

"No, Henry, why don't you just take the day off and get acquainted with that lovely family of yours for a change. That's what I'm going to do with mine and we'll just let this be our little secret."

The next day was another to be compared with the previous family outings for the Martins. It's amazing how much lost ground can be made up when you really put your heart and soul into it. It's funny how you can live in an area for so long and not take advantage of the numerous activities and sights in your own backyard. If this kept up much longer, the Martin family would end up being a veritable travel agency. Both Cathy and Todd had remarked that this was something that they would continue "once this was all over."

Washington, D.C.
Sunday, November 20, 3:22 p.m.

Todd had finished a marathon session at the White House that had started before seven in the morning and had just finished in time for him to grab a quick bite on the way back out to Andrews. This time, however, he would not be leaving U.S. airspace for a change. Two hours later he was in Tampa, heading out to MacDill, where a team of military officers had been assembled to make plans.

General Thompson greeted Todd warmly since it was the former who had been the detachment commander when Todd had shown up as a "shavetail" second lieutenant "way back when." The two men's careers had gone separate paths since then, but there was no doubt that each had achieved success in their own right. The general made quite a fuss about introducing Todd to the rest of the people in the staff conference room and then invited Todd to give a briefing on what was in the offing. The general had purposely kept them in the dark as to the planned operation until Todd could gain the approval of the commander in chief.

Todd began by explaining his background in Special Forces and then related how the mission he had now planned was right out of the textbook with the overall mission of the Green Berets. When he finished there was no doubt that this would be a chance to once more show the value of retention of such a military organization.

"Gentlemen, very shortly we will be putting Special Forces Teams on the ground in the heart of enemy held territory in the Bekka Valley. These teams will be inserted in the most clandestine manner that we possess. That means a night H.A.L.O. (High Altitude Low Opening parachute assault) jump will be required. It's just too easy to be detected if an attempt to insert by helicopter rappelling were tried, so that is out of the question.

"Once on the ground all resupply will be by cargo chutes on prepackaged cargo skids. Radio contact with friendly forces will be next to non-existent except by clandestine methods. Back in 'Nam the SOG guys used to have a pretty effective means of getting their messages back to headquarters. They would make a miniature tape on a cartridge that fit into a plastic box about the size of a pager. Then they would take out another package of similar size which contained a balloon and helium cartridge and inflate the balloon. They would then connect the recorder to the balloon and let it loose. When the balloon reached an altitude approximately fifteen hundred feet above ground level, the cartridge containing the tape activated and sent the message at ultra-high speed in less than two seconds. The guys back on friendly turf would capture the message and play it at low speed to obtain the necessary communication. I've checked and we still have some of those gadgets collecting dust in a warehouse up at Bragg. They will be in your hands by tomorrow.

"Now, guys, I'm not sure if you "007s" have developed any better means of getting and receiving mail, so I'll leave that up to you since I do not qualify for need-to-know. There is, however, one thing I am sure of: Those guys back in Vietnam had as much guts as any man sitting in this room today and I'm sure that trend has continued to the present. This is one hell of a mission to expect any soldier to carry out, but I'm equally sure that we will find ample evidence of that spirit in the coming weeks.

"I want every volunteer who elects to take part in this little party to know every detail of the operation before they make a commitment to be a member of this team. As usual in this type of operation, there will be little glory or accolades to be passed around once the mission is over. Anyone who participates will only have the knowledge and pride of knowing that he has been a true patriot and has accomplished more than ten other men will do in their entire lifetime for the good of this nation.

"Now, I know that you gentlemen are anxious to get busy planning this mission and I intend to remain in the area to provide any assistance I can. I'm pretty good at emptying waste baskets and can even type if you need me. What are your questions?"

The next half hour were used to reiterate the general mission plan and provide as much information as was available to the planners and leaders in the room. During the next five days selected teams arrived at MacDill and were brought into the fold. It still caused Todd to swell with pride to know that there were such paragons of excellence in mind, spirit and body in the ranks of this elite force of men. The names and faces of the men had changed since Todd had left this cherished fraternity, but the same qualities he had seen years earlier were exemplified in the twelve-man A-Teams he now was learning to know.

Todd stayed at the military base for the entire week and even managed to keep up with the guys on the morning runs that were a part of their lives. They had even given a few approving nods to each other when Todd finished the run at the same time they did. He was a little weak when it came to all the other drills they did with nonchalance, but they seemed somewhat forgiving since he had been a member of their select group years earlier and would always be considered a brother in arms.

When he got back home that next Friday afternoon he spent some time with the president and brought him up to speed on what was going on down in MacDill Air Force Base.

"I hear you've been out running with those guys down there, Todd. Don't overdo it trying to be Mr. Macho; I still need you around here, you know. Besides, I hear they have been taking it easy on you because you're an old man," the boss chortled.

Henry understood that his boss was anxious to get home to his family and didn't spare the gas in getting him there.

"Better watch out or you'll get a ticket," Todd mused.

"No sweat, sir; they wouldn't dare as long as you're in the vehicle," his driver retorted with a grin as he pressed a little harder on the accelerator. "Besides, I'd rather face the cops than your wife if I were to delay your homecoming."

These homecomings are getting to be quite the thing, Todd thought as his brood came rushing toward the SUV when it came to a stop in the driveway. A guy could really get used to this honeymoon atmosphere that always awaited him after an absence from his nest. Cathy had prepared a special meal that consisted of his favorite casserole. The kids were not all that excited about it, but now that their daddy was home, they would have eaten sawdust and loved it. Anyone watching the little family during the evening would have thought they were observing "the Cleavers," who never had a bad situation to demand their attention.

The next morning was spent lazing around the house and Todd reading his paper in leisure for a change. The Redskins were doing just fine without him being here to cheer them on. If he could get the tickets it might be fun to go over to RFK tomorrow and watch his favorite team whip the Cowboys. After the game he would treat his family to one of those unhealthy fast food restaurants and listen to his wife berate the terrible food their children were delighting in. Last year, Todd's whole life had seemed to hinge on whether the Redskins would make the playoffs, but in the past weeks his priorities had made a drastic turn.

A couple of telephone calls later, Todd was able to procure the necessary game tickets and felt a little chagrined that his wife did not share his elation over his success. Cathy was one of those women who got more out of watching *Trading Spaces* than anything really important, like sports. She would never sit with him and watch the Friday night fights. He just couldn't figure her out!

By the time Monday morning rolled around the Martins had regained the normal functions of their family and Todd even had to go in and settle a dispute between Becky and Hal. Todd looked up and offered a little prayer of thanksgiving as he left the two children in a state of truce. He was feeling rather domestic and even went out and cleaned off the driveway and walk before the family had left for the game yesterday. This was what life should be like. His mind traveled to the Middle East he had recently left and considered the lot of the average citizen over there. What quirk of fate had made him so fortunate to be born in a country like this?

Todd was sipping from the large cup his wife had filled with the last of the coffee in the pot that morning. He felt the unpleasant texture of some of the grounds as he tipped his cup up to get the last swig. Henry was commenting on how much he and his wife had enjoyed the holiday bequeathed to him by Todd last week. His wife had repeatedly told him to be sure and thank Mr. Martin as soon as he saw him.

When the vehicle made the final turn into the parking lot of the State Department, Todd laid his newspaper on the seat next to him and made ready to face another week of whatever fate had in store for him.

It had been some time since he had talked face-to-face with Mrs. Johnson and she seemed as happy about the reunion as was Todd. She had a lilt to her voice as she greeted him and it was all he could do not to pick her up and swing her around in his elation at seeing the matronly lady he was fortunate enough to have as his secretary.

She pulled out her notepad and gave him a thorough update on all the current events here in his office. Just as she was finishing her report there was a subdued knock on the door. Unseen by either of them had been the approach of Hal Croft, who had taken the time to come down and welcome his protégé back to the home front.

"Mind if I interrupt the two of you and get acquainted with the new guy?" the general quipped as he flopped into the chair next to Todd's desk. "I wasn't sure you would remember where your desk was after this much time." After Mrs. Johnson had taken her cue and left the two of them alone, the secretary of state continued, "You know, Todd, I've really taken some high praise for introducing you to the folks down the street. They think you can walk on water down at the White House, you know."

"Well, I let them all know that everything I have learned of any value was learned at your feet, so you can take credit for the fortune that has fallen upon me," Todd said and meant. "I got to tell you, sir, that I feel like I'm in so far over my head that I must be dreaming most of the time. Have you ever felt that way?"

"Welcome to the world of phonies, Todd. Most of us are in the same boat and only pretend to have the wisdom of Solomon. If you just keep your thoughts pure and work hard, everybody will continue to think that you're brilliant. I am convinced that there are no really great men. There are just average people who make great decisions that cause them to become great. As long as we don't get all puffed up about ourselves we continue to be worth some of the tributes they pay to us. I knew when I nominated you for your position that you would make all of us proud. Your achievements have proven my ability to make such a great decision."

The next hour was spent in bringing General Croft up to speed on all the events of the period since the two men had conversed. Most of it was already known to the secretary of state, but his input on several key issues shed new light on the impact of events for Todd's benefit.

"Sir, I have really put myself on the line with this Syrian thing. I just hope that it was a good call. So much hinges on the success of this mission that I dare not even think about failure. If we can pull this one off as I hope, we will have made this world a much safer place than either of us has known in our lifetime. The Syrians and Israelis feel comfortable with it and General Thompson says he wishes he had been the one to think of it. All the teams who will be in country have bought into the plan wholeheartedly. I just worry about something I may have overlooked and cannot seem to locate. The lives of so many families and the nation are riding upon my plans and I can tell you this much: I'm scared!"

The general rose from his chair and walked over to where Todd was sitting and put his hand on the latter's shoulder. "Son, you have a good plan and you have good men to see it through. Failure or success is in the hands of the Almighty. I just happen to believe He is looking down on you this very minute with great affection and approval. My advice to you is to lean forward in the foxhole and concentrate on defeating the enemy."

— 16 —

MacDill Air Force Base
Monday, November 28, 06:00 hours

Where did this month go to? Todd thought as the formation was making its final turn back to the compound after completing the daily five-mile run that had been as much a part of these special ops people as it was to brush one's teeth or have the morning cup of coffee. This morning had been done at a faster pace now that the "snake eaters" had discovered that "the old man" could keep up with their pace. The smell of bacon permeated the morning air and beaconed to the soldiers as they came to "quick time" and then "halt." Nothing beats a good breakfast after a vigorous workout capped off by a little jaunt in the countryside.

The three SFODs (Special Forces Operational Detachments) had been down here in Florida for a full week now. One of the strange aspects of this was the fact that their families back at Fort Bragg had no idea where their husbands and fathers were. They had simply left for work from their homes one morning and had not yet returned. This, in the world of Special Forces, was known as "isolation." Any civilian who doubted the commitment of these men need only to have experienced this routine aspect of the Green Berets' life to gain full appreciation of these warriors.

A Special Forces Detachment A was comprised of twelve of the finest soldiers on the face of the earth. Much ado is given to other Special Operations Forces, like the Army Rangers and the Navy SEALs, but neither of the latter had experienced even half the basic training that every member of the SF troops had under their belt before they even were assigned to an A-Team. This is not to say that either of the latter troops was short of excellent. It is a simple fact that those who qualified for the designation "3" on their military occupation specialty had undergone some of the most intensive physical and mental conditioning imaginable.

A soldier who desired to become a member of this elite fighting force was first required to undergo extensive evaluation to ascertain the emotional makeup that would be required for the task. The Army wasn't looking for any "Rambos." Those guys will get themselves and their teammates killed without accomplishing the mission. Next, the candidate would be required to be a trained paratrooper or be able to successfully complete the basic airborne course before the Army was willing to send them off to Fort Bragg for training. The first requirement was to complete a training course to develop skills in training others. The purpose of Special Forces was to train indigenous forces to conduct successful operations in their own country.

Once the candidate had completed the initial phase of training they would be sent to master the first of three operational MOS skills required on the A-Team. These job descriptions were operations and intelligence NCO, light and heavy weapons of the world, communications specialist, engineering and demolition, and finally, Special Forces medic. The training in each of these areas was extensive to the point that many of the medics became physicians' assistants once they left the military. Again, each soldier was expected to become proficient in three of these areas.

After the MOS training had been completed the candidate was then sent to a lengthy language course with the goal of learning the selected language sufficient to pass himself off as a native should the requirement arises. If, and when, the successful candidate completed the foregoing requirements they were sent to branch training. This was the final weeding out process to make sure that only the best were selected to wear the coveted green beret. Half the training was accomplished in a classroom where tactics and techniques were taught. The last half was conducted in a realistic setting much like one would encounter in the real world.

The candidates were jumped into the mountainous region along the North Carolina-Tennessee border. The teams were given mission-type orders requiring them to navigate through severe terrain of the Smoky Mountains in a time that seemed nearly impossible and, once at the target site, to successfully attack a target at the destination point. After the attack was completed there was a half hour briefing done by the umpire to rate the action of each individual in the mission and accomplishment thereof. Immediately following the after-action report, the team was handed still another envelope and given half an hour to prepare for the new mission. This could continue for up to ten full days and nights without letup. The course was designed to deprive the candidates of sleep and put them into an environment akin to actual war and see if they could still be effective. The course was one of the most grueling in every aspect that one could imagine. The sad part was that after all this, at least a quarter of those reaching this stage of training would not be selected.

The training for the officers included the same as the enlisted personnel, with the exception of the MOS training. During this period of time the two officers were required to attend a lengthy training course designed to familiarize them with psychological operations and civic actions.

Once the Special Forces soldier is assigned to his A-Team, the training becomes just as intensive as was the case during the initial training. Special Forces soldiers are kept in constant training from the moment they begin until the day they decide to hang it all up. Typical of the skills they learn are scuba, ship bottom searches for mines, scout swimming, lock-in/lock-out procedures from submarines, amphibious operations, cold weather and mountain operations, skiing, H.A.L.O jumping, marksmanship, survival and escape courses, extraction techniques using flying airplanes to snatch a soldier directly from the ground and haul him up to the airplane, and, oh yes, fighting battles while they are waiting for the next training course. Is it any wonder that the Special Forces soldier gets infuriated when he hears some news commentator refer to other military personnel as "Special Forces?"

Ranger training is a very tough course and lasts a total of nine to twelve weeks. S.E.A.L. training is one of the most rigorous courses a Navy man can ever hope to become a graduate of. The S.E.A.L. training lasts six months. The basic truth is that SF training is just as rigorous and lasts a minimum of two years before he is allowed to become a member of the team.

This was the type of people who were being handed over to Todd Martin. These super-human soldiers were the ones he would be sending into the most dangerous battlefield one could encounter. There was no doubt that these men were the best there is in any military force in the world. The responsibility of those who place them in harms way must be absolutely sure that the mission is one that warrants their being placed in that position. By this time, however, Todd was as sure as any man who ever gave the order to send them in, that this was the right time, the right mission, and the right personnel.

175

When you really sat down and analyzed it, those terrorists didn't stand a chance!

Florida
Wednesday, November 30, 01:16 hours

The huge Air Force transport plane stood like some giant dark shadow as it sat on blue ramp of the base. The only light visible was from the red glow coming from the open doors at the rear ramp of the airplane. Occasionally, one could see the glow of lights coming from the forklifts and other equipment scurrying around to place pre-staged platforms into the aircraft in the order directed by the load master. These pallets would be securely fastened to the floor before being cleared for takeoff.

SFODs 237, 238 and 239 were sitting on their personal equipment waiting for the time when they, too, would be summoned to board the airplane. They had done this many times before and were treating it like all in a day's, and night's, work. Their personal equipment included their weapons, of course, and all the gear they would need to survive in the field without support for at least three days.

Before long, the load master called the men forward and they rose to their feet, complaining at the time it took the Air Force load master to get things ready for them. Of course, this was just the normal inter-service rivalry that became a must when various members of the services were gathered together. If any civilian had dared to make a derogatory comment against the airman, he would have faced the wrath of all the Army personnel in the area.

The soldiers moved into the aircraft and found seats that would be their home for the next several hours. If ever a serviceman had discovered the guy who built these seats, the word "mayhem" comes to mind. Whoever the guy was, he hated military people and had used his position to make sure that even the shortest flight would be absolute misery. The frames of the chairs were aluminum tubing with nylon fabric stretched over them in a manner to make sure the person seated in it would feel every inch of the tubes. The back of the chair consisted of woven strips of nylon approximately two inches wide and spaced so as to give only the minimal support. They were connected to a rail somewhere above the passenger's head, but were designed to sag so the point that the back received little or no support. As the Marines are famous for saying, "Nobody promised you a rose garden!"

Shortly after the last trooper boarded the plane the rear ramp rose and interconnected with the fuselage to form a tight seal. The engines were started in the appropriate order and the aircraft lurched forward when the brakes were released. The familiar pattern of blue lights indicated that the bird was taxiing to some predetermined point where the lights would turn full white to indicate and active runway. Within two minutes of the final turn the clunk of the retracted landing gear indicated that they were on their way. This fact was further confirmed when the first cribbage board mysteriously appeared in one area and the decks of cards in others.

"It was really nice of that Martin guy to fly down here just to tell us thanks and goodbye," one of the team members announced to who ever was interested.

"Yeah, he's one of us, you know," another voiced a couple of seats down.

"Nice to know that those pukes up in Washington have a few of us good guys up there protecting us from the politicians," still another stated with finality.

Rhein-Main AFB, Germany
Wednesday, November 30, 16:05 local

The black and green transport aircraft of the U.S. Air Force made its final approach and touched down after the long flight from the states. Normally, troop transports try to avoid air-to-air refueling, but in this case the rules were set aside due to the nature of the mission being flown. Of course, the passengers had no knowledge of the refueling operation due to the limited view from the area of the cargo bay.

On the ground the aircraft took a different course than was normal and soon came to a rest in an area where there were no prying eyes to observe the soldiers as they disembarked. There was a large concrete abutment between where they stopped and the rest of the airfield. Waiting for them were two Air Force mini-buses which were programmed to take them to a dining facility for a sumptuous meal.

"Man, I'm beginning to worry when the Air Force feeds us these huge T-bones before we get on our way. Kind of reminds you of the death row inmates' last meal," he emphasized for the benefit of his comrades.

Once the team members had eaten their fill (they even offered seconds), the mess sergeant came out and took a long look at them. "You guys must really be important to the Pentagon! Some high rankin' mucky-muck named Martin personally ordered all this for you bums." The troopers looked at one another and a pact was made right then and there that Todd Martin would never again have to pay for his own drinks in a bar occupied by "Sneaky Petes."

The teams were transported to an isolated barracks building where clean linen had been made up into beds for their use that night. Many times later those beds and the meal they had just consumed would be remembered with nostalgia. When you travel by military aircraft for any distance it is a tiring ordeal. Before 19:00 hours the sound of sleep was testing the construction skills of the builders of the barracks.

The next morning the troops rose to make their scheduled run and calisthenics before they returned to the dining hall. The run had to be greatly reduced due to the tight security they were under, but they made up for it by extending the repetitions of the workout. By the time they came to the breakfast tables any person observing would have thought that they had been sent to bed without supper. Many chickens and hogs had done their best to make sure that these guys were properly fed.

"Listen up, you guys," stated the senior leader of the teams, who was filling in as both team leader and B-Team commander, when they were finishing their meal. He went on to tell them that they would be leaving this "Garden of Eden" in a couple of hours for a place to be determined once they were airborne.

"I want you guys to take advantage of this time to rest, as it may be the last we'll get for some time."

How in the heck does one bank sleep? You cannot go to sleep in anticipation of being awake for a long time later. "Oh well, that proves this guy is officer material," one of the sergeants whispered to the guy sitting next to him.

God-knows-where in a desert
December 1, 01:15 hours

The replica of the airplane the troops had flown to Germany had landed in some remote place out on a desert location which was indiscernible by any markings whatsoever. This could have been the Mojave Desert, or any number of places like it, as far as the soldiers were concerned when they looked about the perimeter. Finally, though, one of the troops called to the rest of them and directed their attention to a bank of fighter aircraft parked across the runway from them. Each of these fighters sported a large Star of David, which told it all.

"Okay, you men, this is where you get to collect on all the bucks we've been sending over here for most of our lifetime. We are going to have the opportunity to take advantage of these people's delivery crew to our target area. We will be boarding one of their unmarked planes in a short while and taken to our DZ (drop zone). You are not to engage in any conversation with the crew of these birds or leave any items aboard the aircraft when you leave. These guys are really sticking their necks out for us and we're gonna make sure that they don't get them chopped off. That is all."

Half an hour later, the promised aircraft taxied up to the place where the men were waiting and the personal equipment, along with the soldiers, was on board.

"What about the rest of our equipment?" one of the team sergeants inquired.

"Don't worry, it will be delivered to us once we're in place," the B-Team Leader assured them.

"That's good enough for me," more than one of the team members said to nobody.

The troops were loaded aboard the airplane in short order while the air crews nodded in a friendly manner of respect. "At least they know how to build an aircraft seat," one of the soldiers mentioned once they had all strapped in. Since the airplane had already been checked out before coming to pick them up, it was "wheels up" in less than five minutes. Once they were in the air, the B-Team leader was joined by the co-pilot standing at the mid-point of the troop seats.

"Gentlemen, this is the drill. We are going to climb to an altitude of thirty-two thousand feet. At that time we will still be in Israeli airspace. We will then throttle back on the engines to keep them as noiseless as possible and will begin a long glide that will take us to twenty-three thousand feet. At that time you will don your oxygen masks and be prepared to have us open the airplane up to the atmosphere. You have all been issued your cold weather gear and, I see, you all have the suits on. You're gonna need them, I can assure you, when we open the doors. When I finish here, I want each of you to put your parachutes on and all the equipment you will be taking with you.

"When we reach the release point you will all be exiting the aircraft at twenty-three thousand feet. This will give you a full ninety seconds to freefall in the directions of each of your rendezvous points. You will have plenty of oxygen in your bottles to safely get you to the opening altitude, so don't worry about that.

"After you get your parachutes open I want you to release your cargo packs so that they will hit the ground fifteen feet ahead of you. I don't need to tell you how much this will slow your decent. If you try to ride these cargo packs all the way to the ground we're going to sustain casualties and we certainly don't want that!

"As you are in your freefall you will be noting the homing devices that we have placed on the ground this evening. Each of the teams has a different frequency so there will be no confusion. You all have trained for this moment and I'm sure that it will go off like clockwork. If you get bored in the meantime, think of the folks on the ground who would like to have your nuts in a vice. Any questions?"

As promised, the plane continued to climb at a sharp rate of assent and only when they were cruising at what must have been the announced altitude did the sound of the engines begin to abate. The loss of engine roar made it possible for the team members to converse in almost normal tones as the glide path continued.

"Six minutes!" the B-Team commander announced. Once he was sure that everyone had donned their oxygen masks, he signaled the crew chief and within five seconds the clam-shell doors at the rear of the airplane began to open. No matter how many times you went through this process of a HALO jump you never got used to the cold blast of air at this altitude. Without protective clothing you would freeze to death in a short period of time. Of course, you wouldn't even know about it because you would have suffocated well before that time due to lack of oxygen.

"I want each of you to set their altimeter at 29.92. You'll be landing on terrain at approximately seven hundred feet above sea level, so your opening altitude will be six thousand feet. I want you to have plenty of maneuver room to get to the right drop zone, so don't any of you try to be a hero. Stand Up!" Since this was to be a HALO jump there was no need to go through the standard jump orders, which include "hook up" and "check static lines." Of course, there was still a need to order, "check equipment," which came a few seconds later.

"Sound off for equipment check!" the jumpmaster hollered as he assumed the correct sign for each of the jump commands. The trooper standing closest to the pilot's cabin on each side of the aircraft stepped forward toward the rear of the aircraft and into a crouched position and slapped the man closer to the rear on the behind and announced, "Eighteen, OK!" The count continued in descending order toward the rear of the aircraft until the men closest to the jumpmaster announced, "One, OK!"

At this point the jumpers were ready to make their exit from the aircraft and assume the correct posture to maintain some semblance of controlled free fall. This was certainly no easy task, since all of them were encumbered with their slung rifles, their normal basic load, and an eighty-five pound rucksack strapped to their thighs. You won't see that at any skydiving exhibition.

"One minute!" the jumpmaster announced just as the red light next to each door came on. Normally the lights would have come on when the six minute warning had been announced, but due to the clandestine nature of the mission, the Special Forces leader had requested that the pilot wait until the later time.

Right on schedule, the red light went out and was replaced by the green one right next to it. "Go!" the jumpmaster yelled to his team members. They didn't hear the silent comment, "may God be with us," uttered by the team leader as he watched until the last man had leapt from the ramp into the night. Without any hesitation, he followed.

The night was completely dark. This night had been specifically selected to begin the operation when the lunar phase was at new moon. The stars were so bright that it seemed that you could reach out and select a couple for your personal consumption. The beep of the directional beacon had already begun to alert the jumpers that they were in operation and would begin to provide the necessary direction for them to direct their flight. Surprisingly enough, it was still possible to make the necessary adjustments of the body to begin steering toward these beacons. The one danger in a night jump like this was the chance that you would collide with one of your fellow jumpers. That would probably result in an instant fatality.

The spinning altimeters still allowed for the team members to make unhurried decisions and corrections on the decent to the Lebanese landscape below. Even with the lack of any moonlight there is always enough lumination to see pretty well when you are approaching from overhead. At the proper time and height, each of the skydivers assumed the proper position and executed the D-ring pull that caused their airspeed to diminish from well over one hundred miles per hour to a more moderate eighteen miles per hour toward the ground. Next came the opening of the snap fasteners that allowed the rucksack to fall freely until it reached the end of the bungee chord to hang freely below them. It was amazing how much the downward airspeed would be affected once the rucksack contacted the ground. Not that it would be any walk in the park due to all the other equipment being carried, but with a proper parachute landing fall each of them would be ready to stash their chutes and head toward the assembly area. Fortunately, no one was there to meet them.

Once safely on the ground the first order of business after disengaging themselves of the parachutes was to open the rucksack and take out the night vision goggles. After putting them on you could see quite clearly. Next was the disposal of all the air items necessary for the jump. The first thing to go was the thermal suit that had kept them alive in the cold of the upper altitudes. Now that they were on the ground the thermal suits were extremely uncomfortable and the sweat was pouring off each one of them in short order. Next were the oxygen canisters. With the reserve chutes and gauges added in there was quite a pile of items to be hidden. The entrenching tools were put to use right away and the entire pile of air items was soon buried.

All the members arrived at their rendezvous points at about the same time. Each team wondered if there had been any jump casualties in the other teams, but none needed to worry as every member of each team was unscathed by the insertion.

There was no time to hang around and admire their parachute skills as there was still some distance to travel before daylight and they wanted to be completely hidden and camouflaged before that time. Shortly after arrival at the rendezvous point, the members of the party dispersed to their assigned positions in the brush and formed a perimeter to await the coming day.

— 17 —

"They're in!" Todd told the members of his team after hanging up the telephone. The call had come in from MacDill along with a message from the troops on the ground to thank "the old fart member of their organization for the TLC." Todd laughed to himself and was glad that he had the opportunity to send the guys off with a good meal. They sure as heck deserved it.

The caller told Todd that he would keep him informed as things developed and reminded him that the overhead satellite coverage needed to be thorough and constant. Todd had assured the colonel that he was on top of it and there would be no glitches from his end. He mentally tried to place himself in the picture of the Special Forces on the ground and knew instinctively that they would be doing their best to blend into the local population. The team members had been directed to stop shaving the first day of their arrival in isolation, so by now most of them could pass themselves off as the younger brothers of Yasser Arafat.

The team members were carrying AK-47s instead of their TO&E weapons and had changed into local costumes from the moment they had been inserted. They even went so far as to learn the standard Islamic prayers in the event they found themselves in a situation where praying was required. The team had been conversing in Arabic simultaneously with the abandonment of their shaving gear. It was quite humorous to hear the "Jody cadence songs" being chanted in Arabic during the morning runs. These guys really took their jobs seriously as was demanded by the conditions they would encounter and meant the difference between a sleeping bag and a body bag.

During the daylight hours the men would break up into groups of two or three and would go to various places to conduct reconnaissance. The best place was in the open markets where people seem to congregate to exchange gossip as well as their money. The women were more talkative so all you had to do was find a group of them and sit down nearby and pretend to be napping. A lot of the information was "girl talk," but there were those moments that almost made you bolt upright and stare at the one talking.

Constant map study and terrain photos had provided the team members a good background and they were able to move about on familiar paths and roadways as well as the local natives. Of course, you had to be on the ground in order to pick up all the nuances not picked up by the satellite coverage.

Children were the biggest danger that they would encounter. Anywhere in the world the children are prone to venture to places where the adults ignore. The adventurous spirit of these kids was such that they could stumble into the base camp without warning. For that reason, the base camps were mobile and never set up in a manner to indicate that any permanent occupation was evident.

While children posed the biggest threat, they also provided a wealth of information if you handled it in the right manner. A friendly local Arab who gave a little attention to these younger citizens could reap a bounty of information regarding the terrorist activities. The children thought most of the terrorists were quite humorous and in their games they would imitate the swagger and boisterous talk they had observed from them. Given the least encouragement, they would put on a show for the interested adult along with vital information regarding whereabouts and identities. There was, however, the need to be patient when seeking information from this source. You did not want to draw attention to yourself by being too inquisitive.

During the initial phase of the operation no attempts to inflict damage upon the terrorists was even attempted. This was a time to get established as a member of the local community and glean bits of information that would serve you better once you entered into the next phases. When you did hit the enemy you wanted it to be on a large scale basis and not by isolated acts of disruption.

The team had given themselves a full two weeks to complete the first phase of the operation. The second phase would be to start cultivating acquaintances from among the locals and decide if any of them would be suitable for approach. Before any such approach could occur the target would be closely monitored for sufficient time to build a dossier of information on that person. Did he have a family? Did he have children? Was he a devout Muslim? Who did he affiliate with? Did he have friends that were in the terrorist organization? What comments had he uttered to indicate his feelings toward the occupying forces? What about his morals? Was there anything in his background or current activities that could be used for leverage? The list went on and on and must be developed before the actual approach was made.

During the early stages of Phase II it would be necessary to limit the contacts to only a few locals until a foothold was made that would give greater access to the inhabitants. The beauty of this was the fact that like-minded people tend to form close alliances. The friends of the approached person might provide even better resources than the targeted contact. The Special Forces soldiers had been given ample training in this area and had nurtured their skills to a science. It had to be so. The entire operation could be blown if the wrong person was the target of an attempted recruitment. Like Phase I, you just couldn't rush the process.

By the time Christmas had rolled around the operation was in full swing. A total of seventeen indigenous members had now formed the core of what would become the militia. These were a group of individuals who had a strong hatred of the terrorists. When the terrorists had come into the area they treated the locals with disdain and had committed many acts that would bring shame upon them. If you were a local resident with an attractive wife or daughter they were subject to humiliation and even rape if the circumstances were right. Several of the new militia members fell into the category of dishonored husband, father, or brother of one of these young ladies and each of them was anxious to extract Arabian revenge.

The training of the new recruits emphasized the need for caution when engaging in conversations with their families or friends. They were not to approach any one of these sources for the purposes of recruitment. That task was to be the responsibility of the American soldiers alone. Of course, the militia member might be allowed to come along during the actual approach to gain acceptance and encouragement. By the time New Year's Day had arrived the ranks of the militia had swollen to thirty-nine members. It was time to get their feet wet.

Bekka Valley
Saturday, January 2, 19:00 hours

The on-site surveillance teams had returned to the staging area just about ten minutes ago. Each had given their report to the Special Forces team leader with clarity and accuracy. They had spent the entire day in concealed positions to record activities on the target and it was now time to begin the assault.

The target was a motor pool that supplied the majority of the terrorist's ability to move about the countryside. It was also the only source they had to make the runs to the supply points to pick up the materials necessary for their operations. The distribution of food was a major part of the daily trips made to and from the compound.

Like any other motor pool, there were large tanks containing petroleum and explosive ordinance collected in strategic positions throughout the compound. It would be like shooting fish in a barrel. Much of the firepower that would be used in the attack had been pilfered from the stocks located in the motor pool by militia members passing themselves off as laborers working on the site. Little observation was directed to them by the guards since they were "just lowly workers" expected to take care of the menial tasks around the yard. Due to this inattention, the militia members had been able to carry out several RPGs (Rocket Propelled Grenades) and anti-tank weapons. The SF members had provided fuses and other necessary items constructed from improvised materials available in the area.

At exactly 20:00 hours the first RPG was fired into the petroleum storage area. The initial blast from the ensuing explosion was enough to rattle the windows for a mile around. The SF team members had instinctively closed their eyes when the RPG was fired to avoid the sudden flash of light that would come through the night vision goggles and blind them for the rest of the evening. The force of the explosion was such that even outside the camp you could feel the heat and impact of the blast wave as it leveled several sheds in the compound and caused secondary explosions due to their contents.

A part of every successful raid like this was the temporary stun, shock and awe of the enemy forces charged with protection of the facility. This situation usually lasts for up to fifteen seconds before the guards are able to react and do anything effective to repulse the attack. On the other hand, the militia had drilled repeatedly on the actions each was to perform from the very start. A team of three was to go to the ordinance depot and place the charges, set the timer, and make a hasty retreat to their appointed place in the compound. Additional teams consisting of two men each would take their places at strategic points to eliminate the advance of reactionary reinforcements from reaching their objectives. Another set of teams were assigned the responsibility of tossing satchel charges into the buildings where staff or troops were sleeping or eating. Every aspect of the attack was planned and practiced until any member of the team could do their respective jobs blindfolded.

In less than forty seconds the entire motor pool had been completely eliminated. All the vehicles were burning and wrecked with the exception of the three "deuce and one halfs" chosen to make the departure of the attacking force rapid and unscathed. Enemy soldiers were running back in forth in hysteria as many of them had fire coming from their clothing. The last two guards at the gate were killed as the first truck plowed through the barbed wire structure.

The attack was not without casualties among the friendly forces. One of the militia men had sprained his ankle when he jumped from the truck he had just placed an explosive charge on. Other than that, there was not so much as a band aid required among the friendly forces. The elated troops in the backs of the three trucks were yelling and firing off their weapons into the night sky and it took some effort to have them silence themselves into a disciplined force once more.

It would have been nice to have kept the trucks for future operations, however, the risk of doing so would have overshadowed the benefit of keeping them. Once the fighting force had traveled to a pre-arranged point the troops offloaded and when they were a short distance away the Special Forces demolition sergeant tossed his three remaining satchel charges into the cabs of the vehicles and ran to catch up with the dispersing force. Within half an hour each member of the militia was back in their respective homes and in bed. The American forces were at their dispersion locations as if nothing had happened

The first blood had been drawn. From now on the terrorists would be constantly ready to repulse any attack and their anger had been kindled. This would prove to be their downfall. The members of the terrorist organization became more suspicious of the people they were living amongst. They began to mistreat the inhabitants of the local community in the knowledge that some of these people had been involved in their terrible loss. It was a source of great humor to the Americans to see the reaction of these thugs once they became the victims of a terrorist attack. It was beautiful!

Enemy losses were not being reported by the terrorists, but their lack of transportation had forced them to rely on local vehicles to remove the dead from the compound. Surveillance had revealed that not less than sixty members of the enemy had gone to meet with their seventy virgins. If you were to ask any member of the deceased opposing forces you would be informed that furthest thing from the newly departed souls was sexual activity.

During the next few days the Special Forces members had maintained a low profile and were content to allow the angry terrorists a chance to vent their feelings upon the population. This would only swell the ranks of those in opposition to them and make them feel less free to roam the countryside without exercising extreme caution. People in the market places were holding hushed conversations that indicated that maybe these tough terrorists weren't so tough after all. The resentments kept under wraps for so long were beginning to emerge in little comments made in passing among the merchants and their customers.

It was now time to begin Phase III of the operation. That did not mean that Phases I and II were abandoned. They would continue as long as the operation continued and the final outcome had been affected. It just meant that the enemy was going to feel the brunt of numerous crippling attacks upon their positions and put them on the defensive. All the training back at Fort Bragg was being put to good use and it was comforting to know that the concepts, tactics and techniques were right on the money when it came to putting them into practice. The spirits of the Americans were beginning to show through and there was now the occasional joke passed back and forth between the members.

One week later it was time to make another crippling blow to the enemy forces. The team members met and conducted a systematic review of all the targets that might be appropriate for this raid. It was determined that the impact upon the first major offensive was so successful that it would be prudent to make a similar attack that would show the populace that the friendly forces were here and capable of sustained combat against the enemy. The attack upon the motor pool had been effective in putting the terrorists on notice that they were now facing a situation that demanded their full attention. They would have to direct some attention toward their own survival instead of concentrating upon exterior priorities.

The target selected was a headquarters element some twenty kilometers from the initial raid. This objective would be instrumental in disrupting the entire chain of command and would deprive the enemy of its leadership. This factor alone would be a major blow to them since they lacked the ability to develop leaders within their own ranks. Those in leadership positions were reluctant to share any of their skills with their subordinates and, therefore, always left a void in their structure when one of these leaders was captured or killed.

The Americans selected three teams of surveillance operatives to move to the target area three days prior to the attack. Each of the teams was comprised of two indigenous guerrillas and one American Special Forces soldier. This was just enough personnel to maintain a constant vigil while rotating sleep periods were required. It also provided the necessary skills to conduct a proper surveillance and make a useful evaluation of the target.

Schedules of comings and goings of the camp's personnel were noted and times of posting or changing of the guard were recorded. Any special activities were closely observed and habits of the general habitants were well documented. It is surprising how much can be learned about any target by just making observations from a distance of two to three hundred meters away.

During the surveillance mode, the Americans in the teams made several incursions into the perimeter of the camp to make on-site inspections of the key areas of the camp. Even thought there had been the major attack on the motor pool less than ten days ago, the enemy didn't seem to be especially watchful since that attack had occurred some distance away from them. By the time the surveillance teams had returned to the friendly camp a definite battle plan had been developed and needed only be fine-tuned to attain operational readiness.

Once the battle plan has been developed and the surveillance has been withdrawn it is imperative to implement that operation. Each of the teams had left one member of the surveillance team in place on the target site to ensure that nothing would change to the detriment of the plan. The attack force moved into the area from several approach lanes to disperse their advance and avoid detection. When the force met again it was some five hundred meters from the target and the final briefing was accomplished. The remaining surveillance team members returned to join their cohorts as members of the raiding party.

It was decided that the best plan would be to place two ambush sites on the far sides of the camp to prevent elements of the enemy from escape. These two ambushes were established along the secondary roads on the northeast and southeastern side of the camp. The main thrust would come from a two-pronged advance from the northwest and southwest gates. The placement of the ambushes would serve as the anvil of the blocking force and allow the two hammer blows to be the main body of the attack. Each of the main body forces consisted of twenty-five men and each ambush site contained twelve men each.

The ambushes were set up in the "L" formation. A line of firing was placed on one side of the road while a machine gun was placed on the opposite side and above the firing line. The troops on the firing line would inflict a heavy volume of fire on the enemy within the "kill zone" and any who decided to run from the battle zone would move directly into the line of fire parallel to the roadway. There could be no escape once the enemy entered the trap.

At precisely 21:00 hours the attack began. The raiding forces of the main body charged into the unsuspecting camp with fury that can only be imagined in one's worst nightmare. The attack was so violent and the firing so heavy that the enemy did not have the opportunity to react before fully three quarters of them were killed. In the first twenty seconds of the battle the raid had inflicted such heavy losses upon the enemy that the remaining were in a panic rather than a serious fighting force.

That is not to say that there was no resistance. Several of the terrorists fought with bravado and did a credit to themselves and their cause, but the overpowering attack was such as to eliminate these pockets before a full minute had elapsed. Some of the enemy had the presence of mind to attempt an escape. Nine of them managed to reach the ambush site on the northeast corner and seven more were eliminated by the second ambush site on the southeast.

Once the battle subsided, the guerrillas made a rapid sweep of the camp and picked up all the weapons and ammunition they could carry and placed the rest in a pile where they blew them up. A lot of good materials were left behind in the necessity to leave rapidly before any reinforcements might arrive. In most cases, these supplies were burned or blew up so as to make them unavailable for future use. In less than five minutes the second major target had been completely destroyed.

The success gained in this endeavor served to enhance the spirits of the friendly forces to the point that they were now gaining tremendous confidence in their ability to win the war against the terrorists. Their jubilation en route to the dispersion site was difficult to repress, but they now understood the reasoning behind a silent withdrawal.

During the next two weeks the militia forces would participate in three more attacks, with similar results. In fact, it was only on the second of these raids that the militia had sustained their first casualties. Three members of their forces had been killed outright when a mine blew up and another soldier was severely wounded by gunfire. Fortunately, the Special Forces medic had treated the wound and the injured soldier was recuperating nicely.

Two days after the successful raid on the base camp of the enemy, the team intelligence sergeant of SFOD-A237 was conducting a recruiting mission into the neighboring village. He had successfully entered the village and was nearing the home of the recruitment asset when a large contingent of the terrorists came into the same village undetected by the American. Before he knew of the approaching danger, the enemy soldiers were everywhere.

The intelligence sergeant had managed to escape to a large patch of briars near the backyard of one of the village homes and holed up inside deep enough to conceal his presence. Unfortunately, the enemy troops decided to take some R & R in the village and were there for three more days. The American soldier was forced to remain in his hiding place for the duration of their stay.

It was on the second night that two of the terrorists had come to the yard of the home where the American was crouched in hiding. One of the two enemy soldiers walked directly toward the intel sergeant and it appeared as though he had spied him. The hour was late and when the enemy came to the edge of the briar patch, he doffed his backpack and threw it on the ground directly in front of the American, not more than two feet from where the Special Forces sergeant was lying. The terrorist then turned around and laid down on the ground and placed his head upon the backpack for a pillow and within five minutes was sound asleep.

The American was in a stark dilemma. He could have easily taken out his Randall knife and affected a silent kill on the unsuspecting terrorist, but if he were to do so, the other soldier would find his comrade the following morning and the sergeant would immediately be detected and taken prisoner or shot. There was no choice, the American would have to remain motionless throughout the entire night while the terrorists slept not two feet from his position.

The sergeant did not dare to sneeze, cough, or otherwise make a sound. It seemed that the forces of nature had chosen to inflict punishment upon the lone American. There is no torture quite like that of many mosquitoes on the attack for hours upon end while their victim is unable to even swat them away. Just the sound of their approach in the ears of the intended victim is enough to drive a person nearly insane. All night long, the pesky mosquitoes continued their attack until by morning the American was a sorry sight to behold. Every place where bare skin was evident there were large welts from the incessant biting throughout the night. When a person remains in one position for nearly ten hours the muscles of the entire body begin to cramp and, in this case, there was no way to gain relief. The hatred for the terrorists in that individual soldier amplified itself manifold during the next week.

As the sun came up the following morning, the unsuspecting enemy soldier rose from his place of sleep and stretched and yawned in the relaxation and the recuperation that a good night's sleep can provide. Slowly he rose and picked up his backpack, passed an enormous amount of gas, and moved out from the sleeping area.

Fortunately, the commander of this group decided that it was time to leave the village and move on. The American waited for an hour after their departure and then began to track them on foot. He wanted to find their base location and place them high on the list of targets for future attacks. Once he had ascertained their camp he skirted it and made his return to his own base where he found his comrades in great delight to welcome him back. They had just about given up hope of ever seeing him again and the fact that they still had not taken any casualties was a point of great appreciation.

The recent successes in several attacks upon the terrorist organization had been such that it was now possible to conduct resupply in a more overt manner. The militia had been used to man the drop zones on nights when cargo parachutes filled the sky with more sophisticated weaponry and equipment. These night operations were carried out in several locations and the frequency was more often. The added support would assist the opposition forces with greater ability to inflict greater casualties upon the terrorists. Added to this was the fact that the militia now numbered at over a hundred active members and twice that number of support units in the community.

On one occasion when the team medic, who had been accompanied by the light weapons sergeant, was working in a nearby village, they spied one of the terrorists whose identity had been accompanied by a photograph both men had become familiar with. It turned out that this guy was on a food run for the cell back in his own village. The sergeants kept the enemy soldier in sight as the medic continued to administer medical aid to his patient. Only when the terrorist had completed his purchases of food did the American sergeants begin to follow the enemy by using all the techniques for tracking they had learned in the past. The terrorist had no idea he was being followed and proceeded to load up his Toyota pickup with all the food items he had secured. He then went around the corner to relieve himself and the American medic ran quickly to the side of the vehicle and managed to empty three of the packets he was carrying in his medical kit directly into the open container of rice.

When the enemy soldier returned to leave the Americans had already climbed back on the motor scooter provided them by one of the militia members and followed the truck at a safe distance until it reached its final destination. Several enemy soldiers came out to meet the soldier with the food and quickly hauled the entire cargo into a cellar hidden behind a mosque. It turned out that the cellar was the underground bunker where the entire cell of terrorists were living. There was a single entry point and it had a large metal door protecting the bunker. This bunker lacked all conveniences, such as lavatory or basic necessities.

Rather than conduct a raid upon the structure where there was no doubt that friendly casualties would occur, the weapons sergeant calmly walked over to the large door, flipped the heavy latch on the outside, and placed a padlock on it. The two of them then returned to their base camp and reported the entire incident to the team leader.

"What was in that powder you put into their food?" his leader asked.

"Well, sir, it's the strongest laxative you ever heard of, but it has a bad side effect. If you take too much of it, it will give you the worst headache you have ever had for three days," the medic replied.

The Americans waited a full thirty-six hours before returning to the bunker. The weapons sergeant asked, "How will we know which ones are the enemy?"

"Just look for the guy carrying a roll of toilet paper and a bottle of aspirin!" the medic said with a wink. "By the way, you might want to hold your nose when we open that door. It's not gonna be a pretty sight!"

Not all the news was as rosy. The terrorists had begun randomly executing individuals who might have any reason to be opposed to them. The sound of gunfire could be heard on a frequent basis as the marauding thugs moved about the area trying to instill fear in the locals once more. They were successful up to a point, but the more often reaction was to instill hatred and a willingness to do whatever possible to drive them into hell where they belonged. These idiots had failed to learn the most basic factors when living in a guerrilla movement. You must have the hearts and minds of the indigenous if you even hope to be successful. Brute force only works in a totalitarian government. If you do not control every aspect of the lives of the governed then you must work at keeping the governed happy.

It was time to step up the attacks upon the terrorist elements. Failure to do so would be an indication that they were still in control. From now on there would be almost daily or nightly attacks upon the enemy. These attacks were designed to immobilize them and instill fear. The results were doing just that. Terrorist elements were beginning to travel in not less than five or six people on even the most simple of trips. Their progress was always slow and methodical to avoid ambushes that were becoming more and more frequent.

Armed with the order of battle, the Americans had good and reliable intelligence as to where each element was based and the number of individuals in each facility. It was only a matter of making the selection as to which one would be raided and when. The enemy was being deprived of sleep since most of the attacks came at night. Many times the attacking force was made up solely of the Americans since they were the ones in possession of the night vision goggles and the ability to see clearly during the hours of darkness.

When the friendly forces did make these attacks very often the terrorists would kill each other due to their lack of discipline and tactical ability. Their morale was suffering and they had no way to obtain any assistance from the outside. The intelligence sergeant became aware that the enemy leaders were beginning to ration ammunition from dwindling supplies originating from fewer and fewer caches of ordinance.

Elements of the population were beginning to excise a toll upon the enemy as well. Spurred by the recent successes of the militia, the general population were starting to remember all the atrocities committed against them in the past and were making life unbearable by little acts of sabotage that, while lacking much tactical gain, were strategically limiting the effectiveness of the occupying forces.

The Syrian and Israeli governments had been doing their parts at keeping the terrorists off balance. With the shutdown of Syrian support, the enemy was having to dig into their reserves to maintain any semblance of an effective fighting force. The caches of ordinance and materials were being depleted at an alarming rate, with no replenishment on the horizon. It was not a good time to be a terrorist in the Bekka Valley.

The puppet government of Lebanon was having its own challenges. One could not help but feel sorry for the plight of the Lebanese. They had been bombed, beaten and occupied by various factions and external forces for the past three decades. Then there were the political parties who were poles apart in their desires and methods of governing. This beautiful land had been pillaged by whoever the current occupying force was and then left abandoned for the next despot who wanted to humiliate them further. The Bekka Valley had been taken over completely by the most despicable lot of human refuse on the planet. Most of the Lebanese had lost all hope and had resorted to maintenance of their families, who were forced to live in deplorable conditions. The Americans had come to their rescue back in the mid-fifties, but had left too. There had been some hope when the American fleet had stationed itself off the coast to provide fire support for their protection, but then there was that terrible event which left 255 American Marines dead. That had been last straw and the Americans had simply walked away.

When the Syrians had begun to deny access to their materials the terrorists began conducting forays into the western parts of Lebanon to collect the meager supplies needed by the Lebanese people to survive. This resulted in a move by the Israeli Armed Forces to block the path of these terrorist elements. While it was a benefit to the Lebanese people to keep the marauding forces from the Bekka Valley out of their sanctuary, it never was a welcomed sight to see Israeli troops in the heart of Lebanon.

Al-Qaeda tried to use the incursion of Israel as a uniting effort in the Arab world with little success. It seems that all the main backers of the PLO and al-Qaeda were busying themselves with the task of reform that would not be beneficial to either of these organizations. The desertion factor was having a deleterious effect upon the leadership of the terrorist organization as well. Heretofore, the organization had prided itself on the self-sacrificing dedication of its membership. Now, when things were not going too well, it appears that the commitments were not quite as deep as once thought. Several of the deserters had been caught while trying to flee the area and were publicly hung from the street lights of the village as a warning to others who might be contemplating the idea of running. Some of the enemy had even come over to the militia side, but they were relegated to only the periphery of the organization to preclude any "moles" access to the secret organization.

Leaders were emerging from the ranks of the militia and, more and more, control was being passed to them by the Americans. Phase IV was going to occur automatically once the other phases had proven successful. There would come that day when the American forces would pack up and leave the people to begin operating as a separate government, fully capable of administering the course their nation would take. That was not going to happen overnight, but it was refreshing to see the embryonic stages of this happening right before their eyes.

Graffiti was beginning to be commonplace in the public areas of the villages. The terrorists were depicted in the most humiliating terms while patriotic statements extolling the love of their beloved Lebanon were abundant as well. Many of the enemy forces were long past the point of wanting to flee the Valley, but to where? Nobody wanted them anymore. They had two choices: either they could surrender to the militia forces and hope for humane treatment, or they could continue their battle until the day they were either captured or killed. Neither alternative was appreciably better than the other since the terrorists had committed so many atrocities during their reign that there was little likelihood that they would not be executed in a very painful manner regardless of the choice. The morale of the organization was broken, although they each made quite a show in front of their comrades of their willingness to suffer any consequences if it pleased Allah. By now, any reasonable individual would have figured out that "Allah" was definitely not on their side.

The latest development confronting the Americans was the treatment of captured prisoners. It was apparent from the conduct of the militia that "prisoner" was a term that was not in their vocabulary. Persons captured from the enemy forces were tortured until they revealed their innermost secrets and then summarily shot. This was something that America was not ready to condone. The leaders of the revolution were called in and informed in no uncertain terms that the American support would be immediately withdrawn if the condition was not drastically curtailed right now. Certainly, the Special Forces soldiers could empathize with the locals after years of repression, but if a new government emerged that was equally oppressive as the one it was replacing, then all had been for naught. The message was delivered loud and clear.

Lebanon
Tuesday, March 2, 3:19 p.m.

It had been more than a week now since the last known bullet had been fired in the entire Bekka Valley. The Israeli troops, as promised, were finalizing their withdrawal from the nation of Lebanon amid much cheering, both within the departing vehicles and from the citizens who were equally cheering as the diesel fumes hung in the air. It could not be determined if the cheers coming from the sidewalks were for the fact that the IDG soldiers were leaving, or for the role they had played in defeating the hated terrorists who had used the soils of Lebanon for their dirty work. In truth, it was probably a combination of the two emotions along with the strong sense that the days of turmoil were coming to a close in their beautiful homeland.

That same afternoon a ragtag formation of seventy-seven disheveled men came up to where the Special Forces base camp was located with their hands raised high in submission. They were weak from the hunger that plagued their worn-out bodies and the terrible toll the war had taken upon them. These were the remaining holdouts and backbone of the terrorist cadre. One could almost feel sorry for them as many of them had tears running down their faces. Was this the enemy who had caused so much grief throughout the world during the past decades? Could it be true that this frail group of totally beaten men had, up until recently, shaken their fists and caused so much heartache? One could only stand in awe when this defeated enemy held forth their hands pleading for food and the basic comfort items they had denied so many.

Even the militia forces seemed to be taken in by the momentous occasion, and the silence that came over the camp was a cause for near reverence. On cue, the entire group sat down in the roadway and bowed their heads low in complete surrender. The people on all sides had every right to stone them to death on the spot, but that was not what occurred. At first, one or two of the militia stepped forward and offered their canteens of water, then others came forward with cigarettes and food. The defeated enemy was unsure just how they should react to these soldiers who so recently had torn away their entire world. The sign of true leadership is the mercy that is shown to those who are downtrodden. As the Americans stood by and watched the whole affair, they realized for the first time that everything they had endured over the past four months had indeed been worth every minute. A nation was healing in front of their very eyes and there was no doubt that this healing would be permanent. As the prisoners were taken to the holding compound each one was accompanied by one of the militia members, who had their arms about the shoulders of the overcome enemy. Never had any member of the special forces teams seen anything like it. Further, they would never see such a moving experience again no matter how long they lived.

— 18 —

Tel Aviv
Tuesday, February 14, 9:27 a.m.

The city bus had just stopped at the intersection of the busy street and was waiting for the light to change from red to green before making the left turn to the far side of the avenue to pick up the passengers ready to board the city transit system. The usual pushing and shoving occurred as the doors opened and people trying to unload were meeting those attempting to gain entry into the vehicle.

Once the right number had been deposited on the waiting curb and those passengers desiring to leave were situated in their respective seats or holding onto the hanging straps suspended from the ceiling of the bus, the driver removed his foot from the brake and began to push down on the pedal that would signal the diesel engine to accelerate its way into the traffic.

It was at that very moment that a young lady dressed in the uniform of the Israeli Army stood up and uttered a prayer to the wrong God, based upon the garb she was wearing. She then reached into her blouse and pulled on a small ring attached to a device that had not been seen. A chain reaction that took less then one hundredth of a second caused the young woman to disintegrate in a ball of flaming fury that would rapidly spread throughout the passenger section of the bus. In that same period of time the entire bus had become just another in the long list of destroyed Israeli targets attacked in the same manner over the many years since the birth of the nation. Nearly every person on board had been killed outright or were crying out in their final agony. Among those whose lives had been instantly snuffed out were babies, children, young and old, men and women.

The moans and screams of the dying and injured were everywhere as parts of human bodies were strewn around what had once been the bus they were riding on. People outside the vehicle were in a panic as they were unsure of which way they should be running. The smoldering fires in the wreckage were filling the air with an acrid smoke that failed to overcome the aroma of burning flesh. Once again, the people of Israel had been the victims of an act of violence that simply added to the numerous times this same scene had been played out over the years.

Unfortunately, the reaction teams had become so practiced that they had evolved into a science the procedures required in such an event. Within a matter of very few minutes the fire and rescue teams were present on the site and attempting to do the impossible: save the lives of their fellow countrymen when there was little that could stem the dying and pain. The senselessness of the whole incident caused the professionals to go about their tasks in rote and shock.

Within a matter of an hour the local newspaper had a small package delivered to their front door. In it was a familiar repetition of the previous audio tapes that would inform them that the entire incident had been the work of the Palestinian Liberation Organization. Oh, they didn't call themselves that on the tape and had used the name of Hezbollah, but even the most naïve knew that this was just another extension of the PLO.

There comes a time in any situation where the patience of a group of people can no longer hold back the reason and rage. The very name of the PLO provides the explanation as to why there can never be any peace with that organization. How can you deal with people whose very name indicates that their aim is to drive you from your country? They are Palestinians who aim to liberate the land of Israel. Negotiation with such an organization can never be possible. The only solution is to eliminate them.

If the government of Israel continued to allow these senseless acts to continue there would come a time when there were no more buses or people to be blown up. Drastic times demand drastic actions. The only question remaining was how far the people of Israel would have to go to defeat such an enemy once and for all. Should they abandon the heretofore restraint and attempt to seek out the leaders of the cowardly terrorists, or should they accept that the entire race of people were the enemy and should be set upon to the point of extermination?

Nearly four thousand years before the same question was presented to the nation of Israel. Down in the Gaza Strip were a group of people known as the Philistines. They had been in the land for a short time when the nation of Israel crossed the Jordan River and began to take control of the land. This, of course, was not the first time they had been in Canaan. A couple of centuries earlier this same group of people, now known as Israel, had come from the area of Hebron and were known as Hebrews in honor of their place of origin. They were simply returning to their own land to reclaim it.

The God that Israel worshipped had ordered them to kill all the Philistines, but the Philistine women were desirable and caused the Israelite men to spare these people. God had warned the nation of Israel that if they did not eliminate the Philistines that they would become a thorn in their sides for all time.

The Torah is filled with stories of battle and suppression that occurred as a result of the failure to obey their God. The story of Samson and Delilah, Gideon, and Goliath are but a few examples of the continuous strife that has occurred from these Philistines over time. While their name has evolved to the Palestinians known today, the same people, living in the same area, continue to be the constant thorn in the side of Israel. While much of the people of Israel were dispersed among the other nations of the world, these same Palestinians began to move into the legally owned property of the former. This occupation lasted for many centuries until the invaders became convinced that the land now belonged to them. Oh, sure, there were still a smattering of the Israelite people living on the land, but they were reduced in numbers to the point that they could not repel the occupying nation.

That all changed in 1948. The Zionist movement to return to their lands was a direct result of a world war that nearly wiped out the ancient Hebrew race. The only way for the Israeli people to survive was to return to their rightfully owned land and regain the national identity necessary to continue. The Palestinian people were ejected from their "temporary" occupation of the land deeded to Israel.

Since that time the "Philistines" have been in a relentless pursuit to inflict the genocide started by the Third Reich and Hitler. Lacking the ability to effect this atrocity in normal battle, they have resorted constant hit and run attacks designed to destroy the will of the people to continue the battle.

No truce has ever resulted in a peaceful permanent solution to hostilities. It simply gives pause to the factions while they continue to hold the same desires to kill each other. The only successful means to end war is when there is a decisive victor. One of the parties completely dominates the other and both have no doubt that the conflict has been decisively ended. The nation of Israel, having been the recipient of such abuses unheard of in any other nationality, were always reluctant to retaliate in a manner that would solve the problem once and for all. How could they justify the complete elimination of an entire nation when their own history cried out for mercy? This quandary had been facing them since the first day of the rebirth of their nation and could no longer be put off.

The Knesset met once more, but this time there was no doubt that this body would not emerge until a definite plan of action was developed to completely solve the ongoing dilemma. The political parties making up the whole of that body was comprised of the complete array of idealism from those willing to inflict complete genocide to open pacifism. Due to the recent in a series of attacks upon the population, the balance was tilted toward those who were insisting upon direct and open warfare against the Palestinians.

After much debate it was determined that the first course of action would be to take the PLO leader into custody and place him in a confined cell along with his cronies. The argument had been debated that this would only make him into a martyr and would result in even more acts of violence, but this was defeated when reason prevailed.

If the PLO leader were to remain free the conditions would never change from what was now standard operating procedure from his violent organization. The only question was whether or not to kill him outright. It was decided that it would be best to leave him alive. The reasoning behind this was that if he were simply killed he would, in fact, become the martyr the Palestinians would rally around in their continued attacks upon the population of Israel.

During the period when terrorists had been operating within the borders of Lebanon there were numerous attacks upon the Western alliance countries. Terry Nichols and many like him were taken hostage and held in deplorable conditions by the terrorist factions in the region. Finally, however, the terrorists had taken an official of the Soviet Union as one of their hostages.

The results of this operation were much different than they had been accustomed to. Immediately, the Russians had gone out and captured the highest ranking Muslim cleric in the country. The first thing they did then was to film the cutting off of one of the fingers of this Mullah. The photos were provided to the news media along with the warning that each hour that passed would result in another finger being cut off the man's hand. Once they ran out of fingers, they would begin to start the same procedures on the cleric's toes. If necessary, there was still other options of like consequences. This would continue until the Russian dignitary was released, unharmed to his countrymen. Within three hours the Soviet had been found standing on a street corner where he had been allowed to escape from his captivity. Never again was there an incident where a member of that nation was taken hostage by the terrorists.

The Knesset had decided that this same plan would be quite effective in quelling the hostilities against them. Of course, they would not actually inflict the same kind of treatment as had been so effective up in Lebanon, but the Palestinians did not know that. The threat to torture the PLO leader would be enough to stop this violence against them.

That would be only one step in the war against the Palestinians. A state of continuous martial law would be imposed upon them as well. The Israeli Army would move into Samaria, known as the West Bank, and the Gaza Strip in large forces. They would continue to remain there while Israeli intelligence resources could round up all the ring leaders of the opposition and put them in jail. This time there would be no escape. All those children who were constantly throwing rocks at the Israeli forces were to be rounded up and placed in compounds for a minimum of six months. During that time they would be subjected to strong discipline and required to attend school under the watchful eye of the faculty. By the time they were released back to their families their whole attitude would be permanently altered for the better. Those who continued to be rebellious would remain in detention until they were ready to become model citizens.

Many places of national heritage were being occupied by the Palestinians. The birthplace of King David was the town of Bethlehem. This town held even more significance to the whole of Christendom and was currently in the hands of the Palestinians. The same was true of the town of Hebron, which lies in the heart of Judea. How could the Israeli's ever accept that the graves of such as Abraham, Sarah, Isaac, Jacob and Joseph were beyond their control? That would also be rectified with clarity and decisive action.

An argument, however weak, could be made that the Palestinians were entitled to live in Samaria since it was the early Jews who had made the mistake in marrying their women and gaining the scorn well-known to Jews and Gentiles alike. Although they might be allowed to have access to that land, they would be there as the guests of Israel as long as they continued to live in harmony with the citizens of Israel. Their only real home would be the Gaza Strip. While this territory might seem to be limited in size, the strip could easily be extended to the south and west up to the border of Egypt, if necessary, to accommodate the population of the Palestinians.

Once the decisions had been finalized, the prime minister of Israel contacted President Marshall and informed him of the fact. It was anticipated that these actions could cause a huge rift between the two longtime allies; there was no turning back now. How could the Americans continue to ignore the continuous attacks upon their friend and never come to the realization that there would never be any halt to them? Certainly the Americans had taken actions in the past to assist the nations of the Middle East to gain peace, but there had never been any real successes up to this time. It was time to let Israel have a free hand in determining their fate.

President Marshall's reaction was not quite what the prime minister had expected. He listened to the Israelite with full attention and had not interrupted him once while the crux of the call was explained. When he had finished, Prime Minister Alb was treated to a short period of silence before the President began to speak. The tone of the president was one of sorrow and dejection. He had to admit that everything the prime minister had said was absolutely true and there had never been any lasting resolution to the situation, although the United States had played an active role in the peace process. In truth, he could not even honestly refute the actions taken by the Israelis. What were they supposed to do? They were the ones with their collective backs up against the sea with no place to go. President Marshall would have a lot to do now that this situation had reached this level. Todd Martin was going to be a busy man, one more time.

Shortly after hanging up the telephone, the chief executive picked it up one more time. This time it was to summon his closest advisors to the White House once more. An hour later the Oval Office was filled with the major Cabinet members of the administration. Fifteen minutes after that the president ended his dissertation of the call he had just taken from the Middle East. It was now time to hear from his think tank of talent charged with advising him under these conditions.

The first to speak was the secretary of state. General Croft began in soft, but with strong convictions, to state much of the same comments the boss had just heard coming from the Israeli prime minister. The room sat transfixed upon the voice of the secretary since they knew he possessed the wisdom backed up by years of high level service and experience.

"Mr. President, were I in the shoes of the Israeli prime minister I would have taken the same actions you have described to us; only, I would have done this five years ago. We have been guilty of setting a double standard in that area. There is no one in this room who does not realize that the PLO and the PLO leader are the main reasons we have joined the Israelis in suffering during the past decade. The Marines we lost in Lebanon, the disaster down in Africa, the first and second attacks upon the world trade center, the attack of our Pentagon right across the river, the destruction of the Panama and Suez Canals, the attack upon the Alaskan oil pipeline, the murder of our entire Supreme Court, and all the incidents we have suffered in the Middle East, do not compare with the per capita sufferings we have watched happen in Israel.

"We have continued to place restraints on Israel, even when Saddam Hussein was lobbing scuds at them during the first Gulf War. Always, we have urged them to be the "nice guys" while they were dealing with the scum of the earth. When I think of that terrorist, Arafat, being right here in Camp David and the White House, it just makes my blood boil. I, for one, applaud the actions of the Knesset, who have demonstrated courage that we could take lessons from.

"I recommend that we send our congratulations to the Israeli government and ask them how we can support them in this action." With that Harold Croft became silent as he sat back in his chair.

"I fully agree with Hal, but I think maybe we need to do something to assuage the other countries in the Middle East before they do something stupid," the national security advisor pointed out.

"Todd, you've been sitting there in silence for this whole time, but I can tell that you have something you would like to say. Since we're obviously being very candid right now, I don't want you to hold back; this is no time for pussy-footing around this matter," the president said. All the eyes in the room shifted toward the junior member of the group and waited for his response.

"Mr. President, you have asked me to serve you and I know that it is my duty to answer you completely honest and forthright. I have always held great respect for the honor and wisdom of Gen ... Secretary of State Croft. I have never doubted his ability to cut to the chase and tell it like it is. That is why it pains me deeply to say what I must now say.

"Sir, if we stand by and accept the actions of the Knesset I truly believe that it will galvanize the remaining opposition in the Middle East for one last great battle against the nation of Israel. I also have no doubt that the Israeli Army will be victorious in any such war, but at what cost? Right now, the

United States of America is the conscience of the world by default. Every person and government knows this to be a fact.

"While I applaud the decisions made in Israel and concur in every respect, these actions must come from us and not Israel. I would suggest that you immediately call Prime Minister Alb and insist that the planned actions be halted. You should tell him that we all agree with the concept of the plan but it will be us, not them, who conveys this message to the world.

"As soon as you complete that call, I would recommend that you give Yasser a jingle and summon his ass to Washington on the next plane. Once you get that little weasel here he should be informed that his days are over. He will resign his position with the PLO and the organization will be disbanded until they can come up with a better purpose and name for the group. He needs to have the fear of God, or Allah, put into him. He needs to get a good shave and a shower to make him presentable to the rest of us anyway."

The levity of the last remark served to dispel the terseness in the comments and each person in the room turn toward each other while heads nodded.

Beirut
Monday, March 8, 10:26 a.m.

The three A-Teams had left the home they had lived in for the past hundred-plus days and made the trip over to the Beirut airport on the trucks provided by the militia. It must have made quite a parade, because every member of the fighting force they had recruited and trained insisted on accompanying the Americans all the way to the airport. Certainly, some of the residents of the city were frightened when they saw the trucks loaded with armed men coming into town.

The farewells at the airport were lengthy and warm by every member of the American element and their new close friends. Several of the soldiers would be making inquiries about the hour all the way home due to the fact that they had given their wrist watches to members of the militia who had done so much to make the entire operation a complete success. The militia stayed on the edge of the tarmac and continued to wave until the departing aircraft was well down the taxiway and making its turn onto the active runway. There were a lot of mixed emotions among the soldiers as the plane lifted off into the morning sky. Probably none of the new friends would ever be heard from again, but the Americans were on their way home to loved ones and family.

There would be all the parades and speeches made by politicians and generals back at Fort Bragg and most of the men would be getting medals for their actions in the famous valley. But most of all, every member of the teams knew in his heart that something very wonderful had just taken place and once everyone had the time to reflect upon this historic moment in time, the greatest reward would be knowing that the Special Forces had once more done the impossible.

Andrews Air Force Base
Monday, March 8, 7:29 p.m.

A large transport aircraft with no markings except a hardly noticeable U.S. Air Force star on the wings in a subdued charcoal color taxied up to the VIP ramp a short distance from Air Force One. Once the engines were silenced and the ramp on the rear of the cargo bay opened, a group of the nastiest-looking bunch of men you have ever seen emerged. These guys were unshaven and were wearing desert camouflage uniforms that had not been washed for weeks now.

The men seemed quite surprised to see the familiar markings of the huge jumbo jet with the seal of the president of the United States of America on its side.

"What the heck is the President doin' down here in Florida?" one of the more observant troopers asked his teammates.

"I dunno," one of his friends commented, "but I have a feelin' this ain't Kansas anymore, Dorothy."

It took a few minutes for the teams to come to the realization that they were at Andrews Air Force Base and then they observed the United States Army band, dressed in full regalia as it began to play "Hail to the Chief." No, it wasn't for them, but there was no mistaking the presidential limousine as it pulled up to the area and disgorged the president of the United States. Next, out of the vehicle came a face that every man on the teams recognized immediately. Todd walked to the podium along with President Marshall and a full colonel in dress blues rushed over to where the American soldiers were standing in awe.

"Gentlemen, if you will kindly accompany me; the commander in chief would like to meet you and shake your hands," the Army officer said in tones that indicated his honor to be the one to make the introduction. The team leaders showed proper nervousness and embarrassment at the appearance that they would make dressed like this. Quickly, the men doffed their "boonie hats" and pulled out their green berets and placed them on heads that needed haircuts and thorough cleansing. The teams were put into three ranks and the men marched in a manner that would have done a West Point plebe honor over to where the crowd was gathered.

"Group, halt! Left face!" the team leader sounded and then left the men at attention as he turned to the president.

"Sir! All present and accounted for!" At least his salute reflected the discipline inherent in men of his caliber.

The president smiled and gave a waving salute that attempted to be smartly done.

"Have these heroes come to the position of at ease, if you'll be so kind, Major." The senior captain of the team looked down at his tarnished rank insignia just for a second and inwardly laughed at the mistake the President had just made.

"Oh, I see you've been playing around on that R & R trip we gave you and haven't managed to stay in uniform, Major! I see that your men are out of uniform as well; each one of you has been promoted one grade as of this morning according to word I have from the Pentagon. I see that a few of your friends have come out to welcome you guys home, too."

At that signal, a huge ovation rose from a crowd just outside the fence where they were standing.

"I was so anxious to meet you men that I asked your pilot to divert your flight to here in Washington so the folks up here could see what real soldiers look like. I even managed to talk your wives and sweethearts into coming up here and welcoming you home, too. Oh, yeah, will someone open that darned gate over there so these lovely ladies can come in and your children can come and hug their daddy?"

The rush of family members was truly a sight to behold. The disciplined soldiers did not know what to do. They were supposed to be standing in formation before their commander in chief and suddenly family members rushed up to them and began hugging them and kissing them in a manner that reflected all the loneliness and worry that had been pent up for so long. The crowd went wild and the president stepped back from the podium for a full minute before he again stepped up to the microphone.

"My dear, dear friends and members of the most elite group of men on the face of this earth, I cannot express the debt of gratitude this nation owes to each one of you. You have demonstrated all those qualities and characteristics that make this nation the greatest on earth. No one of us will ever know all the terrible moments of fear and valor you have shown the world in the previous five months. Your dedication and self-denial is what makes you elite—not the green piece of cloth you so proudly wear upon your heads. I'll be coming down to Fort Bragg in a few weeks and let your bosses know just how proud I am of you great Americans. But right now I want an old friend of yours to say a few words to you."

Todd Martin, dressed in his complete Army uniform of so many years before and complete with his "badge of honor," the coveted green beret, left the podium and marched over to where the men were standing. When he had come to within ten feet of the now defunct formation, he came to an abrupt halt and then gave his best salute.

"Permission to approach the finest Americans I have ever known," Mr. Martin requested. The salute was promptly returned by the entire group and they rushed forward and surrounded their benefactor with shouts of cheering. Todd made it a point to shake the hand of each member of the teams and thanked them profusely for their contributions. "I bet the next time you guys see me approaching you, you will all run and hide," he told the laughing men. "Now, I think the boss wants to talk to you guys a little more, so if you'll excuse me, I need to get back over to him."

As Todd was making his way back toward the president, the chief executive once more took over the microphone.

"Guys, you sure don't look like what I've always thought you 'green beanies' were supposed to look like. Tell you what, I had your wives scrounge up your class A's and some shaving gear, so why don't you men accompany your ladies back to their hotels and try and get rid of some of that hair before you become a fire hazard? Tomorrow evening, Hazel and I would like you and your families to drop by and have dinner with us. We'll be having a few friends drop by to join us if you don't mind. I hear my Cabinet and the leadership over on 'the hill' are gonna make it, too. I promise that the 'chow' will be to your liking.

"Well, you guys are probably tired of hearing me talk, so I am going to release you to the custody of these wonderful women, who are your strongest support in all you do. As of right now, you guys are on administrative leave and are not to set foot back on Fort Bragg for the next two weeks."

The next few days were a whirlwind of activities for the returning soldiers as they were given free reign in the nation's capitol. No matter where they went or where they chose to dine, the meal was "on the house." Cab fares were denied by the drivers as they were excited to have these folk riding in their personal taxi. Many of them were of Arabic descent and they seemed to be even more grateful to the men and their wives as they drove them about town. Even the barbers who had opened up their shops on their first evening in town provided their service and told the men that it was an honor to serve such people as themselves.

"They should have demanded twenty bucks for the estimate beforehand," one of the NCOs had told his wife.

Each of the soldiers had visited the Supreme Court building expecting to see the ruins caused by people like ones they had just been engaging in combat. They were shocked when they saw that the buildings had been restored to their original condition while they had been overseas.

"I can't believe they got that job done so fast—did you see the pictures in the paper when they first got started?"

The president was determined that any evidence of the crippling blow be removed so the country could get about the task of healing. Apparently it was working.

CIA Headquarters, Langley, Virginia
Tuesday, March 9, 21:00 Zulu (GMT)

The facsimile machine in the secure section for operations was receiving a message directly from an operative in the field in Tehran. The message was coded "Flash," which meant that it was the highest priority designation assigned to a message, regardless of source. The designation caused a red light to begin flashing over the top of the receiver to alert operators to take immediate note.

Grabbing the message out of the tray of the machine, the technician quickly noted the heading of "Top Secret" and reached in the drawer and selected the yellow cover sheet with the same inscription in large letters and placed it on top of the message. Quickly, the administrator selected the appropriate stamp and rapidly marked each page of the communication with the Top Secret indicator and noted the number of copies and which one this particular one fell into. This copy would forever retain the number 1 in the numbered copy ledger. The designation of number of copies was listed as 1 for the time being. In a matter of seconds the document was listed in the log journal with a date/time stamp indicating the time it was received. The latter was really unnecessary since the heading on the fax clearly indicated the time it had come across the receivers, but rules are rules, so the time was repeated in accordance with the appropriate regulation.

As the administrator was leaving the room after signing for the document, the technician was already on the secure telephone to alert the staff duty officer of the flash message on its way to his office. The content of the message could have been from Chicken Little announcing that the sky was falling as far as those in the message center were concerned. They specifically maintained a policy of not reading any message received beyond the aforementioned information and to whom it was directed.

The staff duty officer took one look at the message and let out a nearly silent whistle. He reached for this telephone without taking his eyes off the document he was holding in shaking hands. This had to get to the right people and it had to be done very soon.

Carlos Lopez had been living in Iran now for almost a year. He had graduated from Langley and Quantico nearly three years before and had immediately been sent out to Monterey and the language school. Arabic had not been an easy language for him to learn, but his forensic abilities in the Spanish language had helped him in learning the third language he needed to become proficient in. Not only did the school teach the language, but much of the curriculum dealt with customs and procedures he would need to know in order to survive in a completely hostile setting. There would be no "time outs" or chances to correct mistakes. His Mexican heritage provided him with skin tones that could easily be that of the average native Iranian.

His mission had been quite simple in terminology, but in actual practice, arduous. He melted into the society and began living the life of an average Iranian while he became familiar with those aspects that he would need to master in his craft. It was fully three months before he made his first approach to recruit a spy. He still remembered his feelings of fear when he made that irretrievable approach. You could beat around the bush for only so long before you popped the question. The fact that the man he had chosen was eager to join him didn't ease the tension of the matter.

His selection of the first target was a good one. The recruited agent worked in a governmental office in downtown Tehran and had access to much in the way of usable information. His motivation had been the fact that his father, who had been a loyal follower of the former Shah, had been executed right in front of him and his mother when the Ayatollah came to power. The executioner had actually laughed when he saw the crying son of the fallen man.

With added training provided by Carlos, the agent had become more proficient in his work output and had been promoted to an even more prestigious and advantageous position in the Islamic government. The document that was being given so much attention back in Washington at this very moment was a product of the discovery of the same person. Carlos had broken cover long enough to get the cryptic message back to Langley.

The curtailment of Western education programs had delayed many of the technological activities in Iran. However, that did not keep them from pursuing such matters. Although there was no one in the country with the abilities to create atomic warfare, the government had access to the Arabic nations along the southern border of what had been the former Soviet Union. These border countries had resorted to any means possible to raise funds for their survival. One of the commodities they had to market was plutonium.

The government of Iran had wanted to become a member of the nuclear community, but had no expertise to utilize the materials they had accumulated. There was, however, one nation with the expertise to do so. That same nation was experiencing difficulty in putting their knowledge into practice because they lacked the main ingredient to build an atomic bomb. That country was North Korea.

When two parties with similar aims meet with common goals the outcome is simply a matter of negotiation. Iran had enough plutonium on hand to build nine atomic bombs and North Korea had exhausted its supply of plutonium when they built the third of their devices. In a clandestine meeting of the two national leaders, the satisfaction of both parties were met. The Iranians would turn over all their plutonium to the North Koreans in exchange for the three existing nuclear bombs. That part of the negotiation went rather quickly since North Korea would increase their arsenal three-fold and the Iranians would finally have the needed hardware to continue their international blackmail.

The next hurdle was not so easily planned. The actual exchange of the products would have to be done simultaneously since neither party to the agreement trusted each other. The final plan was that an Iranian ship would be sent to the waters off the coast of North Korea and, at the same time, a ship would depart North Korea bound for the shores of Iran down in the gulf. Once both ships were on station the deliveries would take place while the captains of the vessels were in radio contact. Once the plan was developed all that was needed was to set the date for the transfer. That date had been set and it was then that Carlos's agent had discovered the whole matter. Both ships had already left their home ports bound for their specific destinations and would be passing each other in the next day or so.

Due to the immediacy of the requirement to act, the Pentagon was quick to pick up the ball and run with it. It was decided that this would be handled by the naval forces. The operation would require two submarines to approach the ships while they were both on the high seas and take them by surprise. It needed to be done in a manner that would not allow either of the vessels to get off a radio call. Also, the plan was to take possession of the nuclear materials rather than to have them end up on the bottom of the ocean.

The requisition of the two submarines was a simple matter. The actual boarding party would consist of two SEAL teams, one on each vessel. The boats would approach the two ships during the hours of darkness and come alongside just long enough to allow the boarding party to board the ships and then slip away. The SEAL's would then take the entire ship by surprise and secure the entire crew before they even knew what was happening. Once the vessels were secure, the ships would be halted and the submarines would come alongside once more to off load the crews, nuclear materials and the SEAL teams. Once the transfer was complete, the ships would have their bilges open and allow them to slip silently into the floor of the ocean. No one would ever know what happened to them until the right time.

The South China Sea
Thursday, March 11 22:16 p.m. local

The ship's third officer was on the bridge in control of the cargo ship, *Caliente*. It was a quiet evening, so the captain and first officer had turned the ship over to the junior officer so they could engage in a game of cards down in the captain's quarters. The junior officer decided that he did not need to have the other bridge personnel, which consisted of a single man who had nothing to do but stare at the darkened windows. Wanting to incur the favor of the older seaman, he dismissed him to return to his hammock for some extra sleep.

If he had been more alert he might have detected the submarine as it followed in the wake of his ship some ten fathoms below the surface of the calm sea. That was the furthest thing from his mind as he contemplated his coming arrival in the Persian Gulf and the prospect of engaging in some other activities with one of the local females. He had heard some of the old shipmates discuss the amorous abilities of these Arabian women that, even if half true, would be a far cry from the ladies he had known in his home back in North Korea.

With a degree of practiced stealth, the nuclear submarine continued to decrease the distance between itself and the vessel ahead of it. The wake turbulence caused just enough phosphorous glow to mask the overtaking boat without being detected. Once the desired distance was achieved, the submarine commander ordered a quick turn to port and then back to the original heading. This brought the two vessels into close proximity while avoiding actual contact. The captain had then surfaced his vessel right alongside the surface ship.

Silently, and with the stealth of long practice, the members of the SEAL team had fired the grappling hook over the rail of the *Caliente* at a point in the latter third of the port side of the vessel. One of the members had rapidly climbed the line and when on deck began to coiling the line that had been secured to the rope ladder suspended from the submarine. In a matter of three minutes the full compliment of the team had successfully boarded the ship and had split up into the various elements necessary to complete their mission.

The junior officer on the bridge was more than a little startled when he saw the first member of the team come into the room. At first he thought it was the crewman returning for some item he had inadvertently left behind, but when he saw the individual standing in front of him in a totally black uniform and then saw menacing Uzi, his whole demeanor changed.

The intruder into the bridge silently put his finger to his lips and motioned for the ship's officer to remain completely silent and still. He needn't have demanded this since the helmsman had frozen into an open-mouthed gape with an almost uncontrollable urge to relieve his bladder on the spot.

The stunning shock of the other members of the crew was no less traumatic. Without a single shot being fired the SEAL team had taken complete control of the ship within five minutes of their arrival. Two minutes later the ships engines were at full stop and the vessel began a slow decline in speed as the momentum faded. When the ship had come to a complete halt, a much larger boarding party emerged from the submarine and those responsible for the location of the ship's cargo were making their way to that location. The boarding party had equipment such as Geiger counters to assist them in the search for the dangerous materials

The three containers holding the bombs were sealed sufficiently to avoid detection by the instruments, but since the crew had not expected any difficulty, they were in plain sight as one entered the cargo bay. The Navy team was a little surprised to find that the bombs were not the expected size and only required two men to carry each of them to the port side of the ship. From that point the nuclear weapons were quickly lowered to the waiting arms of the men standing on the deck of the submarine. In short order the bombs were stowed securely in the boat, ready to be transported to a new destination.

The crew of the *Caliente* were certain that they were about to be executed by the American seamen and began to sob and beg in their native Korean language as they were marched to the port side of the ship. Only when the lieutenant junior grade motioned for them to go over the side onto the suspended ladder did they begin to realize that they might survive this night.

The submarine remained on the surface a couple hundred meters away and its captain confirmed the sinking of the ship before leaving the conning tower to rejoin the boat's crew. All the prisoners had been herded to one location mid-ship and were tied up in a sitting position for the duration of the journey, however long that would take.

As it turned out, the journey was not as long as one might have expected. An hour later the submarine surfaced once more, directly alongside a battle cruiser. The SEALs, prisoners and reason for the mission were quickly transferred to the surface ship and the sub silently slipped under the waves to continue whatever mission had been interrupted by the short operation.

At exactly the same period of time a second naval force out on the Indian Ocean had just completed a carbon copy of the same mission executed by those in the South China Sea. The only difference was the composition of the crew. In the latter case, the captured prisoners were Iranian.

Pyongyyang, Peoples' Democratic Republic of Korea.
Friday, March 12

It had been many years since any Westerner had landed in the capitol of North Korea. It was only due to curiosity that the premiere had agreed to allow the aircraft to land on the guarded airfield. The American diplomat was met by certain underlings of the Politburo in order to give an underhanded insult to the hated Americans. The diplomat shook hands with the Korean dignitary, who treated the former's hand like it was in advanced stages of leprosy. The American handed the host representative an envelope and returned immediately to the aircraft and boarded. The pilot moved the aircraft to the appropriate end of the runway and engaged full throttle. The "welcoming party" stood there in silence and disbelief as they watched the departing airplane become a mere speck on the horizon.

The envelope was left with its seal in place as the courier delivered the communication to the office of the premier. Since it was addressed to him, no one dared to open the missive before handing it over to the dictator. When he opened the letter and read the contents, his face became one of confusion. The letter was a short and terse invitation for the premier to come to Beijing the following day for talks that would be beneficial to both counties. He couldn't resist the intrigue of the situation and ordered his staff to begin preparations for his immediate departure.

Beijing, China
Saturday, March 13, 11:00 a.m.

The American contingent seated in the conference hall at Tiananmen Square was headed up by Todd Martin. He had brought with him several members of the Washington diplomatic corps and they, too, were seated at the table in anticipation of the North Korean element. In order to send a thinly disguised insult to the Americans, the premier had purposely made them wait for nearly half an hour before he and his entourage entered the room and moved quickly to their assigned seats. Strangely, there were no Chinese officials in the room.

"To what purpose have the Western imperialists summoned me to this meeting?" the premier questioned, with no attempt to shield his personal animosity toward his sworn enemy.

Instead of replying to the query, Todd passed a folder across the table to the pompous little man without any indication that he had even heard the question. The premier took the folder and opened it, surprised to see that the contents were all in his own language. It was the words written on the pages that caused him to lean forward in his chair and allow the grim facial expression to come over him.

The papers the North Korean was reading informed him that his entire arsenal of atomic bombs had been intercepted and that the expected plutonium would never reach his shores. His anger turned to rage and he screamed across the table, "You cannot steal our national possessions!"

Todd leaned forward and rose to his feet. "Listen here, you little pipsqueak, you've been a painful blister on the ass of the world long enough! Now, sit your butt back down in that chair before I come across this table and slap the kim chi out of you! We have the plutonium you thought you could use to make more bombs with and you'll never see a speck of it. Furthermore, those three atomic bombs you thought we stole from you are still in your possession. Unfortunately for you the whereabouts of these weapons will never be known to you, if you're lucky. You see, we have buried them in three strategic places in your country and we have kept the triggering devices for every one of them. If you so much as fart, we'll set them off and watch you fry like you deserve! We're calling it 'Operation Fried Rice.'

"For decades we have allowed you to remain in power in the hope that you might just come to your senses. This has been a mistake. You have spit in our faces over and over again while we made every attempt to negotiate with you in good faith. When you illegally stole our reconnaissance ship, the *Pueblo*, we exercised restraint while you threw your little tantrums and mistreated our American servicemen. We've put up with your constant encroachment and violation of the de-militarized zone for decades. We have captured your saboteurs on numerous occasions when they were illegally in South Korea. All *that* we have been patient in, but now you have crossed the line by attempting to become a nuclear threat. That we will not tolerate!

"You know, two can play that same game. We have thousands of Korean people who are citizens of the United States. These people have been quite resourceful in maintaining a presence in your land. We have been coming and going back and forth into the very depths of your nation for years now and have developed our sources of information to completeness.

"By the way, don't expect the Chinese to come to your rescue either. They're fed up with your tantrums, too. The Chinese people came to your side during the United Nations conflict in Korea. Millions of these Chinese soldiers lost their lives while trying to be your friend. In return, you have ignored their council, thumbed your noses at them and, in general, have become an embarrassment to them. They, too, are fed up with you and are frightened to think that you could ever pose a nuclear threat. In fact, we have been encouraged to tell you that your standing army is to be reduced by seventy-five percent immediately. You can do that on your own, or we will save you the trouble by flipping the switch on those nasty little bombs you have in your back yard.

"You have literally starved your people to death while you sit around planning your mischief and eating like the pig you are. The whole world is aware that you are a pervert who gets his kicks out of watching 'kiddie porn' and all of us are repulsed by you. You are joke! Don't you realize that the whole world is laughing at you, standing around in your elevator shoes to salve your ego at being not only a mental dwarf, but one in stature as well?"

The North Korean premier began to rise from his chair, ready to stomp out of the room. Todd was not through yet. "Sit your ass back down in that chair before I slap you down," Todd said in a manner that left no doubt that he meant every word of it. "We will be sending a team of controllers into your country tomorrow morning to begin the disarmament of your goons. If we meet the slightest bit of resistance we will immediately pull back and flip the switch. You got that?"

"My comrades, the Chinese people will not stand by and let you do this!" the premier stated with bluffed authority.

"Right now, the Chinese Army is moving toward your border to provide assistance to us if we should need it. Face it, you bastard, you're finished!" Todd said with finality.

At that point, the entire American contingent rose as one and proceeded toward the exit doors, leaving the stunned tyrant sitting in his chair with his mouth wide open. Once outside the room one of Todd's cohorts turned to him and said, "Great diplomacy, Mr. Martin; are you sure that you came from the State Department?"

"I can assure you that what I just told that miserable little man in that room has been needed and wished for for a very long time now. If I were him I think I might choose another destination than to return back to Pyongyang. If he does go back he'll have the whole army out there digging up the whole darned country and going nuts looking for those missing atomic bombs. Too bad he doesn't know that they're sitting back in the states in a warehouse facility."

"Did you see that bastard's face when you let him have it? I really though he would have a coronary right on the spot. It was beautiful!" his assistant said as he re-entered the vehicle that would take them all to the American consulate's compound downtown. "He must be at his wits' end to know that the Chinese have thrown him to the wolves."

"Now all I have to do is pay a little visit on our friends in Iran," Todd remarked in reply.

— 19 —

Over the past five months the entire balance of power had been altered by the events that began on October 12 of the preceding year. That seemed like so long ago when one considered all the major events that occurred since that fateful day. The world had seen the two major shipping routes destroyed and the deprivation of the oil necessary to maintain the world's manufacturing nations caused by the explosion of the Alaska oil pipeline. Then there was the complete realignment of the United Nations when treachery was exposed at the very head of that organization.

We watched as the Egyptian president committed suicide after being exposed as a driving force behind the evil Movement. The huge purge in Indonesia involved trials and mass execution of the terrorists who were part of the world-wide terrorist organization. The former secretary general of the United Nations had fled and was somewhere at sea on a ship that seemed to have disappeared from the face of the earth.

The Syrians, who had long been considered a hotbed of support for terrorists, had suddenly turned the corner and had been a contributing factor in cleaning out the terrible open sore that was the Bekka Valley. There had been that awful day when the terror cell in the United States had attacked and killed all the members of the Supreme Court in one fell swoop.

The world's stock markets nearly collapsed due to the disruption of oil, transport and uncertainty that had been a part of the catastrophic events during this period. In each case, however, the outcome had been a stronger and more determined world population, which was now much closer than ever before. Dictators were trembling in their boots and there were rumors that North Korea and some of the other regimes of repression were finally being put in their place. Unexpectedly, the North Koreans announced that they were abandoning their quest of becoming a nation with nuclear armament. To back that up, the premier humbly stood in the dais of the United Nations and announced that he was cutting his military expenditures by three quarters so that he could free up the necessary funds to provide a better life for his people. Word was, he was being considered for the Nobel Peace Prize.

Now there was talk that the Iranian government was inviting the youth of their nation to become more involved in the running of the country. This had been thought unimaginable only a few weeks prior to the announcement. The United States had even gone so far as to commit significant amounts of relief monies to both North Korea and Iran, according to reports coming out of Washington.

As of yet there were still some parts of the globe where the news was not all that rosy. The PLO had begun to step-up attacks in the Gaza, West Bank and throughout Israel. Leadership of that organization was accusing their Arab brothers of caving in to imperialist pressure from Washington and London. Israel, as one might expect, was retaliating with the usual precision attacks upon the areas known to be in support of the bombings and suicide attacks coming from the PLO factions.

Israel had recently intercepted transmissions from Saudi Arabia directed at the PLO elements that offered financial and material support to them. These reports were expedited to the United States government with a request to re-evaluate their support of the Saudis. The Saudi government began a blitz advertising campaign throughout America, denying these "false and defamatory claims" made by Israel, and urged the citizens of the United States to contact their representatives and repulse these attacks against "America's strongest supporter in the Middle East."

Somehow, the message was not getting through after it was made known some time back that large sums of money were being paid to the "martyrs" that the Western world and Israel were calling suicide bombers. One could almost sympathize with the royal family in Saudi Arabia when one considered their precarious position. While the leadership of the country was very pro-Western in their thinking, the preponderance of the population did not share this affection for the West. The financial support for continued survival depended upon the sale of oil to the West. Accordingly, it became absolutely necessary for the royal family to maintain good relations with the

United States and its allies. By throwing an occasional "bone" to the anti-Western group, the royal family could retain its position of power.

The absolute need to preserve the status quo was made quite clear when the Iraqis made an attempt to annex Kuwait and were poised on the border of Saudi Arabia a few years back. Had it not been for the coalition forces, headed by the United States, there would be no Saudi Arabia today. If the United States ever got tired of putting up with the Saudi government the royal family would be forced to run for cover. It was a no-win situation for the Saudis and they would have to continue to walk the tightrope without losing their balance.

Unfortunately for them, the average citizen of the United States couldn't care less about their dilemma.

The Yemenis were another area of insecurity. The situation that the government found themselves in was almost a copy of that which prevailed in their northern neighbor. Unlike the Saudis, however, they spent much less time trying to appease the Americans. During the years of Soviet power, the Yemen government took great delight at thumbing their noses at the Americans and hadn't yet recognized that their benefactor was no longer in a position to do anything for them. Since they were relatively insignificant when it came to size, the United States had ignored their significance and merely tolerated them as long as they didn't cause problems.

Kuwait, on the other hand, would never forget the debt of honor they owed to the United States. Those in the western hemisphere had no idea of the trauma that nation had endured when Saddam Hussein's troops had attacked them. The infamous Attila the Hun had no edge upon the cruelty inflicted upon the Kuwaitis during that period of time when the occupation was in effect. Certainly, there were small groups of hard-core terrorists still in the small country, but it was an equal certainty that they had better keep a very low profile in order to avoid the revenge that would be inflicted by the population, if they ever became known.

The bottom line was that the entire balance of power in the Middle East was making a huge leap into what could only be described as a tremendous step forward toward democracy. The terrorists among them were losing a death grip that had held them hostage for as many years as anyone could remember. If the deplorable conditions in that area could be overcome there would be relatively few geographic locations where problems could erupt. The days of Castro's Cuba were numbered. Either his age would solve the problem, or the Cubans would take matters into their own hands now that they could see that there was a better way of life. North Korea and Iran had been neutralized by the actions taken when they made that last desperate move toward terrorism.

Oh, sure, there would always be those areas where uprisings of the evil forces could erupt at any given time, but the major powers could handle them in an expeditious manner before they became a force to be reckoned with. The task now would be to conduct "mop up" operations to completely eradicate those elements of the terrorist organizations, and the world was eager to do it. There was only one thing left for the Americans to do and that would happen in the next few days.

A large group of students, representing several of the Arab nations, had made a formal offer to travel to the three attack sites and work to complete the restoration as common laborers in the name of Allah. President Marshall decided to take full advantage of the latest movement and called a meeting of the ambassadors to the United Nations from all the Arab nations—and Israel—to be conducted in Washington. Not one of them dared to object. It was high time that this whole Middle East problem be put to bed forever. If it was ever going to happen, then it would be right now.

"My fellow citizens of planet earth, we have witnessed a lot of history in the past century. Some of it has been very good, while a lot of it has not been what any one of us would have desired. I think most of us have now reached a point where we can no longer accept a condition of continuous strife. If you consider the recent terrible actions there can be no other conclusion than to accept the reason for this attack and the hundreds of others that have plagued every family in the Middle East and here in the United States as well. We will not leave this room until each of us has come to the understanding that we can no longer accept conditions to remain the same.

"The whole matter can be stated in one word—Israel!"

A few gasps escaped from the lips of many present in the room. The ambassador of Israel became alarmed, as he was uncertain of the impact of these words coming from what had always been the closest ally of the world's Jews.

"Whether any of us agrees or disagrees with the right of the nation of Israel to exist, the fact is that it does and will continue to do so." The firmness of this statement left no doubt which direction the meeting was going to go. "You people of the Arab nations have a greater grasp on the history of this world than most even consider. You know that your father Noah came down off of Mount Ararat and the birth of nations began. The very cradle of this history lies in what is today the nation of Iraq. The separation of nations occurred from this birthplace in Babylon.

"Your ancestor, Noah, was the ancestral father of the patriarch, Abram, or Abraham if you prefer. There can be no doubt that he was Iraqi. This ancient leader produced two sons; the first being Ishmael and the second, Isaac. This is where the conflict began and continues to this day. Whether you admit it or not, you people are all brothers. The only question was the inheritance of Father Abraham. Each of you in this room fully accept that God, or Allah, or Yahweh, granted title to this land in perpetuity. He spelled out that the land would belong to the descendants of Abraham and He has always honored His covenants to you. The deed to this property specifies that the descendants of Abraham would own all the land from the Nile River and the Red and Mediterranean Seas on the west, to the Euphrates River on the east and to the borders of Syria and Lebanon on the north. That is exactly where the descendants of Abraham live to this day.

"The grandson of Abraham was given a title to a portion of this land. Jacob was given all the land from Lebanon on the north, the Mediterranean and Red Seas on the west and to the Sea of Galilee, inclusive, Jordan River, and the Dead Sea on the east. That this land was a gift from God is evidenced by the manner in which God has kept the described land under such ownership. The children of Israel (Jacob) were given decisive ownership after being absent from the land for over two centuries in Egypt, and another period of absence extending some seventy years when they were returned to the land of Father Abraham (Babylon and Nebuchadnezzar). In both instances, the land was kept for Israel until they returned

"The third absence occurred as a result of the Roman Empire. Although many Jews continued to live in the traditional lands, the nation of Israel was not present in their inherited land until the return began in earnest after the holocaust of WWII. But return they did. The successful re-establishment of the birthright homeland was once more a fact.

"The terrible clashes of people in this land have gone on from the beginning of time. We know pretty certainly that the original man created by our Creator placed them in the Garden of Eden in what is now known as the confluence of the Tigris and Euphrates Rivers. It was in this vicinity that man began to war with his brothers in the initial act between the brothers Cain and Abel.

"So often, different factions in the Middle East have referred to the United States as the "Great Satan." I'm here today to tell you that the great Satan is not to be found among mankind. No, the real evil has stood by clapping his hands while we humans have sought to destroy each other.

"Another factor so often forgotten is the basic fact that each of us are truly brothers with the same ancestry from the start. We in the Jewish, Muslim and Christian world are aware that the Jewish people were chosen to be God's elect among mankind. Why He did so escapes most of us. Even their greatest leader, Moses, had to stand between them and God on several occasions to keep the Creator from wiping them from the face of the earth. God called the Israelites 'a stiff necked people.' They constantly rebelled from Him for hundreds of years.

"You Israelis were charged by God to be 'the light of the world.' Instead, you chose to be arrogant and hold your favored position over the heads of the rest of the world and treat them as inferiors. On a few occasions, though, there were those among you who excelled in the task assigned by the Creator. Joseph went from the most humble beginnings in Egypt to the highest position in the land next to the Pharaoh. I can assure you he didn't reach this level because of his superior attitude. Then there was a young man who was forced to return to the birthplace of his forefathers back in Iraq. His story is one of great achievement and rise to power akin to that of his ancestor, Joseph. Daniel assisted the greatest king ever to lead what is today Iraq, and became famous and powerful because he recognized that he was put into his position to be the aforementioned 'light.' The great king, Nebuchadnezzar, was led to such conviction that the Torah makes the flat out statement that he will be among those whose dwelling place will be in glory.

"During the time when Israel occupied the land after escape from Egypt and the later years after the return from Iraq (Babylon), there was a small nation which existed in the Gaza Strip. These were the Philistines. Countless wars ensued between the two peoples because the Israeli people failed to remain in obedience to their God. The stories of Samson and Goliath come from these continuous battles. Some of the Israelites began to marry the Philistine women and bring them home to Israel. They were forced to live in near exile in their own land and limited to Samaria (today called the "West Bank").

Today, the Philistines are called Palestinians, a bastardization of the original name. They are located in the same two places as they were in biblical times: Gaza and the West Bank. Somehow, the Philistines thought that they could circumvent the will of God/Allah. They claimed the Israelite land for themselves. It should be noted that although they share a common area with the Arab states, that they are not Arabs at all.

During the realignment of national boundaries under British rule, the question of a homeland for the Philistines (Palestinians) became a matter of much discussion. The Brits decided to end the matter by giving the Palestinians an area of their own. It was called Jordan. As time went on many of these Palestinian/Jordanian people began to cast their eyes to the West once more. They caused so many problems that the Jordanian king rounded them all up and expelled them from his kingdom. That is when they became dispossessed people. Israel had nothing to do with it. However, Israel was in a position to become the scapegoat readily acceptable by the rest of the Arab countries. None of them wanted to give sanctuary to these dissidents and it was easy to blame Israel for all the ills of the Palestinians. That condition has prevailed for many decades now and has never been solved.

"Once more I want to reiterate that Israel is here to stay. No longer will this nation stand by and allow the carnage to continue against your brothers, the Israeli people. There have been numerous attempts to solve the matter by men of good will in the past. Each of these attempts have been sabotaged by a small group of malcontents dedicated to killing every Israeli citizen. Since it really hasn't affected the rest of the Arab nations to any great extent, you have stood by and ignored these criminals who are hellbent upon killing men, women, children and babies. That will stop today.

"Along with that, I want to confirm that the Philistines will continue to be neighbors of the Israeli nation. Since the two of you are going to be perpetual neighbors, it would behoove you to start getting along. You can do that willingly and in a spirit that respects both names of God: Yahweh and Allah. If you cannot do that then you both better start respecting the rest of the world because we have spent enough of our time and resources trying bring you two together.

"I expect each one of you to deliver to your head of state, on an immediate basis, the message I have delivered to you this day. Israel will continue to hold all the land she now occupies with the exception of the following: Gaza and Samaria. Samaria consists of those lands immediately bordered by the Jordan River on the East from a point directly north of the line of Jerusalem and up to the Sea of Galilee. The western border will be the traditional one established during biblical times. People of Palestinian descent will immediately relocate from other territories such as Hebron and Bethlehem and any other areas sacred to the Judean Province.

"Jerusalem has been a place of holiness even before the time of Abraham. The Prophet Melchezadek lived in the same location and was given homage by that Father of God's people. Because of this and the fact that three of the world's religions hold this city to be a part of their heritage, Jerusalem will remain an open city. It will not be controlled by Muslim, Jew, or Christian factions. In that matter there are numerous Christian facilities in the city that are under the direct control of the Vatican. This condition will also cease.

"The control of these sacred places was gained by evil crusaders and belong to the entire world of Christendom. Any attempt to alter these borders will bring down the wrath of this and other peace-loving nations in gigantic proportions. If you have some hotheads in your sovereign nations, I suggest that you get their attention in a hurry. No further acts of terrorism will be directed at any nation in the Middle East—period!

"Now I know that these solutions are subject to rankle the cockles of many in this room. I can only hope that the Creator has been gracious enough to provide this humble servant with the wisdom of Solomon. I can assure you that He has provided this nation with the strength of Samson and a willingness to exercise that power to enforce each edict I have uttered this day. Many have referred to the actions that have taken place in the holy land and elsewhere as a jihad. This is an oxymoron that insults our Creator. There can never ever be a "holy war." By whatever name anyone has elected to call this blasphemy of God, it has never once been holy. It is over this day. May God bless each one of us!"

The silence in the room was absolutely chilling. Certainly, there were those in the room who were thinking, How dare he! There could be no doubt that the decision had been made and would be maintained to the end. The options for the countries involved were: Accept the matter as *fait accompli,* or decide to challenge the military might of the United States of America. The latter was absolutely impossible, especially with the current mood of the people of that country.

Slowly and almost indiscernible at first came the sound of a single person clapping his hands. Heads turned to see where this applause was coming from and saw that it was the ambassador from Saudi Arabia. Within five seconds the applause was joined by the ambassador of Egypt. The next to join in was the Jordanian ambassador and after that came others until every person in the room was standing and cheering. Many, including the chief executive of the United States, had tears of joy flowing down their cheeks. The Kuwaiti ambassador crossed the room and gave a heartfelt hug to his counterpart from Israel. Both men were sobbing. If the terrible incidents of the past month had resulted in this, then the suffering had been well worth it. Never again would the world be the same.

— 20 —

Todd Martin and his family stepped from the VIP aircraft onto the tarmac at Pope Air Force Base to a crowd; the likes of which he or his family had never seen in the past. Off to the side of their plane was the familiar outline of the famous Air Force One that had landed the previous evening on the same runway.

A formation consisting of nearly one thousand men of the various Special Forces groups were assembled in ranks that spread nearly a quarter of a mile wide. Standing there in their crisp uniforms and bloused boots, glistening in the morning sun, and with their distinguished headgear, they were a sight to cause one's heart to beat several counts higher than normal. The pride of America was standing in front of them and the welling up of the same pride could not help but be infectious.

Todd and his family were ushered to the reviewing stand and seated next to the CINC of special warfare. Next to them on the other side was the commanding general of XVIII Airborne Corps and Fort Bragg. Further down the row was the special warfare center commanding general. It made quite an impressive sight to see the best of the uniformed services in the entire world in such a small setting.

Off to the left front was the band of the 82nd Airborne Division in their distinctive maroon berets and bloused boots only authorized for paratroopers. At a signal from the podium the band took up the strains of the familiar "Hail to the Chief" just as the president of the United States of America and his wife stepped onto the red carpet provided for their walk to the podium. A large crowd of spectators on either side of the podium broke out into a standing ovation that lasted a full five minutes, unabated.

The parade adjutant directed, "Colors, post!" and the color guard stepped forward from the troop line and moved to a point in front of the reviewing stand and reversed to face the troops. This was followed by "Adjutant's call," and the individual Special Forces groups moved forward in turn, starting from the far left to the far right, to the designated point on the field half the distance from the starting point. The formations moved with complete precision so as to appear as a single body as the unison of their march was equally precise.

Once the parade had formed on line, the adjutant exchanged salutes with the group commanders and took their reports of "All present or accounted for," across the formation from left to right. He then turned to the reviewing stand and rendered a smart salute to the reviewing stand.

The commanding general of the United States' Special Warfare Center moved to the podium and returned the salute and called, "Persons to be decorated, front and center." From the rear of the reviewing stand, three Special Forces Detachment A's came forward in single file until they reached the front of the reviewing stands and then formed into three ranks of twelve men each. Unlike the rest of the uniformed soldiers, who were dressed in their class A dress uniforms, these men were dressed in their field uniforms, which had received the extra attention to ensure proper military creases and press. Detachments A-237, 238 and 239, the same ones who had distinguished themselves before the whole world in the Bekka Valley, were once again assembled to be honored in a befitting manner. Somehow they seemed to be not as tall as one would have expected as they took their places in the formation. They appeared to be just ordinary men who you might just pass by on the street. Of course, that was what it was all about. America has produced men of this caliber many times during their short history on the world scene and, no doubt, would continue to do so until there was no longer any need to do so.

"Give the units the order to present arms," the commander of troops ordered. Once the entire parade of soldiers was in compliance with the order, the band began playing the national anthem while every person rose to their feet and either saluted or placed their hands over their hearts. At the conclusion of the hymn the crowd seated themselves and the units were given the command to, "Order arms and come to the position of parade rest."

It was then that commander of troops stepped forward and made the official introduction of the president of the United States of America. As

President Marshall stood and came to the microphone, a huge roar of applause rose from all over the field, from the reviewing stands and from the crowds on either side.

"My soldiers and friends, it is indeed an honor to be in the presence of greatness, of some of the finest people of the face of this earth this morning. Mere words cannot reflect the pride I have in my heart as I look out across this field and see the talent, professionalism, commitment and patriotism you so eloquently exemplify. I want to personally thank each one of you for the sacrifices you make on a daily basis so the rest of us do not have to.

"It is not just the soldiers standing on this parade field that deserve the deep appreciation of this grateful nation. The families of these men are also present here this morning and deserve no less credit for the sacrifices they also make. Think of the wife who has to fend for the family while her husband is sent off to harms way, not knowing if he will return to the safety of the family again; the wife who must stand in line at the commissary or in the hospital to provide for her children and be both mother and father much of the time; the wife who must make the pay go around each month in the knowledge that there will always be financial challenges. Think of the families who are asked to pick up their homes and relocate every few years and leave behind friends and loved ones and go through the ordeal of reestablishing a home. There are so many sacrifices that these families endure and, for that, no nation can give adequate thanks. I can assure you that this one individual is well aware of your gift to the nation and I will never let you down as long as there is breath in my body."

The president then paused and turned toward Todd Martin and said, "Mr. Martin, would you please take your place down on the field and join your fellow soldiers so that you might be recognized." As a shocked Todd Martin rose in embarrassment and strode down toward the friends he had made some time before, the president reiterated all the actions Todd had been responsible over the past year.

Once Todd had found his place, that the troops of the three detachments insisted was at the front of their formation, the president said, "Folks, if you'll excuse me for couple of minutes, I have the honor of presenting some medals to these fine young men."

With that, the president, accompanied by the entire chain of command for the honorees, stepped down off the platform and went directly to where the soldiers to be decorated stood. As the president went through the formation and presented medals, the announcer's voice came over the loudspeaker and

JIHAD!

read the citation for each medal awarded. Todd stood at the front of the formation and the tears streaming down his face would not stop as he heard the words to each member of the elite group as the president pinned on the medals. He just hoped that the guys behind him didn't see their "sob sister" bawling in front of them. He glanced down at the Medal of Freedom hanging from his lapel and then directed his attention toward his wife in the reviewing stands.

When the medals had been awarded, the president and his entourage returned to the reviewing stand and the honored soldiers and Todd moved to a place directly in front of the platform and turned to face the troops.

The president stepped to the podium once more and then said, "My fellow Americans, I want to introduce you to some of the finest Americans you will ever meet. Would all the wives who have supported these honored men please stand so we can give you our appreciation as well."

With that, each of the married men's wives from Detachments A-237, 238 and 239 rose to their feet and another wife joined them as Cathy Todd stood with a heart full of pride that could not be contained. The applause led by the president did not stop for a full minute.

All across the nation, television sets were tuned in to watch the proceedings that were held at Pope Air Force Base and Fort Bragg. If one had the opportunity to go into the homes of the millions of viewers that day they would have observed many different responses from all walks of life. Many veterans, unable to restrain themselves, rose from their chairs and rendered a salute. Others sat in silence to take in this hallowed moment while many shouted in glee and pride in their nation. More tears of joy were flowing that morning than had been shed during the terrible times endured over the past six months. The nation had healed.

"Pass in review," the commander of troops ordered once the president had completed his remarks. At that point the 7th Special Forces group (Airborne), and specifically Todd's old detachment, led the troops as they made the turning move and began the lengthy procedure of turns that would bring them past the reviewing stand. As each element reached the platform the commanders would direct, "Eyes right," and every head in the formation would turn forty-five degrees to the right as the formation passed the honored soldiers, the colors, and the dignitaries on the dais.

Once the last element of the Special Forces groups had departed the field, the president stood once more and, as customary, went to the crowds of people who had gathered for the occasion and mingled with them, shaking hands and exchanging greetings. Not for a long time had there been a more beloved chief executive in this nation or any other. He had presided over America during the worst situation since the World Wars and conducted himself with dignity and wisdom. He would continue for a second term nearly without opposition.

Todd Martin returned to the family who had stood by him over the past months and did not restrain himself from hugging his wife and kids in front of the whole world. The president had directed the pilot of the VIP aircraft to fly Todd and his family to Hawaii and drop them off at Honolulu, with instructions to remain in that state for not less than the next three weeks.

"You're gonna need all the rest you can get, Todd, 'cause when you get back to Washington, I have a few things in mind I want you to do for me."

The president smiled to himself and joined his party heading for Air Force One while Todd, Cathy, Becky and little Hal scurried off in the direction of their own private jet.

Printed in the United States
30716LVS00004B/127-153